AF414274

Also by Susanna Shore

The Reed Files
The Perfect Scam
The Perfect Hoax

P.I. Tracy Hayes
Tracy Hayes, Apprentice P.I.
Tracy Hayes, P.I. and Proud
Tracy Hayes, P.I. to the Rescue
Tracy Hayes, P.I. with the Eye
Tracy Hayes, from P.I. with Love
Tracy Hayes, Tenacious P.I.
Tracy Hayes, Valentine of a P.I.
Tracy Hayes, P.I. on the Scent
Tracy Hayes, Unstoppable P.I.
Tracy Hayes, P.I. for the Win

Thrillers
Personal
The Assassin

House of Magic
Hexing the Ex
Saved by the Spell
Third Spell's the Charm
Magic by the Book

Two-Natured London
The Wolf's Call
Warrior's Heart
A Wolf of Her Own
Her Warrior for Eternity
A Warrior for a Wolf
Magic under the Witching Moon
Moonlight, Magic and Mistletoes
Crimson Warrior
Magic on the Highland Moor
Wolf Moon
Magic for the Highland Wolf

THE PERFECT HOAX

THE REED FILES: BOOK TWO

SUSANNA SHORE

CRIMSON HOUSE BOOKS

1

ELIOT

Of all the things I would miss when I left Lyon, I hadn't thought the old ladies of my yoga class would be among them. There were three of them, each more delightful than the other, making the afternoon yoga sessions with students, pensioners, and stay-at-home mothers something I looked forward to.

The youngest of them was Mademoiselle Morel. She was in her late sixties, I guessed—a gentleman never asks a lady's age—a former nun turned kindergarten teacher, now retired. As a very lapsed Catholic since my childhood, now a firm non-believer, I was in awe and a little frightened of her.

She was best friends with Madame Fabien, a seventy-something sturdy matriarch of four children, eleven grandchildren, and two great-grandchildren by the latest count. She would talk ceaselessly of them given half a chance, and we usually gave it. Mademoiselle Morel had taught most of them and she was as devoted to them as Madame Fabien herself.

And the cherry on the top was my absolute favorite, Madame Benoit, eighty-two. She'd volunteered her age herself the first time we met.

She had buried three husbands and was on the lookout for number four. She'd set her eyes on me. "I like a big, strapping man in my bed," she'd told me with a teasing smirk.

I'd blushed, to the great glee of all three. I don't even know why. I'd been propositioned by older women hundreds of times, especially when I'd been the manager of the casino-spa hotel in Brooklyn, New York, and regularly mingled with the guests. They'd been customers I needed to entertain, and I'd usually taken their advances in stride. These women were … well, friends as it turned out.

Madame Benoit was a tiny, lively woman who wasn't bothered by her age at all, thanks to a life-long yoga habit. Her white hair was tinted purple, and her black eyes were twinkling.

"You were particularly energetic in class today, Monsieur Reed," she teased me in French, the only language we had in common. They always called me Monsieur Reed, even though I'd asked them to call me Eliot. I, of course, only called them by their last names. I wasn't sure I knew their given ones.

We were in the café of the gym, a bland space on the ground floor lobby, enjoying our after-yoga refreshments, a healthy kale smoothie in my case, cappuccinos and cakes in theirs. "When you're as old as we are, it's absolutely vital to indulge," Madame Fabien had said once, giving me and my smoothie pitying looks I wholeheartedly agreed with.

There'd been a time when I'd indulged too, especially Italian food, but that was double my body weight in muscle ago. I was happy with my new, lean form, but occasionally I missed some foods almost as much as I missed my mother. I especially missed my mother's food.

She wasn't dead. I was. As far as she knew anyway.

Madame Benoit leaned closer to me. "I nearly had a stroke when you did that downwards dog."

I turned my eyes to the ceiling and bit the inside of my cheek not to laugh aloud, but they noticed and doubled their efforts at teasing me, Mademoiselle Morel included. A nun really shouldn't be so good at innuendo, even a former one.

I'd already finished the smoothie, which was my usual signal to say my goodbyes and return to my office in the next building. But I was in no hurry to leave. I'd sold my business and terminated the leases on my office and apartment. I had my getaway bag ready, and I'd emptied the apartment of everything personal and wiped all the surfaces clean of fingerprints. I'd only wanted one last yoga session before I left.

And then it had dawned on me that I would truly miss these women; a small ache that unfurled in my chest, threatening my composure.

Pity I only realized it when it was already too late. I would've brought them chocolate—or the excellent port they'd introduced me to.

I kept a smile on my face as I listened to the outrageous comments the old ladies made, but all I could think of was that this would be the last time I saw them. And that made me not want to leave.

I squeezed my hands into fists under the table, annoyed with myself. This was exactly the reason for *never get attached to what you have and who you're with*, the rule number three in my list of how to stay alive and undetected after faking your death to escape a life as a mafia first. Because that's what I'd done—successfully, I might add.

And then I'd put everything in jeopardy by breaking it. Maybe I needed a new rule: *Don't start any hobbies where you might accidentally befriend someone.* Or maybe it was more of a subrule; 3.1 or something.

It was a good rule, and not solely because I would miss those I left behind. I had to be able to ditch everything and leave without anyone noticing I was gone.

These women would definitely notice. And then they would meddle. Before I knew it, there would be a full missing person search. And that would lead to trouble with the police for me when they realized I'd disappeared on purpose.

I also had a rule about not being noticed by the law enforcement; rule number eight for those keeping score. Another solid one—and one that I'd already broken too, thoroughly.

I would have to say proper goodbyes, but every time I opened my mouth to tell the ladies I wouldn't be coming back, I froze. The mere thought of upsetting them made me want to stay instead. Knowing that it was my own fault I had to leave didn't make this any easier.

A year after faking my death and making a clean escape from my life as the right-hand man of Craig Douglas, in a major New Jersey drug organization fast expanding to other areas—geographically and business-wise—I'd had a good thing going in Lyon, Southeast France. I had a nice home, good job, new face and body, and identity that I liked. And then, like an idiot, I'd first gotten involved with the police, and then I'd garnered the attention of even an bigger crime lord, Salvatore Bosco; Italian who operated on Mediterranean. He'd believed I was a cop investigating his drug smuggling business and had tried to kill me outright.

My only hope was that he believed he'd succeeded. It was the only reason I hadn't fled immediately and had put my affairs here in order first. Because men like him didn't leave things half-finished. He would try again until the job was done.

One way or another, Eliot Reed would cease to be. I intended it to happen on my terms.

I would no longer be a thirty-two-year-old businessman with American and Italian nationalities but would adopt a new identity and disappear. I had several ready, complete with passports that were as genuine as a world-class hacker could make them. I only had to choose.

I hadn't chosen a new one yet though. I was about to go after Bosco before he came after me. I might not survive it, so why bother changing.

The only real thing about my identity was my American nationality, though I did have Italian heritage from my mother's side. Likely from my father's side too, but I didn't know him. I'd made Eliot a couple of years younger than my true age, and my looks were radically different from my original self, Jonathan Moreira. He had begun his career in crime as an enforcer and had had looks to match: six foot three and almost 260 pounds of solid muscle—or 120 kilos and 190 centimeters in local.

It had taken years, a thorough lifestyle change, and a nose job, but my profile was now elegant, I was about 80 kilos with nice, lean muscles that didn't bulge all over the place, and an inch shorter. The latter I'd achieved by giving up wearing shoes with false bottoms. I'd been short growing up and got used to wearing them even after a growth spurt.

But apart from maybe growing a beard—I'd already stopped shaving, much to the delight of the old ladies—dyeing and cutting my hair—currently light chestnut, slightly curling and longish at the sides, shorter at the back—and wearing colored contacts over my green-grays, I couldn't go through a change as radical as when I became Eliot Reed.

Luckily, I had the ability to learn from my mistakes before anything permanent happened, like death. I would do better staying hidden in the next location. I just needed to go.

I opened my mouth once again to say my goodbyes, when a new person walked to our table. My heart sank.

THE WOMAN WAS IN her mid-twenties, short and wiry, with multiple piercings and full-sleeve tattoos revealed by her black tank top. Her hair was dyed blue and teased into a low faux-hawk. She looked like a frontwoman of an underground punk band, or a post-grad student of intersectional feminism, both of which might be true.

Her name was Laïla Diab and she was a cyber security expert at Interpol, the headquarters of which were in Lyon. Back when I settled here, I'd thought I could go under their radar. I'd been wrong, and breaking the rule number three was to blame for that too.

"Sensei!" the old ladies greeted her, delighted. She smiled and bowed in Japanese style in return. She had a black belt in ju-jitsu, and the ladies and I had recently attended an introduction class. The ladies had continued. I hadn't been back.

Laïla turned to me, her eyes concerned. "Have you seen Ada?"

I tensed, trying to figure out what she was after with the question. Ada Reed—the last name was a coincidence; mine was false after all—was an Interpol analyst about my age, highly intelligent and very attractive, which alone would've guaranteed my interest. But she was also a successful cat burglar, which I'd discovered by accident. For a career criminal like me, it was like catnip.

"No, not since our … adventure."

The euphemism was for the old ladies. I hadn't told them what had happened a month ago in Monaco, when Ada and I had barely escaped human traffickers—in addition to Salvatore Bosco, who had tried to kill me.

My euphemism failed. "You're having a romance with Sensei Reed?" Madame Benoit demanded, but her eyes were lit in delight so she wasn't truly upset.

I bit my cheek again, but couldn't help the smile. "No, I'm not."

In fact, I'd kept my distance from Ada ever since we returned from Monaco to avoid any sort of romance with her. I couldn't afford one, knowing I would be leaving. I hadn't called her or answered her calls, and I hadn't attended the self-defense classes where she was one of the teachers.

She had taken the hint.

Laïla's brows furrowed with worry, making the piercings sway. "She didn't come to work today and she isn't answering her phone. She's never done that."

I didn't know Ada well enough to offer insights, but what I did know was that she took her career seriously. She couldn't afford to draw attention to herself if she wanted to keep her criminal activities hidden.

"Have you checked her home? Maybe she's fallen ill and is too sick to contact you." It was perfectly feasible that she would have caught pneumonia after our freezing escape through nighttime Mediterranean in wet clothes. René Bellamy, a lyonnaise detective who'd been with us, had caught a flu. But it had been a month already, so it wasn't likely Ada would have done so too.

"Or maybe she's tripped and hit her head or something."

It was a lame suggestion and Laïla looked dubious. Ada had the body and dexterity of a gymnast. But the old ladies were instantly worried.

"My neighbor fell and broke her hip and couldn't even call for help," Madame Fabien said. "If I hadn't gone over to ask her for a cup of coffee, who knows how long she would've lain there."

"You have to go check her home," Mademoiselle Morel urged Laïla, who gave her a decisive nod.

"I will." Then she turned to me. "Will you come with me?"

I had no reason to, if curiosity didn't count, and she didn't need me for a quick check. But I had nothing pressing to do until my train to Rome left later today. I had my affairs in order and my bag packed. I nodded and rose.

"Of course." I turned to smile at my companions. "Until next time."

It wasn't until I was outside that I remembered there wouldn't be a next time.

CENTRAL LYON WAS ON a long and narrow peninsula between two rivers, the Rhône and Saône. At the southern tip where the rivers converged was a neighborhood called Confluence, where my apartment and office were. Or had been until today.

Tram and bus lines ran through the old town, but we took a taxi outside the Confluence train station around the corner from the gym. The station, and the mall above it, was a convert from an old warehouse, like so much of the area that had been transformed in the past couple of decades from an industrial area to a trendy residential neighborhood.

I had no idea where Ada lived, and I was both reluctant and curious to find out. Reluctant, because I knew she didn't want me to know, and curious for the same reason.

Our destination turned out to be Quai de la Pêcherie by Saône in the old town. The distance was less than four kilometers and traffic was light, but most of the old town had one-way streets that were illogical to navigate. We couldn't take the most direct route, so the journey took closer to twenty minutes. I paid the taxi despite Laïla's protests that she'd invited me, and we climbed out.

The riverside boulevard was lined with five- and six-story brick or stone buildings from the eighteenth and nineteenth centuries, built attached to each other. Each building was painted a different color and had different trimmings around the windows, with restaurants and small boutiques at street level. It looked pretty and very French.

Ada's building was beige, or maybe pale yellow covered with grime of the past two centuries; three windows wide and six stories high. The ground floor had two tall, arched display windows that had had marble coating around them once, but it had shed long ago. They belonged to two antiquarian bookshops, one of which looked to have gone out of business some time ago.

The residential entrance was between the shops. Laïla let me into a narrow hallway that led to a staircase at the back. It was dim, and the walls were faded green and yellow. There was no elevator, so we climbed to the fourth floor.

Each floor had two apartments, one facing the river and the other the back yard. Ada's was toward the river, which had to be expensive, but if Laïla wondered how Ada could afford it with her salary, she didn't say it aloud. If I knew Ada at all, she'd already given her a logical explanation, like wealthy parents.

My gut tightened in unexplained anxiety when Laïla opened the door to Ada's apartment. Did I fear we'd find Ada injured inside? Or worse.

I tensed when a notion that Bosco might have found her hit me. Then I remembered that she'd been in one of her disguises when she met him, and my muscles eased. But the brief scare strengthened my resolve to go after him to make sure he wouldn't retaliate on her.

Taking a calming breath, I followed Laïla in. Maybe I was simply reluctant to get a glimpse of Ada's private life like I would be reluctant to show her mine. Our double lives were only possible if we kept our privacy.

A short hallway that doubled as a foyer opened onto a one-window living room. A small but functional kitchenette was on the left and could be entered from the foyer and the living room. To the right was a bathroom and door to a bedroom, also one window wide.

Everything was elegant and neat, but a bit impersonal, as if Ada hadn't wanted to make this place a home. I could relate. The bed was made and the kitchen didn't have dirty dishes. Fridge was empty of perishables. And there was no Ada.

"Maybe she went away for the weekend," I noted to Laïla, who frowned.

"She didn't say anything to me. And she would've informed us if she weren't coming to work today."

"Maybe she was called home for an emergency," I suggested, but I was starting to have a notion of where Ada had gone—or at least why. She was a cat burglar, after all. That she hadn't come back made the ache in my gut return.

Laïla bit her lower lip. "Her mother is rather needy, always demanding she come to London to look after her. But surely she would answer her phone?"

I didn't know if the needy mother was real or just a handy excuse for Ada's other activities that regularly took her all over the world, but I shrugged. "Plenty of reasons why she wouldn't. Maybe her mother is in a hospital, and she's switched it off."

Neither of us brought up that Ada would've called if she could.

Laïla sighed. "I guess I can only wait that she'll call."

"She will," I said with more confidence than I felt. I didn't like this one bit.

I saw Laïla back to the street. "I'll be in Rome for the rest of the week. Can you contact me if Ada comes home?" I hadn't planned to tell her where I was going, but if both of us went missing at the same time, she'd launch an investigation. With her skills, she'd find me in no time.

"Absolutely," she promised, heading to the nearest bus stop with a wave of her hand.

I went in the opposite direction and rounded the corner. There I paused and waited for the bus to arrive. I peeked around the corner to make sure she was gone. Then I went back to Ada's building and entered her apartment using the keys I'd lifted from Laïla. I'd leave them with the janitor when I was done.

I went straight to the bedroom and started looking around. The building was three windows wide, yet Ada's apartment only had two. So where was the last window?

The bedroom had a large walk-in closet that would extend out of Ada's apartment the way it was laid out—unless it wasn't what it seemed. I felt behind the clothes that hung in neat rows, all suitable for an Interpol analyst. Several pairs of surprisingly whimsical shoes were in their rightful places too.

My hand met a lever, and the back wall swung open on silent hinges. I moved the clothes aside and stepped through.

It was the missing room. The curtains were drawn, but enough light came through to show me a tidy space that seemed to be a study, with an ordinary desk and a computer. The walls were lined with racks full of clothes, shoes, and accessories suitable for disguises. Drawers contained wigs, rappelling ropes, and night vision goggles.

The lair of a cat burglar.

I switched on the laptop, but it was password protected and I didn't have time to start guessing what it could be, so I looked around the neat desk. There was only one paper, with flight numbers scribbled on it, along with a word that made my heart jump.

It was a hotel. I knew it because I'd booked a room there myself.

I guess we would both soon be in Rome.

2

ADA

ROME. THE ETERNAL CITY. Or a very old one anyway, much of which was visible for tourists to gawp at. It was chaotic and beautiful and I loved it. I'd been there several times and would return regularly until the day I died.

That day might be closer than I wished for.

Or maybe I was already dead and this was hell. I wasn't terribly religious and didn't believe in hell, but maybe it believed in me. It certainly felt like it.

Rome in mid-June was a boiling, windless cauldron. It didn't used to be this hot this early in the season, but times changed and the climate along with it.

It was four in the afternoon and the sun was battering me through the west-facing windows of my hotel room. They had curtains, but no one had bothered to close them.

I was currently unable to.

The Tiber River, a short street down from my hotel, was running low, and the stench of mud and millennia of sediment was overpowering even through closed windows. Before the stink reached me, I'd wished they were open. Not that it would've made much difference in the room's temperature. The room should have air conditioning—the building was centuries old, but my room was in a new part purpose-built atop it—but either it had broken or it was deliberately shut off.

My money was on the latter, but the first was possible too. It wasn't exactly a five-star hotel.

The tiny, family-owned place stood by a small, idyllic piazza in Trastevere—literally, a neighborhood on the other side of Tiber—about a kilometer from Forum Romanum and Pantheon across the river, and two kilometers downriver from the Vatican. I'd chosen it for its anonymity and lack of surveillance, and had been lucky to get a room on a short notice at this time of year. Or maybe others had known about the smell. It was popular among tourists and visiting academics at nearby universities alike, the latter of which I was pretending to be.

Had pretended, anyway. Currently I was a prisoner bound to my bed. A naked prisoner, but the lack of clothing did little to relieve me from the discomfort of the heat.

I'd been held here for thirty-six hours, yet in that time I hadn't been able to figure out what had happened. Well, I knew *how* I had ended up imprisoned in my own hotel room, but not *why*. My captor hadn't seen fit to tell me his plans.

I'd come to Rome on Friday to do a quick B&E Saturday night to steal a specific item from a safe I'd been commissioned to do. It should've been an easy job. It had been an easy job. *Too easy*. Because it turned out to be a trap. One set by my late husband.

I guess he wasn't as dead as everyone thought.

I'd known Danny was alive. I just hadn't known where he was, despite spending the past five years trying to find him. Then by chance I'd come across his moniker, Hand, in connection to a drug and human trafficking case I'd been investigating for my day job at Interpol. I hadn't wanted to believe he would get mixed up with such things, especially human trafficking, but here I was, captive.

He had found me first, catching me red-handed opening the safe he'd commissioned me to open so he could record me doing it. I had no idea why he had gone through all this trouble and why I was his prisoner now. Surely there were easier ways to catch people you wanted to traffic. Like the party-boat I'd ended up on in Monaco a month ago that belonged to the crime organization I'd been after.

Was this payback for ruining the operation? It was the only explanation that made sense.

It would also have made more sense if our places had been reversed. Five years ago, out of the blue, Daniel Reed had faked his death during a bank heist—one we'd been pulling together—and disappeared with the money. I'd managed to flee, seething with rage and hurt for his betrayal, only to be treated like a grieving widow by our families and colleagues at the Metropolitan Police in London who thought he died a hero in the line of duty defending the bank.

I still couldn't understand why he had done it. I thought we were happy. And if he hadn't been, there were better ways to handle things, like divorce.

To say I'd spent the intervening years fuming was a bit of an exaggeration, but I had been tracking him in order to get even. I wouldn't have tied him into the bed, naked, though. I would've put a bullet through his head.

Or probably not. I'd never killed anyone and I wasn't even comfortable with firearms, but his betrayal merited some kind of revenge. I was the injured party here, so why was I the captive?

I wiggled on the bed, trying to get comfortable. My arms were stretched above me and tied to the bedpost, and blood wasn't circulating properly anymore. The sheet under me was soaked with sweat, but it didn't make me feel any cooler. And I desperately needed to use the loo.

Danny had visited a couple of times since he confined me here in the early hours of Sunday morning, bringing food and letting me use the toilet. But he hadn't been back since breakfast this morning. I was hungry and so parched my tongue was sticking to the roof of my mouth. Evidently, I was being punished here, but for what?

At first, I'd tried to open the ropes, but I hadn't made any progress by the time Danny came by to see to my needs, after which he redid all the knots, forcing me to start anew. Today, I hadn't even bothered anymore. It aggravated me that I gave up so easily, but my arms were numb, my wrists were chafed raw, and it turned out I wasn't good at withstanding pain.

Here lies Ada Reed, quitter, in her own sweat. May she rest in eternal agony.

I snorted a laugh and it made me feel a bit better. Then a muscle in my shoulder cramped and the laugh turned into a groan of pain. I couldn't take this much longer.

The door rattled just then and I tensed, absurdly getting my hopes up. Maybe it was housekeeping, wondering why I hadn't checked out the previous day like I should've.

But when the door opened to admit my jailor, my stomach tightened in disappointment—and fear.

DANNY CLOSED THE DOOR swiftly behind him and crossed the floor to me, carrying a plastic bag that I hoped contained food. He paused to stare at me, running his gaze up and down my naked body, his head tilted in appreciation.

I forced myself to lay still but I wanted to cover myself. I used to be married to this man, and had been comfortable being naked around him. The way he looked at me had been enough to arouse me back then, but he wasn't my husband anymore. I didn't know who he was.

He looked pretty much the same. He was tall and lean, with tightly coiled, ropy arms that his T-shirt bared. His dark blond hair was slightly overgrown and messy, as if he'd run fingers through it to ease the sweating, and his face was handsome with an angular chin and brown eyes. He used to make my heart skip a beat in delight, but not anymore. And not merely because he looked a little worn, as if he'd aged more than he should've in these past five years.

I made a quick calculation in my head and realized he would be turning forty this year. Maybe this was what he should look like.

The biggest change, however, was the barely hidden anger just underneath the surface. The Danny that I remembered had had an easy smile despite his taxing job at the Metropolitan Police in London by day and bank robber by night. Now his brows were furrowed and there was a permanent divot between them that didn't exist before.

"I guess the money didn't make you happy."

The words were out before I realized I was about to speak. His appreciative gaze tightened.

"You could say so…"

He leaned over to untie the ropes. I wanted to hit him, but my arms were burning needles now that the blood flow returned to them, and I had no strength. No opportunity to either, as he kept a tight hold on my upper arm, adding to the pain.

He allowed me to use the bathroom alone, but he was already banging on the door as I was about to shower. Ignoring him, I stepped under the cold spray, almost moaning as my overheated body began to cool. I could've stayed there for the rest of the day—there was no window to escape through, so Danny couldn't object—but his impatience forced me to emerge.

To my surprise, there were clothes on the bed. Mine. Danny gestured at them. "Get dressed. We're leaving."

"Where to?"

But he wouldn't answer. I didn't expect him to.

I didn't test his patience more, and quickly pulled on the plain underwear, linen trousers, white T-shirt, and a sheer, long-sleeved linen blouse I'd meant for protecting my redhead pale skin against the sun. Now it would cover the bruises in my wrists that were throbbing with my heartbeat.

There were a couple of slices of pizza waiting on the table with a can of coke. I grabbed the latter and emptied it as fast as the bubbles allowed me to. It was warm, but I didn't care. Only then did I eat the food. It was already cold, but I didn't care about that either.

What a good little captive I was.

When I was done, Danny gave me a large-brimmed straw hat and my sunglasses. It wasn't much of a disguise, but it covered my short strawberry blond hair and most of my face. Maybe it would suffice for where we were going.

He grabbed me by the upper arm and walked me out of the room. I paused with a startle. A large, Italian looking man was waiting in the hallway, leaning against the opposite wall with his arms crossed over a meaty chest. It gave me a glimpse of a weapon under the unbuttoned shirt he wore over his T-shirt. The muscle, I presume.

I kept my mouth shut and didn't try to run.

A white Fiat 500 was parked outside the hotel, and the armed man took the wheel. It was a tiny car, with barely room for him, but it had only two doors, which made it a good choice if one wanted to keep the backseat passenger from fleeing.

Danny let me onto the back and took the front seat. The car glided out of the piazza before he'd put on his seatbelt, as if the driver was protesting how long we'd taken.

I studied him curiously, but he wasn't anyone we'd worked with in the past—or anyone I recognized from Interpol wanted lists for that matter. He was about Danny's age, with curly black hair, and a prominent nose. Danny didn't introduce him and I didn't ask.

We drove across the river, the tiny car proving its usefulness in the Monday evening rush as it zigzagged between the lanes. We headed southwest, following the river and keeping to the main streets despite the traffic— or maybe because of it. The smaller streets were probably completely jammed.

After about half an hour we reached the part of Rome I wasn't very familiar with. It was a district called EUR, a brainchild of Mussolini that his regime hadn't been able to complete because of the Second World War.

The town plan had been inspired by fascist imagining of ancient Rome, with wide boulevards and large piazzas, an artificial, geometrical lake, and imposing limestone and concrete buildings that resembled ancient temples with tall columns, but stripped of any trimmings and ornaments to suit the fascist ideals of rationalism.

The original buildings had been completed in the sixties when the place had been transformed into a commercial district with high-rises that housed government ministries and headquarters of international companies. Even to this day though, it was sparsely built, making the area look spacious and kind of half-completed.

The nameless muscle who hadn't spoken a word during the drive—if you didn't count shouting at idiotic fellow drivers—drove us down a wide boulevard to a black-walled high-rise that didn't have any neon signs on its walls naming the companies occupying it, so it was likely a government building. The near-empty parking space behind it seemed to confirm my notion, as no self-respecting Italian government worker stayed overtime. He pulled over underneath a large tree that offered shade from the early evening sun and cut the engine.

We've arrived, I presume.

I remained silent. If Danny wanted me to know why we were here, he'd tell me. I wouldn't volunteer any interest.

Danny exited the car and pulled his seat forward to let me out. I obeyed, with stiff legs. It wasn't a roomy car, to put it nicely, and I had long legs that I'd had to fold tightly to fit behind his seat. The evening air was hotter and more humid than the air-conditioned air in the car and it pressed on me uncomfortably. It was still better than my hotel room.

Danny took a hold of my upper arm. I didn't yank myself free or attempt to flee this time either. I was faster runner than him, but not in my current condition. I would bide my time.

"We'll have to hurry. The place will close in half an hour. And don't try anything funny. Enzo's carrying."

I took it Enzo was the driver who had exited on his side and was now waiting for us to move.

I was surprised Danny wasn't armed. He'd always loved guns, a constant cause of strife between us, as I preferred to avoid bloodshed at all costs. His faked death had involved an explosion that had killed people.

We crossed the street and a small plaza outside the building to the main entrance. The glass door had the name of the place in discreet letters on it: *Banco Posta*. My stomach fell.

We were here to rob a bank.

3

ADA

THERE WERE MORE PEOPLE IN THE spacious lobby of the bank than I would've thought for that late an hour. Definitely more than I was comfortable with for a robbery.

Over-the-counter robberies hadn't been Danny's style back in the day, and they definitely weren't mine, especially with my own face. I was more a breaking into the vault after hours kind of girl, though even then I preferred private safes to bank vaults. I'd only helped Danny on occasion—like that last fateful time.

"Go to that desk and ask after the safe deposit boxes. You want to open one for a client," Danny ordered me, nodding discreetly in the right direction. Enzo had taken a seat near the door, so maybe we weren't here for a robbery after all. "And you want to see the vault."

Or maybe we were.

"In English?" I didn't speak Italian, so the question was justified.

"Speak Chinese for all I care, just do it."

I didn't look at him as I crossed the lobby to a special desk at the end of the counter. If there was some kind of queue or number system, I ignored it and just greeted the young man behind the plexiglass with my best smile, taking off my sunglasses. It was a risk, especially since I wasn't wearing any makeup to alter my looks, but he would find it odd if I kept them on.

"Hello, do you speak English?" I asked in my best Boston accent. It wouldn't fool natives, but it was distinctive enough that even Europeans would make note of it, even if they couldn't accurately place it.

I remembered the last time I'd used the accent and my heart jumped. It had been a month ago when I'd been surprised while emptying a private safe.

That was twice in a month that I'd been caught red-handed. Maybe I should consider retiring. The next time it might be a cop instead of a vindictive ex-husband or a former security expert who for some odd reason hadn't turned me in.

If I'd known that Eliot Reed, the man who walked in on me, was American, I would've kept my mouth shut. My carelessness had led to a chain of events that had culminated in us fleeing for our lives from human traffickers in a RIB through a vast open sea.

I wondered briefly what Eliot was doing, but pushed the thought aside. He wasn't my problem anymore. I purposefully didn't think of Laïla either, even though I knew she would be worried when I hadn't shown up to work this morning.

My problem was Danny and whatever scheme he was concocting.

The young teller smiled and checked me out. If I was lucky, he would remember my body and not my face. I had a nice body, a remnant of my childhood as a gymnast, until the breasts popped out, but I hadn't done anything to accentuate it today.

"Of course," he said politely in very good English—and a definite American accent. My stomach fell, but I only deepened my smile.

"You're a fellow American?"

He shook his head. "I went there as an exchange student. How may I help you?"

"I need to open a safe deposit box for my client. This is the correct desk?"

"Yes. Although we prefer that the person opening the account does so in person."

"Oh, that won't happen," I said with a brush of my hand. "He's not the kind to bother with such details, but I'll have the power of attorney. Will that do?"

He looked hesitant, so I pressed on: "At any rate, I'm not going to open one right this minute. I just need to see the safe to assure him that his valuables will be secured."

His mouth pressed into an offended line. "Our safe deposit boxes are very secure, I can assure you."

I leaned my elbows on the counter, arms crossed under my breasts. I'm not a voluptuous woman, but it pushed what I had up without giving an impression I was deliberately showing my breasts. His eyes lowered from my face instantly.

"I'm sure they are, but we're Americans. I don't know if you're aware, but modern banks there don't really bother with private safe deposits anymore and the law doesn't protect the contents, so he's a tad anxious. Truly, all I need is to take a peek so that I can look him in the eyes and say I've done it."

He drew his eyes away from my breasts, reluctantly enough to please me, and reached for keys. "I guess we can take a quick look. We're closing, so there won't be time to open one today anyway."

I flashed him another smile. "Sounds perfect."

He let himself out from behind the counter through a security door and I followed him down two flights of stairs to a basement, keeping an eye on the cameras. I didn't want to be caught in them, but I needed to know where they were.

We entered a short corridor that had a large vault door at the other end. I gave it a professional assessment and deemed it too difficult to break into even with explosives.

Well, the door might open, but the floor above would likely collapse too.

We didn't go there but paused outside another safe on the adjacent wall. This door was an older model and doable with the right tools, but the alarm system was topnotch and custom made. If Danny wanted to break in here, he'd better find a different safe-cracker.

The door unlocked with two large keys, so the best option would be getting the keys. They'd been in a drawer behind the counter, but I was reasonably certain they would be held in a more secure place after hours.

The heavy door opened soundlessly, if you didn't count the small grunt the young man made as he pulled it with both hands. Lights came on automatically and I detected two different cameras at a glance. There might be more.

Rows and rows of steel lockboxes covered the walls on both sides. There had to be hundreds of them. "It's much larger than I anticipated," I said, trying to sound admiring while my mind was racing. What could Danny want with this place? Unless he knew the exact box that he wanted to rob...

The young man gave me a pleased smile. "We're an old bank and have been here since the building was finished in the sixties. *We* take our safe deposits seriously."

I ignored the slight emphasis on "we" that was meant as a jab at Americans. I was British, so I didn't have to care.

"If it's been here so long, are there any empty boxes left?"

The man stepped inside the vault and I followed, keeping my face away from the cameras. He walked deeper and disappeared around the corner. I went to take a look and my mouth dropped open in genuine surprise. There was an even larger vault there. One side by side with the main vault of the bank.

So that's what Danny was up to.

DANNY WAS IN THE lobby, with Enzo still sitting by the door, when I emerged from the basement with the young man. I said my chirpy goodbyes and promised to be back soon, all the while scanning discreetly behind the counter for where they secured the keys for the night.

I left the bank without looking at the men. I wanted to run, but instead I crossed the street to the car. I might as well see this through. I'd been trying to find Danny for five years and I hadn't even had my revenge yet. Besides, he had that video of me robbing a safe.

Enzo unlocked the car and I reached for the door on the passenger side but Danny beat me to it, startling me. But I kept my reaction to myself and just climbed into the back seat.

We didn't speak until Enzo had turned the car the way we'd come. I presumed I was headed back to my hotel confinement, which made sense from Danny's point of view. I wouldn't bring an outsider to my base of operations either, if I were him.

"So?" Danny finally asked.

"So what?"

He turned to glare at me over his shoulder. "You're not this stupid."

"Maybe I am…"

"Can you get into the safe deposit vault?"

And there it was.

I gave him a calm look. "No."

"Why not?"

"I don't want to."

His brows furrowed, deepening the divot between them. "You don't seem to appreciate the situation you're in."

"Nothing to appreciate…"

"Is it doable?" he asked, angrily.

I heaved a heavy sigh and gave in. "The door is easy. All you need is the keys, which are kept in an ordinary lockbox behind the counter. It's the security system that's the bitch, and not only on the vault door. Plus, cameras everywhere. But if you can get a topnotch security expert to handle the alarm, you can pretty much walk in."

"And you're saying you can't handle the security?"

"It's custom made and I haven't familiarized myself with new bank vault systems in recent years."

He snorted. "Don't try to pretend you've retired."

It annoyed me that he knew me so well, but we'd been married for three years and dated over a year more before that. We'd been happy and close, connected by our mutual double lives. He knew what drove me to the life of a cat burglar.

"Of course not. Just from bank jobs."

"That's where the big money is."

I leaned closer. "I don't need money. I need my freedom."

"That's not happening."

My gut tightened. "You don't need me anymore."

The cold look on his face was nothing I'd seen there before. Had this person always existed and I'd simply been blind to it, or had he changed that much?

"You have no idea what's going on."

"So enlighten me."

But he turned to face the front again and didn't speak the rest of the drive.

Traffic had eased, and we reached the hotel before my legs turned wooden for being crammed into the tight space. But I had to stifle a groan as I unfolded myself out of the car, and I didn't try to run. Moreover, I needed a place to run to first.

Danny walked me in and Enzo followed us with his gun, though it was still hidden. The middle-aged lady receptionist gave us a delighted and meaningful smile and didn't start demanding I vacate my room immediately. I glanced at Danny as we walked past her to the lift.

"Did you extend my stay?"

"Easiest thing in the world when I told them I'm your husband," he said, as we entered the lift. "I told them I had something romantic planned, and since the room was free and I was willing to pay extra, they let you have it."

I shuddered. How many women were trapped in a situation like mine because people were fools for romance? When I got free, I would make sure this hotel never made the same mistake again.

He leaned closer, as if reading my mind. "Incidentally, the entire staff knows not to bother us. No one is coming to your aid."

I'd have to free myself, then.

"As long as you know you're not my husband anymore." I sounded calmer than I was. To my satisfaction, he startled.

"Of course I am."

"You died. I have a legal paper to prove that I'm a widow and free of you." Legally anyway. I arched a questioning brow. "Unless you're willing to return to the land of the living?"

"Do you have someone new?"

"None of your business. You're dead."

The doors opened and I marched out of the lift without a glance at him, but he grabbed me by the upper arm and yanked me around. He glowered down at me.

"Let's make one thing clear. I am and always will be your husband."

It took all my composure to meet his gaze without showing my unease—and anger. "You betrayed me as my husband and as my partner in crime. There's no coming back from that."

He sneered. "What, no room for forgiveness?"

I gave a meaningful look at his hand still squeezing my arm and he released me. I wanted to rub the bicep but I wouldn't give him the satisfaction.

If I'd wanted to have revenge on the man I'd loved, I absolutely needed to best the man he'd become.

THE AIR CONDITIONING was back on, and the room was blissfully cool. For a further measure, I closed the curtains. I wouldn't bake if the system broke again during the day.

The bed had been made too, so Danny must have given the housekeeping permission to enter. He didn't immediately tie me onto it again, and I was embarrassingly relieved for it. If I never laid on that bed again, it would be too soon.

I was relieved too, that Enzo was waiting in the hallway and not in the room, though it puzzled me. Did he trust Danny to keep me in line unarmed? Then why was he here at all?

Danny had the blueprints of the bank. He spread them on the small table by the window, and we went over them with meticulous detail. It was achingly familiar, and I had to steel myself not to fall into the emotional trap it opened. If it hadn't been for the tension between us, it would've been like the old days when we spent months planning his every heist together, even those I didn't take part in. My private jobs I planned and executed alone. I needed to be in total charge of them.

I marked all the cameras that I'd noted and added a few possible ones inside the vault. Then we went over the alarm. I made a few suggestions about what kind of system it might be, but custom-made alarms always had a few surprises in them.

"If we can't get the keys, how do we open the door?" Danny asked. I studied him from under my brows.

"What's with this *we?*"

He tapped the blueprint with his index finger. "You're handling this."

His stubbornness was frustrating and aggravating. "I already told you, it's out of my area of expertise. I'm a liability." I had no interest in getting caught breaking into a bank, but it would be doubly infuriating if it happened because of my incompetence.

"Let's put it this way: either you open the vault or your boss at Interpol will get a video of his star analyst breaking into a safe."

My entire being froze. How did he know where I worked? I'd been at the Metropolitan Police in London when we were married and we hadn't exactly caught up on our lives these past two days.

But I only shrugged. "He'll also be informed that Daniel Reed, deceased, is not only alive, he's the notorious bank robber, Hand."

He was unfazed. "Unlike me, you don't have proof."

"Easiest thing in the world to get it now that I know where you are. All I need is to access the surveillance systems in this city and *voilà*."

"Gone native, have you?"

It took me a moment to figure out that he meant my use of the French word. "Surely you haven't forgotten that my mother is French?"

"You didn't used to make it obvious."

Did he have something against my background? This was the first time he'd brought it up. He had liked my mother.

In truth, I had no recollection how I'd spoken back when we still lived together, but I wasn't about to admit it. "French is what I use daily."

That wasn't entirely true, as our office was international and we used English most of the time. But he didn't need to know that either. He didn't need to know anything about me. Though it seemed he was much better informed about my life than I was about his.

I decided to change the topic. "Why this bank?"

"Why not?" he countered with a careless shrug, but I wasn't fooled.

"You've chosen this especially, an odd government bank in Italy. Either it's easy to break into or there's something you really want inside. Since it's not the first, it has to be the latter. And it's not money, because you can get that from any old bank."

"Maybe there's a shitload of money."

I leaned back in the chair and crossed arms over my chest, studying him. "Let's say I believe you. How do you plan to move that much money?"

Bank notes in large quantities were heavy. You crammed a duffel bag full of them and the weight soon exceeded your ability to carry it. And it never yielded quite as much in profit as you hoped, unless you brought a large crew to carry it.

"It's not gold, is it?"

His lip curled in amusement. "No."

"Then what's my cut?"

He dipped his chin, studying me in return. "You'll get the video back."

That was priceless as far as I was concerned.

"How many men are you bringing?"

"Just you, me and Enzo."

My mouth dropped open. "That's … ridiculous. You can't pull off a bank heist with three people."

His jaw flexed. "It's how we'll do it, and that's final."

"Why does this matter so much to you? What is going on?"

"None of your business."

I studied him, really studied him for the first time since our abrupt reunion. Beyond the changes I'd already noticed, there was something I hadn't noticed in him before. Fear.

"You're not in charge of this, are you?"

He lifted his gaze from the blueprints and didn't say anything, but I knew I was right. It explained Enzo too. He was here for Danny, not me.

"You've become involved in something you shouldn't have. Something bad." I inhaled sharply. "Is it Dobrev?"

He startled. "Who?"

"Please… I found your moniker in connection to his operation. You've become a drug and human trafficker, haven't you?"

He looked incredulous and then angry. "Don't you know me at all? Why the bloody hell would I get mixed in that shit?"

"I don't know, but here I am, prisoner, a month after I got Dobrev's right-hand man killed."

Technically, Dobrev's men had killed Melnyk, but we'd been there with Eliot. We'd even locked Melnyk up, which had made it easy for Dobrev's men to kill him.

He threw his arms up. "I have no idea what you're talking about."

"Right, and all this is just coincidence." I gestured around.

"No. I need a job done and you're the only one I can trust to help me."

I gave him a fed-up look. "Touching. I already told you, I can't do it."

"Maybe another night tied on that bed will change your mind."

He made to stand up and I went cold all over. "Can't I sleep in the bathroom?" I pleaded and wasn't even ashamed of it. I would not be tied on that bed again. "You can block the door from the outside so I don't need to be bound. I'll have the use of the facilities, and the sun won't scorch me tomorrow."

I was sure he would refuse, just to teach me a lesson, but he ground his teeth and nodded. "Fine."

He only waited for me to carry the bedding into the bathroom before closing the door. I could hear him move the furniture, and a moment later he asked me to test the door.

The handle wouldn't move at all and when I put my best effort into ramming the door, I only hurt my shoulder.

"It'll hold," I told him, and managed not to sound disappointed.

"You'd best be there when I return in the morning, or your boss gets interesting mail."

I ignored his threats, and a moment later I heard him leave. I made myself as comfortable as I could on the floor, and prepared for the first decent night since he'd captured me, although he had left the lights on. It was practical for me, but it made it slightly more difficult to fall asleep.

Or so I thought. Because before I knew it, I woke up to the sound of the furniture being moved again. I sat up, bracing myself for another annoying day with Danny when the door was yanked open.

But it wasn't Danny. My jaw dropped.

4

ELIOT

THE OVERNIGHT TRAIN TO ROME arrived at the Roma Termini, the main railway station in central Rome, at six in the morning on Tuesday, half an hour late. I could've flown and been here already the previous evening, but airports meant tighter security, and even with my new face and body, I wasn't willing to take the risk.

Moreover, I had packed a couple of handguns in my bag—courtesy of Artem Melnyk, a drug and human trafficking asshole from whom I'd liberated them—and I wasn't willing to disclose those.

I'd travelled by train in Europe before, and the first-class experience was as enjoyable as ever, even though the travel time was over twelve hours, with one change of trains. I'd even had a chance to sleep in the double bed in my compartment this time round. I'd been alone, but if a suitable candidate had sashayed up to me in the excellent restaurant car like on my previous journey, I might have changed my mind. Random casual encounters were the only way to get laid for me. I couldn't afford to get attached.

I took a taxi outside the station. This early, there was no traffic yet, so the driver decided to take me down the scenic route as an impromptu travel guide. He drove me past all the major sites between the station and the hotel, like the Colosseum and the Forum Romanum, talking ceaselessly, testing the limits of my Italian. Since the map on my phone indicated it wasn't much of a detour, and it would probably be the only chance I had to see the sites— I'd been to Rome before but not for sightseeing—I let him. I even gave him a good tip when he let me off outside the hotel half an hour later.

The tiny place by a sleepy piazza was already open, the early leavers enjoying breakfast on the small terrace outside. Since I was in no hurry, I joined them.

The morning was warming up, but the sun that reached down the east-facing street wasn't glaring yet. With its flower arrangements and small tables, the terrace was a lovely place to sit with a cup of excellent Italian coffee and a pastry that I'd been craving practically ever since I knew I was coming here.

By the time I was done, the people checking out had cleared the reception area and I made my way there to see if I could check in early. Having been a manager of a huge casino-spa hotel, the small antique desk with one computer seemed quaint, but I'd chosen the place on purpose.

Yes, you could be completely anonymous in a large five-star hotel the way you couldn't be in a small place like this, but the surveillance here was aimed at keeping people out, not monitoring those staying.

And I had an additional task here as well, one that I shouldn't forget. Knowing Ada, she likely hadn't checked in with her own name. Describing her wouldn't work either, if she'd altered her looks like she usually did for a job. She was so good at her disguises that even knowing it was her could still fool a person.

But I was in for a surprise, because the young woman checking me in gave me a bright smile when she read my information. "Are you having a family reunion here, Signor Reed?"

I took a split of a second to translate her Italian, which was nothing like my grandmother and mother spoke. Then I smiled. "Yes. Have others arrived yet?"

"Mr. and Mrs. Reed are already here. Mrs. Reed arrived on Friday, and her husband on Sunday."

Husband? I didn't like the sound of that. But I only deepened my smile. "Wonderful. Would it be possible to get their room number? I'd rather not call and wake them up this early."

I tried to keep the disapproval off my face when she eagerly gave the information. If she'd been working at my hotel, she would've been fired for such a security breach.

"I booked you in the adjoining room," the girl said, handing me the keycard, oblivious of my thoughts. "The balconies connect too so you can have lovely time there together."

That was convenient.

I thanked her and headed to the elevator. The room was on the top floor, a modern addition at the top of the building that couldn't be seen from the street. It was basically a rectangle of steel and glass that sat atop the original medieval building without the charm of its terracotta walls and red tile roof, but it fit there surprisingly well.

My room was sparsely and inexpensively furnished, but it was clean and spacious, with a large enough bed for me. I dropped my bag on the floor, crossed to the balcony and pulled the heavy curtain aside.

The balcony facing the back yard stretched over the roof of the original building below and had a red tile floor and dark brown wooden pergolas with canvas roofs to offer some shade from the sun that would reach here in the afternoon. There were partitions between the rooms to provide privacy, but they were easy enough to round if one so chose.

And I did.

The curtains were drawn across the windows in the adjacent room, so the occupants were likely still asleep. I hesitated. The receptionist had mentioned a husband, which had to be a ruse for the Catholic sentiments. Ada was a widow, so it couldn't be her actual husband but likely a romantic partner of some kind. Nevertheless, she wouldn't thank me if I barged in on them.

The idea of Ada with a man caused me unease I had no right to feel. I was about to change my identity and disappear from her life for good. She would go on like I'd never existed. I didn't have to like it, but it was a choice I'd made.

The only choice I could make.

But I couldn't help wondering who he was. Detective René Bellamy from the Lyon police? He'd certainly indicated his interest when we'd been together in Monaco. He would be a good match for her too, if it weren't for her other life. It would be impossible to live a double life as a criminal with a cop in her life.

Then again, hadn't her late husband been a cop too?

That gave me pause again. Ada had checked in with her own name, which meant she wasn't here for a job, so a romantic getaway sounded more likely. But why hadn't she told Laïla where she was going and why? Surely good friends like they were shared everything about their romances.

Something didn't add up here, and the only one with answers was Ada. Feeling indignant—though why and for whom, I had no idea—I reached for the balcony door and pulled. It wasn't locked, which was careless of her, and it glided silently aside. I paused to listen, but there were no sounds of sleeping people—or people engaged in more vigorous activities for that matter.

I pulled the curtain aside and peeked in. The room was dark, but the open balcony door let in enough light to see well. The bed was empty—of everything. No pillows or blankets. The sight baffled me so much I didn't immediately notice it had been dragged out of place too, and was blocking the bathroom door.

That was not normal…

Two possibilities ran through my head and I discarded the first immediately. If Ada had captured someone inside the bathroom, she would've called authorities to handle it and she would be here. So, the only other option was that Ada herself was held inside.

I didn't wait to act on my reasoning. Crossing the floor, I took a good hold of the double bed, bent my knees not to break my back, lifted…

…and almost fell on my butt when the bed turned out to be lighter than it looked. I took a hasty step to find my balance, moved the bed and lowered it down. Then I went to the bathroom door and yanked it open.

Ada was sitting on the floor in a pile of bedding, wide awake and baffled.

"YOU COULD HAVE KNOCKED."

Ada's dry remark made me grin in relief. I dropped on my knees on the bedding and pulled her into a hug. She fit my arms nicely, and I rested my chin on her head.

"Jesus, woman, you had us so worried."

She squeezed me tightly and spoke against my chest. "I had myself worried too."

"Why were you locked in the bathroom? And by whom?"

She sighed and pulled back, and I released her. We weren't at the hugging stage of our relationship.

We *weren't* in a relationship.

"It's a long story. How did you find me?"

"Laïla." Her pale blue eyes grew large in horror, so I hastened to calm her. "She merely told me you were missing and we searched your home. But she doesn't know about your secret room."

It didn't relax her. "But you do?"

"Yes." There was no point denying it. "I found the name of the hotel there."

"That was careless of me…"

"I'm glad of it, otherwise we'd had no idea where to look for you."

"You didn't bring Laïla, did you?"

I lifted a reassuring hand. "No. And I'd already booked a trip here, in this hotel even, so she doesn't know I had a lead on your whereabouts."

She rubbed her face, looking tired. I noticed her wrists and inhaled sharply. They were chafed red with what obviously had been ropes. My hands tightened into fists in anger.

"You were tied up?" My voice was almost a growl.

"Yeah…" She studied her wrists. "And not in a good

way. The bathroom was an improvement to that."

"Who is holding you here?" I demanded in a tone that used to make people working for me quake with fear when I was a mafia enforcer—and occasionally as a hotel manager too—but she met my eyes squarely.

"My husband."

The floor beneath me suddenly dropped, making my stomach dip. "What?"

Her smile was bitter and didn't reach her eyes. "Could you give me a moment to put on my clothes?"

She was wearing only a spaghetti-strap top and panties, but I shook my head. "No, you can dress in my room. We have to get you out of here." I rose and made to pull her up, but she didn't take my hand.

"I can't leave."

"The hell you can't!"

She wouldn't budge. "He has a video of me breaking into a private safe and he'll send it to my boss if I'm not co-operative, or here when he returns. Which might be soon. What time is it?"

I glanced at my wristwatch. "Seven thirty in the morning."

"He won't be here before nine. Wait in the room."

I wanted to demand she tell me everything immediately, but I exited the bathroom and closed the door. While she showered, I called reception for breakfast. Ada was dressed by the time it arrived, but I met the waiter at the door so that he wouldn't see the state of the bed.

"Should we sit on the balcony?" I suggested, but she hesitated.

"The neighboring room might hear our conversation."

I smiled. "I'm your neighbor."

But she was right about curious ears, so I merely pulled the gliding doors and curtains completely aside so that we could enjoy the morning air without being overheard.

She attacked breakfast like she hadn't been fed in days, and my anger intensified. But I let her eat in peace, only pouring myself a cup of espresso from the pot.

"You're not eating?" she asked when she had polished off half the offerings. I gestured her to finish the rest too, ignoring my craving for the chocolate filled pastry on the plate.

"I've already had breakfast."

When she couldn't eat more and the coffee pot was empty, she leaned back on her chair with a sigh. "I guess you deserve an explanation."

I gave it some thought. "You don't owe me one, if that's what you think. But I'd really like to know who I'm killing and why."

She startled. "You mean that."

"Yes."

She didn't tell me not to, which gave me a pretty good notion of the level of her anger.

She dipped her chin and studied me. "I told you about my husband, Danny, didn't I? How he died during a bank heist?"

I nodded. "In the line of duty."

Her mouth twisted. "None of that is true. He didn't die and definitely not in the line of duty."

My brows shot up, but I only nodded for her to continue. She shifted into a more comfortable position and leaned her elbows on the table.

"We were robbing the bank."

If she'd hit me in the head with a baseball bat, she couldn't have stunned me more. "I thought you do private safes."

"I do. Danny does banks."

My earlier thought of her dating René returned. "No wonder you were comfortable with being married to a cop."

Her smile was bitter. "Yeah. It was a shared hobby, and I occasionally helped him with his. The last one was a small branch in London that didn't have all that much money in the vault on a normal day, but it was the night before pension day and the Grand National was that weekend. People in that neighborhood want their money in hand, and several booking agencies used it too. So, the vault was more than usually loaded."

Making it an alluring target.

"The job went exactly as planned. The security was easily dealt with, the alarms were old, and the vault child's play. There was more money than we'd anticipated, and we filled our bags with as much as we could. Danny and Thom, a fellow cop turned crook, carried the first bags out, and John, the fourth in our team, and I were about to follow with the rest when the cops arrived."

She sighed, lost in her memories. "I couldn't understand what had gone wrong, but we had planned for it, and the plan was to ditch the money, run and disappear, so that's what John and I did. It wasn't easy, mind you, as the cops had the place surrounded. We couldn't have managed it if it hadn't been for the explosion at the front of the bank that drew their attention."

Her lips tightened with anger. "I thought it was a diversion planned by Danny. And in a way, it was just that. But when the emergency responders finally got inside, they found two bodies, Danny's and Thom's. All the cops there swore that they'd been the first two to enter the bank." She shook her head. "I still don't know how it went down and I've spent five years going through the events in my head."

"They had their SWAT gear stashed somewhere nearby and made a quick change?"

She nodded. "It's not SWAT with the Met, but yes. And not only that. Because Danny didn't die, and Thom probably didn't either."

"How do you know?"

"The money was gone, even the bags John and I had abandoned, as was the getaway car. But no matter how long John and I waited, following the protocol we had in place, they never returned."

"They faked their deaths by planting two bodies in their gear?" This was starting to sound eerily familiar.

"Yes. And since there was no way they could've dressed up the bodies so fast, those had to be in place already too. And the explosives."

"Or the bodies had the explosives."

"Yes. So, while John and I were in the vault, Danny and Thom set the stage, changed their gear, called the cops, joined them and went in first, triggered the explosives and escaped through the back, taking the money John and I had abandoned with them."

It was a lot to take in. "But … why?"

She spread her arms, aggravated. "That's what I've been asking myself these past five years."

5

ELIOT

I STUDIED ADA, TRYING TO picture her breaking into a bank vault dressed all in black like a ninja, avoiding the cameras. I'd witnessed her as a cat burglar and had been impressed, but for some reason I couldn't imagine her as a bank robber. I smiled and her brows furrowed.

"What's so funny?"

My smile deepened. "You as a bank robber."

"Hey! I was pretty good. I was a good member of the team." She pressed her head down and sank fingers into her short, strawberry blond hair, pulling it as if punishing herself. "And I truly believed we were a team. Yet Danny, and possibly Thom, betrayed us. Danny betrayed me as my husband too."

I hadn't thought of that angle. When I faked my death, the only person it truly hurt was my mother, and let's face it, she knew what her son did for a living and had probably feared the day I'd die for a long time. And I made sure she had no reason to doubt my death. Sorrow would fade over time, even a mother's—I hoped—but betrayal…

Betray an Italian mother and you'll wish you were dead.

"What happened here, then?" I asked, gesturing at the room. She looked around, as if seeing it for the first time, shaking her head, annoyed.

"I was set up. I accepted a job to break into a vault in a private home here in Rome. It went as planned, and then Danny showed up. I was too stunned by his sudden appearance to flee. Then he told me he had a video of me in my criminal activities."

My jaw tightened. "The fucker. Why would he do that?"

"I think it's payback for Monaco."

"What?"

She grimaced. "I didn't tell you at the time, but I found Danny's moniker among the names in Dominique Fabre's phone when we checked the money laundering files."

Fabre was a businessman who had been shot right after Ada had emptied his safe. Trying to find who killed him had caused all the trouble with the drug smugglers in Monaco.

"What does it mean?"

"I think he's part of Dobrev's operation." She reconsidered. "Well, I thought he was, but he denied all knowledge. It could be he's forced into doing this too."

"Doing what?"

She lifted her eyes to meet mine. "He wants me to break into a bank vault for him."

I could only stare. "That's ... optimistic of him."

She laughed and the tension inside me eased a little. "Very. Also very foolish, because I'm not familiar with that system."

"Did he used to be foolish?"

Her gaze sharpened. "No, he didn't. Blackmailing me into a certain capture is completely out of character."

"Meaning, he has no choice."

"Exactly."

I ran fingers down my beard, marveling at the odd sensation, as I'd never had a beard before. I tried to come up with an alternative explanation, but it was too much a coincidence.

"Maybe he already got involved in drugs before he died and that's why he had to fake his death."

Her face went taut with upset. "That would mean I knew him even more poorly than I thought."

"Why in Rome, then? Dobrev operates from Bulgaria."

"No idea."

"And why would Dobrev want him to rob a bank? It's not usual for drug traffickers. Did we cause more trouble for the operation than we believed?"

"We didn't cause any trouble. It was Salvatore Bosco."

My mouth tightened. With our murder investigation, we'd stumbled into a turf war between Bosco and Dobrev, where the first had played the latter into attacking his right-hand man, Melnyk. Bosco intended to take over the Mediterranean smuggling route and that had been his first move. That we knew of.

"Maybe Bosco's been disrupting Dobrev's operation longer than we think, and Dobrev's run out of money."

She spread her arms. "Then why that particular bank? It's Banco Posta, an ordinary government bank that mostly provides savings accounts and insurance. I doubt there's all that much money in the vault, even if it's the main branch."

"That is odd. Run it by me."

Her lips quirked in amusement. "You're an expert on bank robberies now?"

She knew me as a former security expert, not as a former mafia. If things went well, she'd never learn about the latter.

"I can't say I've ever robbed one…" It was true too. My criminal history involved robbing a liquor store or two in my teen years, but once I was made an enforcer, I gave up those activities. I'd had an image to uphold; people to beat up.

Her smile deepened and then disappeared. "I only know half of his plans anyway, if that. He wants me to break into the vault that has the safe deposit boxes. It runs parallel to the main vault, so I think he wants to get through the connecting wall."

I didn't know anything about robbing banks, but I knew one thing: "Drilling is too slow. And he'd have to use so much explosives it would destroy the contents of the vault."

"And possibly the ceiling above too." She sighed. "It must be something in the safe deposit boxes, then, and that can be anything. But unless it's raw diamonds or similar, I don't know what could be profitable enough."

I drummed the table, running possibilities in my mind. "A government bank, you said?" She nodded. "Then maybe he's stealing government secrets."

Her eyes narrowed as she considered it. "That's the only possible explanation. A smuggling operation might need that kind of intel. But would a government have classified information in a bank vault and not their own archives?"

I shrugged. "I've never done espionage either. But whatever the target, I'm pretty sure it's in the safe deposit boxes."

"Well, it doesn't matter much anyway. Because I can't get into that vault."

My phone rang, startling us both. "It's Laila."

"Don't tell her I'm here."

The request surprised me, but I only nodded as I answered the phone.

"I'm sorry to call this early," Laila said, sounding apologetic. "I hope I didn't wake you?"

"No, I'm finishing my breakfast," I assured her. "What's up?"

"I made a search of flight manifests, and it turns out Ada flew to Rome on Friday."

My brows shot up—not for the news, but that she'd been worried enough to track Ada. "She's in Rome?"

Ada's eyes grew large, but she managed to keep from exclaiming aloud.

"Yes. I don't have access to hotels though, and since you're already there, I was wondering if you could look around?"

"I absolutely will," I assured her, even though it would've been an impossible task for me if I didn't already know where Ada was. There were hundreds of hotels in Rome and none of them volunteered information about their guests—except the one we were staying at, apparently. "But I can't promise fast results."

She sighed. "Should I alert the police, then?"

"That's a bit premature, don't you think," I said hastily. The last thing we needed was the police actively looking for Ada when she was about to rob a bank. "Maybe she's only having an overly long weekend. Maybe she's fallen so madly in love with a handsome Italian fellow she's forgotten the time and place." I winked at Ada, who rolled her eyes but smiled too.

"She wouldn't go AWOL for something like that," Laïla said, her tone admonishing.

"You're right, but give me a couple of days before calling the police. I can't devote my full time for this, you know. I'll call you if I'm unable to find anything."

"You have until Thursday. Then I'm putting a missing person alert on her."

"I'll find her before that."

That I could guarantee.

"SHE'S PERFECTLY CAPABLE of launching a search for me if I don't contact her soon," Ada said with a sigh after I finished the call.

"She is your friend," I said warmly, but I shuddered inside. It was a reminder that I couldn't disappear on these people or I'd be hunted with the same determination.

She covered her eyes with tight fists, aggravated. "I've been so careful, never giving her a reason to doubt me, and now Danny has destroyed that trust. Even if I manage to get myself clear of this, Laïla will always be on edge whenever I leave town from now on."

"You'll have to stop safe-cracking for a while."

She lowered her hands and faced me. "Reputation is key in my line of business. If I disappear, I'll have to start anew."

Since I was preparing to disappear to start a completely new life, again, I could sympathize.

"Return home with me, right now," I pleaded, even though I didn't have a home to return to. "We'll claim the video is a deepfake if Danny actually sends it to your boss."

But she shook her head. "Laïla is an expert on deepfakes. She'll know. She might lie for me, though it's not her style, but she'd know."

And that would be the end of their friendship.

"Then we'll disappear. Change our identities and live on our savings in a tropical paradise somewhere." I was amazed how tempting it sounded, but she gave me a slow look that didn't brook argument.

"I'd be a hunted criminal for the rest of my life. And if my integrity is questioned, they might open all the cases I've been working on at Interpol and challenge them. Criminals would go free."

I wasn't sure that would happen, but I let it be. "I'll have to destroy the video, then."

She straightened, startled. "How would you do that? Why would you do that?"

I leaned closer to her for emphasis. "Because you're my friend. And friends help each other." It would be the last favor I did for her before disappearing. "As for how … I have no idea. Maybe I'll steal Danny's phone or something."

"He's not easy to fool." Her shoulders slumped. "I'd best get back in the bathroom before he shows up. Can you put the room back the way it was?"

I hated that I had to leave her at the mercy of her captor, but there was no point in saving her if it only ended up destroying her life.

"Just remember that I'm in the adjoining room the whole time. If things get bad, scream and I'll come."

She gave me a small smile that almost broke my resolve to leave her here. It was such a far cry from the confident woman I'd come to know.

"Thanks. Be careful. He has an armed guy with him. *Enzo.*"

My hand went to my side where I was used to carrying, only to come up empty. I'd have to remedy that.

Ada went to the bathroom and I moved the bed back the way it had been. Then I cleared the table and pulled the curtains back across the windows, but I left the balcony door open a little. Maybe Danny wouldn't notice.

I took the breakfast tray with me as I exited to the hallway and left it outside my room so that Danny wouldn't realize it had come from Ada's. In my room, I dug the pocket-sized 9mm handgun I'd taken from Melnyk's yacht from my bag. I made sure it was loaded, put the safety on, and slipped it in the inside pocket of my linen blazer. It wasn't an easy draw, but it wouldn't be noticed there. This wasn't exactly a concealed carry country—or an open carry one for that matter.

Feeling better now that I was armed, I went to the balcony, placed a deck chair as close to the partition between the rooms as I was able, and took a seat. I didn't have long to wait, maybe fifteen minutes, before I heard the sound of the bed being moved in the adjacent room. A man spoke, but I couldn't hear the words, and I cursed. I should've opened the door more.

I was contemplating a stealth operation onto Ada's balcony to remedy it when the voices came closer and I could hear what was being said.

"Really, you have no idea what she's capable of if I don't show up at work for the second day in a row," Ada was saying. "It's Interpol we're talking about. You really don't want them to launch a missing person's search when you're trying to pull a heist."

"You're not getting your phone back," Danny said. His voice was low and firm, and it had an accent I placed to industrial towns of Northwestern England, based on British detective series.

"I'm not giving you access to it either," Ada stated. "Just give me the phone. You can watch and make sure I don't do anything stupid with it."

"What would you even say to her that would sound believable?"

"I don't know. That I've fallen head over heels in love with a charming Italian and I need to see it through?"

Her use of the story I'd come up with made me smile, but Danny growled. "I'm your husband and you're not having a romance."

"My husband is dead. I don't know who you are. Now, give me the phone." Apparently, he complied, because the next thing Ada said was, "You could've kept it charged."

"Just send the message."

"Oh, we're beyond messaging at this point…" There was a pause while she clearly rummaged for the charger. Then she spoke in a louder voice. "Why are you pointing the gun at me for?"

I tensed. Was that my cue to barge in? But if the gun was pointed at her, he might shoot her before I could kill him.

"Insurance."

That was in a different voice, speaking in accented English, so likely the armed guard, Enzo. I couldn't take both him and Danny before they hurt Ada. Squeezing the armrests of the chair, I stayed put.

"And put it on speaker."

Ada huffed and I judged it to mean she wasn't afraid and I didn't need to act yet. A moment later, Laïla's delighted screech came through the phone.

"Ada! Where are you? I've been worried sick."

"I'm sorry. I've been … undercover."

"Ada…" Laïla admonished her. "You're not a field operative."

What most people didn't know was that Interpol didn't go after the criminals themselves and they couldn't make any arrests. They analyzed data, acted as liaisons between law enforcement agencies of different countries, and asked the local law to make arrests.

"I know, but I had a lead that was too good not to follow."

"Is it about the drug trafficker case?"

"Yes."

I nodded to myself, impressed. It was probably the only story Laïla would believe. And if we were right about Danny, it was even true. I was in Rome because of the same case, though for more personal reasons.

"Has it led to anything?"

"Not yet, but I have a new lead. I need a couple of days. Can you cover for me, pleeeease?" Ada pleaded like a schoolgirl who didn't want her friend to nark on her to the teacher.

Laïla's sigh was audible through the speaker. "I don't know… What would I even say? You won't get time off to do criminal investigation."

"Tell Laurent I went to London to see my mom and now I have pneumonia."

"He'll want to see the sick note from the doctor."

"I'll think of something."

Laila sighed again. "Fine. But you owe me. And I don't like how you've taken up these investigations. They're illegal, and dangerous."

"I'll be careful. And I definitely owe you. I'll be back by Monday."

"You'd better be. And you'd better call Eliot."

"Eliot?" Ada's voice broke, as if she hadn't known I was here.

"He's in Rome and I asked him to look for you."

"How did you know I'm here?"

Laila huffed, amused. "Because I'm brilliant. Call him."

"I will."

The call ended and I heard the unmistakable sound of a gun being cocked. I guess it hadn't been primed before, but since it was now, it didn't really make me think better of Enzo.

"Why didn't you speak English?" Enzo asked, and I realized the women had spoken French. Apparently he didn't.

And neither did Danny. "What did she say?"

"She would've been suspicious if I had used English, because she's French," Ada said, sounding amazingly calm for a woman with a gun pointed at her. "And she promised to tell my boss I have pneumonia. But I have to be back to work by Monday."

"We'll be done before that. Now, let's go."

Hearing that, I exited the balcony and hurried silently to my door to be ready to follow them. Or perhaps I should go to the lobby ahead of them…

I was about to open my door when the door to Ada's room opened. I pressed my ear against the door to hear them pass, and almost had my eardrum burst when there was a sudden knock on it.

I waited a heartbeat to recover and to not reveal that I was standing right behind the door, and then I yanked it open.

A man was standing outside, older and a bit shorter than me, dressed in jeans and a T-shirt. Behind him stood a larger Italian fellow, pointing a weapon at me.

The first man sneered. "Eliot Reed, I presume."

6

ADA

THE STUNNED LOOK ON ELIOT'S face would've been comical if the situation hadn't been so dire. I stood tense, prepared to act if he did. Enzo was armed, but I'd seen Eliot in action and he was good. He was as big as Enzo and had half a head and a lot of muscle on Danny. I had a first dan black belt in ju-jitsu. Between the two of us, we could take them.

But Eliot only spread his arms in a calming fashion, which opened his linen blazer as if to show he wasn't carrying a weapon underneath it; a very American thing to do. No perp I'd arrested back when I was working for the Metropolitan Police ever thought to voluntarily show what they had under their clothes, as concealed carry wasn't a thing in the UK.

He glanced at me over Danny's shoulder and his brows shot up as if he was surprised to see me. I hadn't known he was such a good actor.

"Ada? Why are you here? What is going on?"

If he was going to pretend, he could've pretended we didn't know each other, but it was too late for that. I only shrugged apologetically as Enzo gestured with his gun for Eliot to back up into his room. We followed, and Enzo leaned against the door as if to make sure none of us escaped.

Danny pushed a bit too close to Eliot. "You do know my wife. How?"

This jealous act was getting old. If he'd behaved like this when we were married, I would've divorced him long before he had a chance to betray me.

"I … can't really say I do," Eliot said, bewildered and a bit scared, still holding his hands slightly up. "She's teaching a self-defense class I've been attending."

"Yet you followed her to Rome?"

Eliot pulled straight, managing to look offended. "I did no such thing. I'm a businessman, I'm here on business."

"This isn't a business hotel."

"I didn't say I was a successful one…"

I had to bite the inside of my cheek to stifle a laugh.

Danny's lip curled. "And you just happened to be in the same hotel as my wife?"

"I am not your wife!"

Danny didn't spare me a glance, but Eliot looked at me, baffled. "He isn't your husband?"

"No," I said with emphasis just as Danny said, "I am."

Eliot turned his attention back to Danny. "I believe it's the lady's choice," he said in an admonishing tone. Where he got the nerve, and the poker face, to pretend he didn't know exactly what was going on, I had no idea.

"Why did her friend tell her to call you?" Danny demanded, but I'd had enough.

"It's none of your bloody business who I know and what they do. You have no right to interrogate my friends."

Danny turned his face just enough to glance at me. "You're both Interpol and he's here to find you. It's definitely my business."

"He's not my colleague," I huffed, and he gave me a slow look.

"Yet he pretends his name is Reed and that he's family. The reception was delighted for our *family reunion*."

There was a twisted logic there, but Eliot shook his head. "Reed is really my name, and I'm not from Interpol. Whether we're family or not, I have no idea. It's not exactly a rare name. And us both being here is a coincidence."

Danny's jaw tightened. "I don't like coincidences. This isn't a hotel that people just randomly find."

Eliot shrugged. "Maybe it isn't a coincidence, then. Maybe I mentioned the name of the hotel when I planned to come here, and she subconsciously chose the same place, or the other way round. As for her friend, she asked me to look for Ada yesterday at the self-defense class because she knew I was coming here."

The lie was so smooth it amazed me, though I don't know why. I'd witnessed him concoct stories on the fly before.

Danny finally backed up a step, and Enzo put the weapon away. I felt my muscles relax and Eliot looked calmer too.

"Too bad you found her. Because now you're in this too," Danny said. "Pick up your bag. We're leaving."

My stomach fell. "You don't need to involve him."

"Involve me in what?" Eliot asked, curious, but Danny just gestured him to exit the room.

"I'll tell you when we get there."

Eliot gave me a questioning look, but I could only shrug. I felt bad that he was in my mess again, but since he had managed the previous time, I wasn't terribly worried. *Yet.*

We made our way out of the hotel, acutely aware of Enzo and his gun following right at our heels. The same tiny Fiat 500 was waiting for us and Enzo sat behind the wheel again. Danny opened the passenger side door and pulled the seat forward, gesturing for us to climb into the back seat. Eliot's eyes grew large.

"I don't think I'll fit…"

"You'll fit," Danny stated. The "or else" was implied.

With a sigh, Eliot folded himself in two and climbed into the back seat, the car swaying with his weight. Sitting on the same side as Enzo who was also a big man, the car was visibly tilted that way.

He looked pained as he tried to fit his legs behind the driver's seat, only to give up and stretch them to the footwell behind the passenger seat. His large bag was on his lap and he reached to take mine as well. I had to place my feet between his legs as I climbed next to him, my knees sharply bent after Danny put his seat back into its place.

"Reminds me why I hate flying…" Eliot muttered to himself. I grinned and he grinned back, the crinkles at the corners of his eyes easing my tension a little. Then mine turned to an apologetic grimace, and he gave a calm nod in return. We'd survived Dobrev. We'd survive this.

We didn't drive downriver like the previous day, but towards the Vatican and up the Gianicolo Hill, winding through the narrow medieval streets of Trastevere. A nice view over Rome opened from the top, still clear this early in the morning before the haze of the heat hid it, but I didn't pay attention. I was beginning to suspect where we were going and I didn't like it.

When the car pulled over on the circular driveway of a Renaissance villa, I knew for sure. It was the place I'd been commissioned to break into. I kept my mouth shut though as I folded out of the car, if you didn't count the slight moan of relief.

Eliot emerged rather nimbly for a man of his size and he winked at me. "Yoga."

I couldn't help smiling, which made Danny frown. He really had to ditch the jealous husband act.

I studied the villa curiously, seeing it in daylight for the first time. There were a couple of these Renaissance villas on Gianicolo, the only place in Rome where they were still up and livable, though most of them belonged to various cultural institutions.

Beautifully symmetrical, as befit the style, it was three stories tall and five windows wide, and had light pink walls—or faded terracotta—with white Doric half columns on both sides of the door and each corner. Five low steps in a half circle led to the door in the middle, and I knew from my previous visit that there was a loggia at the back with a view over Rome.

The entrance hall was dimly lit and cool. It had black and white tile floor, stucco walls painted in dark terracotta, and a wide marble staircase in the middle leading up. I was familiar with the layout of the house from my reconnaissance, and knew that the study with the safe was on the next floor.

We didn't climb there but entered a room on the right that turned out to be an elegantly furnished parlor with a wooden floor, dark green walls filled with art that made my brows shoot up and fingers itch, and a ceiling painted with rococo cherubs and pastoral scenes. The furniture was comfortably faded, formerly dark green Empire style, though likely post-war copies and not genuine early nineteenth century pieces.

A silver coffee set in art nouveau style was placed on the coffee table, and seated behind it on an armchair, facing us, was a man in a well-fitting, expensive suit. He was in his late forties with black hair combed slickly back and a gaunt face that brought out his patrician nose. He smiled, and I shivered in fear.

"Welcome, Mr. and Miss Reed."

IF I EVER WAS IN the presence of Italian mafia, he had to be it. It wasn't the man's appearance; it was the fear he ignited in me simply by being there.

He gestured at the seats and we dropped down, Eliot and I side by side on the sofa, closer than we normally would. His thigh pressed mine and the warmth comforted me.

Danny took the last armchair, trying to look at ease, but I knew him well enough to detect the tension in him. I'd known he wasn't in charge of this operation, but I was surprised to learn that the man who was wasn't Genadi Dobrev like I'd assumed but an unknown entity. My gut tightened anew.

"I must say, I'm intrigued by your presence, Mr. Reed," the man said in a conversational tone to Eliot. His English had an Italian note in it, but it was otherwise good.

Eliot startled. "You know who I am?"

I, too, had thought that the man had meant Danny with his greeting. My tension intensified.

Our host poured himself a cup of coffee, but he didn't offer us. There was only one cup anyway. I didn't mind, as the strong scent didn't make my mouth water like normally. It made me nauseous.

"I know everything." He downed the contents of the small cup in one, and then studied us over the rim. "I'm Aristide Falconi."

My bones went cold. I knew that name. He was on Interpol's most wanted criminals list. He was the biggest arms dealer in the Mediterranean, selling to warlords in Africa and terrorists in the Middle East, as well as to drug lords in Eastern Europe. He was untouchable as far as the police were concerned, his public front squeaky clean, the vassals handling the day-to-day operations. But we were keeping an eye on him.

I could've done without this close an eye.

Eliot clearly had no idea—and why would he have— because he nodded calmly. "I'm not entirely sure why I've been brought here."

"You are a surety."

Eliot's brows shot up. "For what?"

"For the cooperation of Miss Reed."

As if the video wasn't enough. But I kept my mouth shut. It had gone so dry I couldn't have spoken if I'd wanted to.

"And what is it that you want her to do?" Eliot asked.

Falconi put the empty cup back on the table. "Rob a bank."

Eliot sat still for a heartbeat. Then he threw his head back and barked a laugh. "That's a good one." He laughed for a while, then wiped his eyes and turned to me. "Can you imagine it, you robbing a bank?"

It was difficult to remember that he knew everything, the way he was acting. I cringed with a hesitant apology. "Well…"

"Well what?" He pulled straight, stunned. "You mean you're actually going to rob a bank?"

The cruel sneer on Falconi's face was chilling. "It appears you don't know everything about Miss Reed."

"I know nothing about her," Eliot said, turning back to him. "I met her a month ago at a gym. Have seen her only a couple of times since and never socially, but nothing will convince me she's a bank robber."

"In that case, it might trouble you to learn that Miss Reed is—"

"No!" The word was out before I could consider it, but it was how I would've reacted if Eliot hadn't known about me. Falconi ignored my protest.

"—a renowned cat burglar name Hummingbird."

A stunned silence fell. Eliot faced me again, studying me bewildered and disappointed, the reaction so genuine that tears of shame sprang to my eyes. It was a stark reminder of how people would regard me if they ever found out.

Then again, Eliot had known and he hadn't judged. I had no idea why, but until this moment I hadn't realized how much it meant to me.

"I see…" he said after a while. "I can't say I believe it though. And now you want to rob a bank?"

"Want is a wrong word…" I said in a dry tone.

Danny placed a phone on the coffee table and pressed play on the video there. The image was dark, but we could see the form of a woman climb a trellis onto the loggia, disable the alarm, and pick the lock on the door there. After she disappeared into the house, the person shooting the footage followed nimbly the same way, and hurried after her through a dark house. A light was on in the study, and the footage cleared, showing her expertly opening a safe. The man filming spoke and she faced him, stunned.

The video ended and Eliot gave Danny a questioning look. "Is that supposed to be Ada?"

I blinked, but didn't relax. I'd been wearing a balaclava and night vision goggles until I'd turned the lights on, and my back was turned to the camera during most of the video. But once I faced the camera, you could tell it was me. It wasn't obvious if you didn't know me, and the light was dim and the goggles on my forehead pressed my brows down and distorted my face a bit, but I couldn't risk it being shown to my boss.

Falconi nodded. "Indeed, it is. It's one way to ensure her cooperation, but I hear she's being stubborn. And that, Mr. Reed, is why we need you. You're someone she cares about."

I froze. "I barely know Eliot."

"Yet he followed you here?"

Eliot huffed and pointed at Danny. "I already told him that it's a coincidence. I'm here on business."

Falconi sneered. He pulled out a weapon, cocked it, and pointed it at Eliot's head. He gave me a cold look. "Then you won't mind if I shoot him."

"What is wrong with you? Of course I mind!" I exclaimed, horrified, almost crawling backwards on the sofa to get away from the gun. "Even if I'd only met him today, I would mind."

He lowered the weapon. "Then this will work."

Bugger.

Eliot sighed. "Just tell me, what is it exactly that you want us to do?"

7

ELIOT

Enzo took Ada and me to a room on the top floor. The gun wasn't out, but it was visible enough for us to go nicely. Danny followed, and even though he wasn't armed, I wasn't counting him out as a threat either.

The room was small and it had a slanting ceiling that reached almost to the floor, with only low strips of windows that would be impossible for even Ada to fit through. Not that anyone would be foolish enough to try climbing a straight wall three stories down without ropes.

The floor was parquet and the walls were yellow stucco that had started to crumble. There was a double bed from the '50s that looked too short for me and too narrow for two; a baroque wardrobe, and a small bathroom that was clearly a later but not a new addition, with a tiny shower I'd barely fit in, and a commode from the '70s. At least it was clean.

Danny eyed the room with his brows furrowed. "It was meant for Ada alone, but now you'll have to share. We don't have another room prepared."

He didn't sound happy about it. For a man who had abandoned his wife five years ago, he was amazingly possessive of her. But I didn't suggest he and I share a room instead. I wouldn't leave Ada alone.

"As long as you don't snore," I said to Ada, who gave me a small smile in return. She'd been incredibly tense ever since we'd been introduced to Aristide Falconi.

I was tense too. Even New York mafia were familiar with Falconi's reputation, and he was bad news. A second-generation Sicilian arms dealer, although his father had moved the base of their operations to Milan in Northern Italy where they ran a respectable casino, a money laundering front of their operation. The actual business happened elsewhere, in desert villages in Africa and the like.

My old boss, Craig Douglas, admired Falconi, which was why I knew so much about the man. Craig had even modelled his operation after Falconi's, although Craig was in the drug business. If weapons weren't so readily available in the US, he likely would've become an arms dealer too.

When he started dabbling with human trafficking, I left.

That I kept collecting crime bosses like it was a hand in poker amazed me. Maybe there was a prize if I had a royal flush of them.

I used to be the tenner, but that was behind me. Craig and his new business partner, the human trafficker Patrick Crow, were the jack and the queen, but I'd left them behind too—permanently, I hoped. I'd added Salvatore Bosco since moving to France, and had believed him to be the ace, but that now turned out to be Aristide Falconi, making Bosco the king. I hoped it was so anyway, because if there was someone even worse out there than those two, I didn't want to meet him.

I should've retired to a tropical island when I had the chance…

We dropped our bags on the bed. If Falconi's men searched them, they'd be in for a surprise, because not only did mine contain one more handgun, it held a fake ID and a prepaid phone. Enzo had confiscated my other phone, but he hadn't frisked me, so I still had my weapon.

"Let's go," Danny ordered impatiently. He didn't wait but exited the room and was halfway down the stairs before we followed.

I put my hand gently between Ada's shoulder blades, less to guide her than to assure her of my support. We were in this together.

"I hope your businesses won't suffer because of this," Ada said in a low tone. I blinked, then remembered my disguise that I'd already begun to shed. I'd have to be Eliot Reed for a little longer.

"No. It's just a startup event to make connections," I told her without a telltale pause that would've revealed I came up with the explanation then and there. I'd been to a couple of such events since I assumed my businessman persona—a man had to make a living, after all—and knew that those were held regularly. And she wouldn't be able to check whether one was held in Rome this week.

"No one knew I was attending and no one will miss me."

She nodded, then leaned closer. "Keep your guard up with Falconi."

I squeezed her shoulder in comfort as we entered a room the floor below with windows facing the street. It was more of the same faded elegance and opulence as the parlor downstairs, with walls filled with expensive art that made Ada stare in awe. A grand piano stood at one end, and in the middle was a large billiards table covered with a wooden lid, creating a table. Falconi wasn't present, which was a blessing, but Enzo was sitting by the door.

A blueprint of a bank—I presumed—was spread on the billiards table. It was held open with knickknacks placed on the corners, like a marble ashtray and a bronze statuette of a woman that was likely the most expensive item in the room, if the pained expression on Ada's face was anything to go by when she noticed it.

There were some markings on the blueprint, probably identifying cameras. I gave it a cursory look, not wanting to show any interest. It would be best if these people didn't learn about my alleged past as a security expert. They were suspicious of me as it was.

"This is the headquarters of Banco Posta," Danny said, tapping the blueprint. "I need Ada to open the door to the safe deposit vault and you're going to convince her to do it."

Ada growled, frustrated. "There isn't anything or anyone that can convince me to do it. I mean, I can get to the vault door if you absolutely want me to, and if you get me the keys, I can even open it. And then the police will come, because I can't disable the bloody security system on the vault door."

I propped a hip against the billiards table and crossed arms over my chest. I studied Ada as I mulled it over. "What do you need to be able to do it?"

My question baffled her, as if she couldn't believe I was taking Danny's side, but until we figured out how to get her out of this mess without risking her future, we'd best play along.

She spread her arms. "I don't know, an exact replica of the alarm on the door and a month to practice?"

I shot a questioning look at Danny, who shook his head. "I don't know where we'd find a replica of a custom security system, and we don't have a month."

"The straightforward approach is out, then…" I mused, racking my brain for an alternative, but I was out of my skill zone here.

"We need to get into that vault," Danny said. He sounded angry—and scared, if I wasn't mistaken. Ada detected it too, because her eyes sharpened as she studied her one-time husband.

"I thought this was about Dobrev. How did you get involved with Falconi? Are you dealing arms now?"

"None of your fucking business," Danny growled. Ada sneered.

"You're the one insisting we're still married, so prove it."

Danny leaned closer to stare down at her. "Couples don't need to share everything, you know."

"As you so elegantly demonstrated five years ago."

Ada sounded so bitter that I began to feel uncomfortable witnessing their relationship drama. I straightened and adopted a conciliatory tone. It didn't come naturally to me, but I'd had some practice mediating fights back when I ran the hotel. Kitchen staff especially were prone to fights and they had easy access to sharp objects, making it imperative that I learned fast.

"Regardless of how it happened, we're risking ourselves here for people we don't know or trust. So how about you tell us why you want to get into the vault. Is it worth it?"

Danny studied me, as if assessing my worth. I tried to look harmless, which definitely didn't come naturally to me. He glanced at Ada and then back to me. "Financially, no. In terms of our lives, as in being able to keep breathing, priceless."

"I KNEW IT!" Ada huffed. "You didn't used to be this stubborn and stupid when it came to heists. What does he have on you?"

Danny's lips curled, as if he were tasting something foul. "We tried to rob the wrong place. Falconi's men showed up. I don't know why they let me live."

"Meaning the rest of the team didn't make it?" Ada asked sharply.

Danny glanced at the ceiling, gathering himself, before nodding.

"Thom?"

Danny nodded again and Ada looked briefly sad. I recalled that Thom was the other crooked cop on their team who had faked his death with Danny, but since I wasn't supposed to know about it, I changed topic.

"I presume that this robbery isn't just a fun exercise for you to prove your worth to Falconi? That whatever is in the vault has value for him."

"He needs the contents of a specific deposit box," Danny said.

"And who owns the box?"

He spread his arms. "I have no idea. I'm not exactly a trusted insider here. Falconi needs a bank robber and that's what I am."

"He trusts you enough to operate on your own," Ada pointed out.

"Hardly." He nodded at Enzo. "Besides, Falconi knows I have nowhere to run where he couldn't find me."

As someone who used to do the hunting, I knew he was right. As someone who would be hunted if my boss knew I was alive, I could sympathize.

I turned to study the blueprints of the bank, but no matter how much I stared at them, I couldn't come up with a plan for how a person without the required skills could do the job.

"You're going about this the wrong way," I finally noted aloud. "You're thinking like a bank robber."

"I am a bloody bank robber," Danny growled.

"But Ada isn't."

He brushed my words aside. "She's robbed a few. She knows how it's done."

"But it's not what she's best at, is it. I saw the video. She was an excellent house burglar." I'd witnessed it firsthand too.

Danny gave me a slow look. "We're not robbing a house."

"We can't exactly rob a bank either."

Ada propped her elbows on the table, and leaned to study the blueprints too. "You're saying that the only way we're getting into that vault is with permission."

I nodded, pleased that she figured it out immediately. "If you can't disable the alarms, then someone needs to do it for you."

"And then I'll pick the lock on the deposit box…"

But Danny shook his head. "If it were that easy, people would be opening other people's boxes all the time. There's an alarm that will go off if it's not opened with the key. And we can't disable the alarm on the boxes in the middle of the day without it being immediately noticed. I have thought of other angles too, you know."

Ada pursed her lips, ignoring his comment. "If a key is needed, then we need to get the key." She straightened. "Who does the box belong to?"

"I told you, I have no idea," Danny said. "I'm on a need-to-know basis only."

"Well, we need to know. Find out, or at least who holds the key."

"And then what?"

"Then I'll steal the key from the owner and go with it to the bank, posing as the owner of the deposit box."

Danny gave her an annoyed look. "You need IDs to match the key too."

Ada growled, frustrated, but I nodded. "Then we'll pretend to be opening a box of our own and gain access to the vault that way."

Ada bit her lip. "I've actually already asked about opening a deposit box for a client."

"Excellent. I'll pose as your client, then."

She didn't look happy. "But then your personal information would be on record if there's an investigation about a robbed safe deposit box."

I brushed her concern aside. "There's no reason why they would suspect me for it."

"Not many people open new deposit boxes these days," she said, still not warming to the idea. "You'd be the first one they look into."

I liked that she was concerned for me, and she was right: I couldn't afford to be investigated. I scratched my beard that had begun to itch—I'd had no idea it would do that—while pretending to give it thought. "I'll need a fake ID, then."

Ada and I turned to Danny who pulled back. "I don't have contacts like that in Rome."

"I'm sure Falconi has," I said, but Ada gave me a stern look.

"We will not give him any ammunition against us."

I would disappear right after this and adopt a new identity so it wasn't much of a concern for me, but I nodded. "Fine. I'll think of something."

Danny sneered. "What, a *businessman* knows people who fake IDs?" You could practically hear the quotes around businessman, so he clearly still believed I was from Interpol.

"Of the three of us, I've never worked for any kind of law enforcement," I said with a fed-up tone. "I'm not going to go to the cops and ask for fake IDs in exchange for handing over Falconi."

Even if I did, the police wouldn't move against him with such flimsy cause. There were reasons these mafia bosses were so powerful.

"How are you going to get them, then?" Ada asked, baffled, and slightly suspicious too.

"It's amazing the kinds of people you meet at the tech start-up scene," I hedged with an easy smile. "There are some really good hackers among them, though I'm not supposed to know about it."

Ada's face cleared. "Right…"

"How soon would you be able to get the IDs?" Danny asked. I shrugged.

"I really have no way of knowing, but I'm sure I'll get them by the time we must go to the bank."

"Stealing the key and getting your IDs will slow things down," he said, frowning.

"Better to go slow than end up being caught," I said, and he sneered.

"Let's hope your IDs are good enough to avoid that, then."

I could barely keep the answering sneer off my face. Oh, they were. They so were…

8

ADA

ELIOT AND I WERE CONFINED to our room while Danny
went to talk with Falconi—or whoever here represented
him, because I doubted the man himself stuck around. I
didn't mind. It was better than staying with Enzo and his
gun in the billiards room, and it was straining to be around
Danny. I had so much I needed to say to him, to clear the
air, but the man I was dealing with felt like a stranger and
I didn't want to talk to him.

I studied the small room. The windows were towards
the neighboring villa, so the view was nothing to write
home about, but at least the house blocked the sun and
the heat, and the room was pleasantly cool.

"We should probably ask for an extra mattress," Eliot
noted, staring at the bed in dismay.

"You'd sleep on the floor?" I asked, and he grinned,
easing my tension.

He had a beautiful smile, though currently obscured
by the beard he'd grown. I didn't like how it hid his
features, but I had to admit that the neatly trimmed full
beard in slightly darker shade of chestnut than his hair—
which I'd thought was dyed but I guess not—made him
look even more handsome.

"I was hoping you'd sleep on the mattress. The bed is just about the right size for me alone."

I rolled my eyes good-naturedly but didn't argue. I didn't mind sleeping on the floor. I could move the mattress to the window and open it for extra coolness.

Eliot opened his bag and went through the contents meticulously. "I don't think they've searched this."

It hadn't even occurred to me that someone would go through our bags. My gut tensed. I had all my break-in equipment there.

Then I huffed to myself. These people already knew I was a cat burglar. I had nothing to hide.

But I hadn't thought Eliot would have.

"There's something in there you don't want them to find?"

He pulled out a phone and a charger, and I perked. "You anticipated this?"

"No one could've anticipated this." He spread his arms, as if encompassing the whole situation. "But you never know when you need a new phone fast when you're travelling. Drunken escapades with water tend to happen and pickpockets are everywhere."

We looked for a socket for the charger that Falconi's men wouldn't notice and found one behind the wardrobe. We now had a way to communicate with the outside world if the need arose. The constant ache in my gut eased a little.

"Do you have anything else useful in your bag?"

"I do indeed." With a flourish, he dug out a semiautomatic pistol that I instantly recognized. I inhaled, stunned.

"You kept Melnyk's gun?" I don't know why I was so dismayed by it. I was a criminal surrounded by worse criminals. This was no time to get hung up on legalities.

He put the gun back into his bag and began to take out toiletries and clothes, as if he were settling in. "It's a Makarov," he said like that justified it. The name didn't mean anything to me, and it wasn't the point here anyway.

"I don't care. You should've handed it in."

His lips quirking, he slipped a hand into the inner pocket of his linen jacket and gave me a glimpse of a small 9mm. "I guess I shouldn't have kept this one either, then."

My mouth dropped open. "You've been armed the whole time?"

"Yep. Good thing your husband didn't search me."

"He's not my husband," I said automatically. His answering smile was slow, his gaze heating as he measured me.

"Good."

I had to fight the full-body flush his appreciative look ignited. "Since we're not sharing the bed, it doesn't matter."

He glanced at the double bed and then back at me. "I could be made to change my mind…"

The temptation was real. I hadn't been with anybody in years, and I'd been fantasizing about his body and what it could do ever since we shared a shower in our hotel in Monaco, a necessity at the time. But he hadn't contacted me since, and I'd convinced myself he wasn't as interested in my body as I was in his.

I guess I'd been wrong.

"Why didn't you call me, or answer my calls?"

I hadn't realized I was about to ask it before the question was out. I hadn't even thought that it mattered to me, after having convinced myself that he was laying low to avoid Bosco.

His grimace was awkward, the look uncharacteristic. "I … may have to leave Lyon soon. I didn't want to start anything I can't make good of."

My heart stopped beating. "Leave?" My voice caught and I cleared my throat. "Why? Where?"

He glanced down. "Home. I … probably should've gone already. My … mother is poorly. But I needed to wrap things up here first."

"I'm … sorry to hear that. You're not coming back?"

He shook his head and it felt like a gut punch. "It's dementia. Who knows how long it'll take her, and I'm the only one who can look after her."

I realized I knew nothing about him. "You don't have siblings?"

"I have a sister, but she has children and a full-time job. I'm free and I have money to keep going even if I don't work for a while. It's still cheaper than putting Mom into a care home. Though it might come to that in the end anyway."

The excitement I'd felt about the shared bed was wiped away. "You're a good son."

He made a face and I felt like there was a story behind it. "Hardly." He glanced at the bed again as if reading my mind. "So … it's a no on the bed?"

His smile was wistful, but I liked that he didn't pressure me. "I think that's best. No need to complicate matters."

"Sex isn't complicated," he said, but I knew he couldn't mean it. He would've called me when we returned from Monaco otherwise and we would've slept together already, even if he knew he was leaving.

I looked around, desperate for a change of topic. My gaze landed on the door. "I could easily pick that." Enzo had locked the door on the outside, but it was an old lock, easily opened with even rudimentary tools.

"I probably could too," Eliot admitted. I gave him a curious look.

"It's a skill that a security expert needs?"

He shrugged. "More often than you'd think. But let's leave the door locked for now. We might have to make an escape eventually, and it's best if they don't see us a flight risk until then."

Good point.

"So … what shall we do meanwhile?" I asked and he gave the bed a suggestive look, wiggling his brows. I grinned. "Other than that."

"Shame."

It really was.

We sat on the bed anyway on our respective sides, as it was the only place to sit. "So … it's not Dobrev after all," I noted, turning to face him over the bed. He grimaced.

"Falconi isn't better news."

My brows shot up. "You know who Falconi is?"

"I used to be in the security business," he reminded me, as if that explained it. But it didn't, unless…

"Were you one of those contractors that work for the military in Iraq and Afghanistan?" That would explain so much. But to my disappointment, he shook his head.

"No, but we had connections to those people. Maybe Danny has too?"

I pursed my lips. "He said he was blackmailed into this like I am. But his moniker was on those papers we found on Fabre."

He scratched his beard. He did it a lot, as if it annoyed him. "Could Dobrev have sent him to steal something from Falconi, only for Danny to get caught?"

"As a commissioned burglar?" He shrugged and I gave it thought. "Could be. That would explain why he didn't recognize Dobrev's name and why Dobrev only hand his moniker. I don't usually know who's commissioning me."

He leaned against the headboard and closed his eyes as if about to take a nap. "Well, whatever the reason, he's as stuck here as we are."

I sighed. He was right. But unlike Danny, I had something to lose if I didn't get out of here, and fast.

WE WERE RELEASED for lunch. A late lunch, but at least they were feeding us. We'd whiled the day away by watching videos on Eliot's phone, though we had to keep it on mute and put on captions. It was mindless entertainment, but I'd spent two days bound to a bed, my mind churning in circles. Anything was improvement to that.

My stomach was growling as I followed Danny and Eliot to a dining room on the ground floor. It was a smallish room at the back with a mahogany table seating eight and a view over Rome, though the afternoon haze had already obscured the hills in the distance.

"Does Falconi own this house?" I asked, curious. The man or his guards weren't present, which made me braver.

Danny shrugged. "I have no idea. I didn't ask and he didn't volunteer information. But would a capo wanted by the law really live in the middle of Rome where everyone can find him? Or have his name on the deed?"

I'd forgotten that Danny had been a cop too, and tended to think like one, though he'd been at the Specialist Firearms Command and not a detective like me.

"Falconi has a good, law-abiding front. But whoever owns this place has a lot of money and good taste in art."

He sneered. "Art's always been your thing."

"Money is yours."

He didn't say anything to that.

Lunch was simple, Italian, and so good it was likely prepared by a cook. "Did they fetch this from a restaurant?" I asked Danny, enjoying the taste of delicious pasta carbonara.

"No. There's an in-house chef working for Falconi."

Of course there was.

Eliot looked curiously pained as he ate, taking small portions and chewing every mouthful carefully, as if he had to work for it. Finally, I couldn't keep silent anymore. "Don't you like pasta?"

"I *love* Italian food," he said with a moan. "If I don't watch myself, I'll lose all control and blow up like a balloon."

He didn't look like a man who had to watch what he ate, but then again, a perfect body like his didn't exactly happen on its own. I hoped he wasn't starving himself on purpose. I'd been a gymnast as a child and unhealthy eating habits had been common there. I wanted to tell him he'd be just as fine if he were bigger, but it was none of my business.

"In that case, Italy probably isn't the best place for you," I said dryly, making him laugh.

"I guess I'm a glutton for punishment too."

Danny finished first and pushed his plate aside. "What do you need for your fake IDs?" he asked Eliot.

"My phone."

"I can't let you contact the outside world," Danny huffed. "Think another way."

Eliot gave him a steady look. "This isn't exactly my area of expertise, you know. Or my town."

"Then you'll just have to go with your own ID."

Eliot pursed his lips. He didn't look happy, but he nodded. "Fine."

I wasn't happy about it either, but we couldn't risk him getting caught acquiring fake IDs either.

"Do you have any information about the owner of the safe deposit box?" I asked Danny, who nodded.

"I know where he lives but not his name. We'll go case the place tonight and plan a house burglary instead of a bank heist. That should be right up your alley."

It was. I felt better about this ordeal already.

After lunch, we returned to the billiards room to study the map of Rome on a laptop. The house I would break into was in Parioli, an affluent neighborhood upriver where the Tiber made a hard turn to the east. The area was filled with large villas in various styles from the seventeenth century baroque to nineteenth century revivals as well as postwar estates made to look like them. A couple of huge parks gave the area a verdant look.

There were also several embassies, one right next to the house that was our target. I made a face, pointing at it. "That's going to mean extra surveillance." Some embassies had a military presence too, but fortunately it was an embassy of a small country that probably wouldn't.

"They're only a problem if they're willing to release the security footage," Danny dismissed my concern.

"Embassies aren't as against helping local law as movies give to understand, especially if the matter doesn't concern them."

Eliot placed a hand on my shoulder as he studied the satellite image. I wanted to lean on him, the strain of the past days starting to get to me, but I steeled myself. I'd best not get used to relying on him, since he was leaving.

I couldn't rely on anyone. Danny had taught me that lesson well.

"All these back gardens are connected," Eliot noted. Not only were the houses large, they had large gardens too. "The fences between them look low and scalable, and there are plenty of trees and shrubs to offer cover."

I also tended to forget that Eliot was a security expert. He would be more helpful planning this than I'd anticipated.

"That could be a good route to approach," I said, nodding. "But we need to get closer to check the security on the ground floor doors."

"And to find out whether the whole house belongs to one family," he added. "Most of these old villas have been divided into apartments."

The terracotta baroque villa was huge: four stories tall plus one below ground, six windows wide, and almost as deep. It could have several apartments.

"So how do we find the correct apartment if we don't even know the name of the owner?"

We turned to Danny, who shrugged. "Let's worry about that once we find out if it's divided or not."

Since none of us wanted to go to Falconi to ask more details, we nodded and turned back to the satellite images and Street View.

Eliot pointed at the screen. "The wall on this side looks easy enough to climb. Maybe you could enter through that balcony."

"I am not scaling a wall that high in the dark. Besides, it's towards the embassy."

"That tree blocks the view."

"Provided it's still there. This image is two years old."

We studied the map for a long time, but the second-floor balcony seemed to be the only option, unless the doors had old alarm systems.

"What are the chances that the house belongs to an institution or similar that doesn't care for security all that much and doesn't occupy it at night?" I asked Danny, who shrugged.

"I have no idea. All I know is that the key to the safe deposit box is there."

"And you just happened to find that out in such a short time?"

He sneered. "People like Falconi get the information they need. Screw a few thumbs, grease a few palms. You know how it goes."

Right…

"Suppose they couldn't intimidate a blueprint out of their contacts as well?" Eliot asked, not at all fazed by Danny's colorful description. "If it's a one-family house, the key could be anywhere. We need a way to narrow down the search."

I pursed my lips, thinking. "We have the address. We can take the official approach." Two baffled faces turned to me and I smiled. "It's a historical building. The blueprints are bound to be in the state archives."

Danny glanced at his wristwatch. "We'd best get going, then."

IT TOOK A BIT OF googling to figure out which building belonging to the state archives held the historical blueprints. It turned out to be a huge sixteenth century palazzo built for Pope Gregorius XIII. It was near Piazza Navona, down the hill and across the river by the Vatican, a fifteen-minute drive according to the GPS. But nothing ever went that fast in Rome.

"I hope they don't ask for references," I muttered as we sat stuck in traffic.

At least we were in a proper size car this time, a black Audi with a more comfortable sitting position, if not exactly ample room for Eliot's legs. Danny had to sit in the back with us, with me stuck in the middle, because Enzo was driving, and there was an additional guard who sat at the front. He was a tight looking man in his late twenties with fashionable black hair and a beard shaped with geometrical precision. He wasn't openly carrying— his black T-shirt was so form hugging it couldn't have hidden a needle—but that didn't mean there wasn't a weapon in the pocket of his cargos.

"Can't you use your Interpol credentials?" Eliot asked, and I grimaced.

"I guess I could, but if there's an investigation about the break-in, it'll come back to bite me in the buttocks."

"Why would there be?"

"I haven't lasted this long in this business by taking unnecessary chances," I said with a pointed look. He dipped his chin, agreeing with me.

"Shouldn't you have worn a disguise, then?"

Danny perked and I grimaced, but Eliot looked calm, as if he hadn't indicated that he knew I wore those all the time.

"I wear them occasionally," I said lightly. "But I didn't bring any for the job I came here to do." I'd travelled with my own name and passport even. I usually did, as I couldn't risk getting caught using false IDs.

"Maybe we could get you a disguise for the bank."

"I already went in with my own face. But we'll need a disguise for you," I reminded him. "Did you bring a good suit? Because I let the clerk at the bank to understand that my client is a very rich, very important man."

He groaned, as if pained. "I had to leave it behind. The start-up scene is relaxed. You see hoodies more than suits."

"We'll have to go shopping, then."

That cheered him. "Maybe an Armani…"

"You'll never get an Armani suit fitted for you this fast," Danny noted. Eliot nodded, resigned.

"Off the rack it is, then."

9

ELIOT

THE ARCHIVES BUILDING WAS huge. It took an entire large block, the high outer walls toward the streets plain stone and mostly windowless, as if it was a fortress built to resist a siege. All the beauty was hidden within. A modest gate through the western wall led to a vast, paved courtyard that was surrounded by a many-tiered cloister like a medieval monastery. It even came with a church at the other end.

"How are we supposed to find anything here?"

Ada and I were standing in the middle of the courtyard, our mouths hanging open as we tried to take the place in. Tourists were swarming around us, taking photos. I was itching to take one myself, but without my phone that I'd left in our room, I couldn't.

Even if I'd had it with me, I couldn't have taken it out as it would've been confiscated.

"I'm pretty sure they won't let us go look by ourselves," Ada said as Danny propped a hand at her back to prompt her to move on.

I was surprised that the guard accompanying us— Enzo had called him Ciro, though he hadn't been officially introduced—had allowed all three of us to come here. If I were him, I would've left me with Enzo in the car as the surety I was supposed to be or back at the villa. But he was young. He'd learn.

Then again, at his age I was already my boss's most trusted man. This one was more flash than brains in his too-small black T-shirt that squeezed his muscles and gave a peek at a tattoo on his shoulder.

There was a museum shop on the left and we headed there. A quick enquiry sent us back across the courtyard to an old oaken door under the cloister that almost disappeared into the wall. It was locked; annoying, but smart of them, if they didn't want all the tourists randomly walking in.

Ada pressed the call button and a moment later a fed-up-looking older man in a museum usher's uniform opened the door. He glared at us from beneath bushy, graying brows and demanded to know what we wanted in Italian.

"Do you speak English?" Ada asked politely.

"No," the man said, ready to pull the door closed. I stepped forward and addressed him in Italian.

"We're not tourists, we're here to conduct research in the library. Could we get in?"

"Appointment only."

Shit.

I relayed it to Ada, who sighed and took out her Interpol ID from her shoulder bag. "It's police business," she said in English, showing it to the man. I translated, embellishing a little to give the man to understand that it was an urgent matter. He grumbled, but stepped aside and pulled the door open.

"It's on you if the archivist throws you out."

I nodded my thanks and made to follow Ada in, when Ciro pulled me to a halt. "Metal detectors," he said, pointing at the foyer. "I can't go in."

I spotted the weapon in the cargo pocket of his pants. "Maybe they're security gates to stop people from stealing priceless books," I suggested, although I was carrying too and couldn't risk going in.

"Or maybe they're there for guns. I can't let you in without me," he countered.

"Ada has to go in," I reminded him, and he gave it a brief thought.

"She goes; you two stay." He didn't look happy, but he couldn't make a scene.

Ada turned to look at what kept us and I nodded at her. "You go alone, we'll be waiting in the museum shop."

Her brows shot up, but she didn't argue and just went in alone before the usher changed his mind and threw all of us out.

Danny sneered at me as we crossed the courtyard. "I would've thought you'd insist on going with her."

I shot him a puzzled look "You really believe we're closer than we say we are?"

"I believe you're her colleague and ready to protect her."

The last part was true anyway.

"What is it about me that makes you believe I'm a cop?"

I genuinely wanted to know. I'd been automatically profiled as a criminal since my teen years, which had led to dozens of altercations with the cops, whether I'd done anything or not. The change was baffling, even if I'd worked hard to achieve it.

He swept his gaze up and down my body. "It's either that or ex-military. I know a killer when I see one."

Fair enough.

"I've never been a soldier either," was all I said as we entered the museum shop. I wasn't interested in anything they had to sell, but Ada might take a while to return, and it was something to occupy myself with.

Moreover, it was air-conditioned. The courtyard was baking in the late afternoon sun, the stone walls and paved courtyard reflecting the heat. I would've taken off my linen blazer, but since my gun was in its inner pocket, not to mention my passport and wallet, I didn't dare to, in case they came tumbling out.

Soon though, the sanctuary was invaded by tourists when a busload of my fellow countrymen swarmed in. As a former hotel manager, I was used to masses of Americans on holiday, but Danny's face darkened as he listened to them make loud comments on everything on display. I thought it best we exited the shop before he, or Ciro, lost his temper.

"Bloody hell but I hate Americans…" Danny muttered.

"Gee, thanks," I said dryly, but his mouth only quirked and he didn't apologize.

I guess I wasn't his favorite person either.

We moved a little away from the shop and the tourists, and leaned against the relatively cool wall of the cloister where the sun didn't reach. Danny took out his phone and soon became absorbed by it, but without my phone I had nothing to do except observe the people and think.

I'd come to Rome to hunt down Salvatore Bosco, but obviously that would have to wait. It wasn't like he knew I was coming for him, so I wasn't inconveniencing him in any way. Besides, the lead I had on his whereabouts simply pointed at the offices of one of his legitimate side-businesses, and he probably wasn't even here but on his yacht. I could take my time and see this through, and the moment I had a chance to take Ada safely away, I would.

Then I would change my identity and lay low for a while to avoid Falconi. Bosco would have to wait.

Ada emerged from the archives, and Danny and I straightened to cross the courtyard to her, Danny pushing the phone into the back pocket of his jeans and me tugging my shirt back in place. She looked satisfied, so I presumed her task had been successful. But we couldn't talk here.

The place was closing and the ushers were herding the several busloads of tourists out. The gate was maybe three people wide and the mass exodus was too much for it, creating a blockage that slowed us down.

"Keep an eye on your bags," the loud, shrill voice of a woman shouted, the sound echoing underneath the cloister. "This is exactly the kind of place where pickpockets like to hunt."

I would've been embarrassed for my countrywoman's suspicions if the taxi driver hadn't warned me of the same thing: "They're especially active in the Vatican."

Not even the Holy City was sacred.

The throng sucked us towards the door, jostling us from both sides. Heeding the lady's command, and knowing from experience how pickpockets operate, I kept a hold on the lapel of my blazer, my arm pressed against the inner pocket where the gun was. The last thing anyone needed was a pickpocket getting their hands on it in this crowd.

We were already near the gate when a commotion broke out at the entrance. A lady tripped on the steps down to the street, which made people either step in to help her or halt and step back as not to trample on her. The ripple effect was large, and the people in front of me were pushing against me as they retreated. I wrapped an arm around Ada to steady her, but people behind us trying to get through pushed me against Danny.

And you know how opportunity makes a thief…

"YOU TOOK YOUR sweet time," Enzo grumbled when we finally reached the car. "Twenty more minutes and I would've gone."

"No, you wouldn't have," Danny countered. "Because your boss would kill you if you let us disappear."

Enzo yanked the manual shift in answer, making the gears shriek. That was no way to treat an Audi.

Traffic hadn't eased at all while we were away. If anything, it was even worse. It didn't help that Piazza Navona was full of tourists whose buses were waiting for them and blocking the narrow streets.

"So, how did it go?" Danny asked Ada, who smiled. For all that she was here against her will, she was starting to enjoy this. Planning a break-in really suited her.

"It took some digging, but I got what I needed. And the good news is, the house isn't divided into flats, so we don't have to find out who the key belongs to before going in."

Danny nodded. "Good. We'll study the blueprints, and once the sun sets, we'll head there for some recon."

"We're not breaking in tonight?" I asked. Ada pursed her lips as she gave it thought.

"We'll see. If the place is empty, maybe…"

And if it wasn't … well, then this became more complicated.

As we approached the main street, I spotted a familiar bank by it in the opposite direction of where we would head. When I was preparing for my exit from Craig's organization, I'd created one contingency plan after another. I had money and IDs hidden all over the world in safe deposit boxes. And in Rome, that bank held one of them.

"Do you know what we need?" I said aloud as an idea took form. "A practice run."

"Practice for what?" Danny demanded to know, turning to glower at me. I pointed at the bank.

"How to open a safe deposit box. And that branch is still open."

He didn't look convinced. "How difficult can it be? You ask to open one, and you open it."

I shrugged. "It's the main weak point in our plan so far. But fine…"

Danny growled, but he directed Enzo to head to the bank instead, which he did, reluctantly. "Signor Falconi won't like this…"

"Then don't fucking tell him."

Enzo pulled over outside the bank and I exited the car. Ada and Danny did the same, as did Ciro. I lifted a hand to halt him. "I'm not marching into a bank with an armed man."

"You're not going there alone either," Ciro stated.

"Then ditch the gun." As if I wasn't carrying.

To my amazement, he complied, throwing the weapon rather carelessly on the front seat. "No funny business and no trying to run." He pointed at Danny. "And you stay in the car."

I guess he could be made to learn after all.

It was cool and dim inside the bank after the early evening heat. I paused to look around, as if I hadn't been here before. Then I addressed Ciro. "You wait here. It's best we don't go in as a group."

He glowered at me but took a seat on a wooden bench by the door and picked up a newspaper someone had left.

I led Ada to the counter that handled the safe deposit boxes. "Do we try the same routine we'll do in the real bank?" she asked. "You a businessman, and me your assistant?"

I glanced at her, but kept my face and gestures neutral, just in case Ciro was watching us. "No. Just follow my lead and don't look suspicious."

I felt her tense next to me, but her step didn't falter. In times like these, it was good to be paired with a person who knew how to improvise.

The clerk behind the counter was a woman who had handled my affairs before and she smiled when she spotted me, addressing me in Italian. "Signor Reed, *buona sera.*"

That she recognized me even with the beard was problematic, but it was an issue for later.

"*Buona sera, signorina.* I'd like to visit my safe deposit box," I told her in English. She gave a curious look at Ada and I smiled warmly. "This is Signora Reed." The truth, even if she wasn't my wife.

The woman's brows shot up and her smile turned more professional. "Would you like to add her as a person who has access to the safe deposit box?"

I gave it a quick thought and nodded. "Excellent idea." Who knew, she might need the contents one day.

I took out my wallet that held the key to the safe deposit box, and a passport from the inside pocket of my blazer, careful not to disturb the weapon there, and passed them to the clerk. Then I nodded at Ada.

"Give her your passport, dear."

Her eyes grew large at the endearment, but she just smiled and dug out her passport from her shoulder bag. The clerk took our passports and turned to click her computer to check my ID against the number on the key and add Ada there too.

A moment later, the printer behind her spewed out a paper and she handed it over for us to sign. We did as we were asked and she gave Ada a key of her own. Then she rose.

"This way, please."

I could practically feel Ciro's eyes on my back as Ada and I followed the woman to the basement of the bank. The vault was as I remembered, and much more modern than the one in Banco Posta, because it was opened with a code on the keypad that the woman entered with ease of practice.

The door opened automatically on silent hinges, and she gestured for us to enter. She followed us in, and entered another code on a pad there. One of the hundreds of narrow doors filling the walls opened at the other end of the vault, and she nodded before stepping out of the vault.

"You may access your deposit box now."

We walked to the open door. I pulled out the steel box from its slot and placed it on the long table that ran through the room. I took my key and inserted it in the keyhole. Then I hesitated.

"Could you please turn around?"

Ada startled and turned her back to me in a hurry. "Sorry. I'm still reeling from the fact that you have a deposit box here. I didn't come to think you might not want me to see the contents."

"Well, you have a key now, so if you're ever curious…" I muttered, opening the lid.

Inside, there was about twenty thousand in euros and dollars, a weapon, a phone, and a couple of passports, driver's licenses, and credit cards with matching names and nationalities. I selected the passport I wanted and other IDs going with it, and slipped them into the already full inside pocket. Then I took a wad of euros and put them in my pants pocket. Cash might come in handy.

I contemplated taking the gun and the phone, but left them. I might need them later, if Falconi's men found the current ones.

Before closing the lid, I took from my pants pocket what I'd pickpocketed earlier, and put it in the box with a smug smirk. I locked the box, put it back in its slot, and closed the door. It was as secure as the bank could make it, provided no entrepreneurial people with ill intent showed up. Other than us, I mean.

Five minutes later, we were back in the car. "Well, was it necessary?" Danny asked with a sneer.

"Yes," Ada and I said in unison. She continued.

"Turns out the key only opens an actual box that's behind a door of the pigeonhole. The clerk opens the door. In this bank, it's with a keycode."

Danny furrowed his brows. "Is it a different code for each box?"

"Could be, as only one door opened," I said, and Danny cursed. Ada didn't look discouraged though.

"But in Banco Posta, they didn't have electronic anything inside the vault, so we don't need the code to the door we want opened. It could be that the client's key opens both, or maybe the clerk opens the door for the client with a universal key."

"And we can easily lift the key from the clerk," I said, nodding.

Danny gave me a contemptuous look. "You know how to pick pockets?"

Did I ever...

"I was kind of hoping Ada does," I said with a calm smile. She shrugged.

"Not very well, but I'll do it if we must."

We returned to the villa relatively fast, the traffic having eased a little. The dinner wasn't set yet—they served it late in this country, and who could eat in this heat anyway—so we climbed to the billiards room.

"Show us the blueprints of the villa," Danny ordered Ada.

"They emailed it to me, so I'll need the laptop."

"You gave them your Interpol email address?" he asked, stunned.

"I pretended to be there for Interpol," she said, sounding fed-up. "What else was I supposed to do?"

"I don't know, take photos of the blueprints?"

She threw her arms in the air in a huff. "I didn't have my phone, did I, because someone confiscated it."

"You could've borrowed mine," he stated, putting a hand in the back pocket of his jeans, only to come up empty.

"Where the fuck is my phone?"

10

ADA

DANNY WAS GLOWERING AT US, as if it was our fault that he'd lost his phone. "Where did you use it last?" I asked in a reasoning tone.

"The car?" Eliot suggested, but Danny shook his head, then gave it a thought.

"I had it in the archives."

Eliot tensed. "Did you keep it in your back pocket?" When Danny nodded, he cursed. "In a place full of stupid tourists that lure pickpockets in troves?"

My heart stopped beating. "You had your phone stolen?" I inhaled. "With my video on it? Which is now in the hands of criminals who won't hesitated to use it?"

Danny actually looked stricken. Maybe he wasn't as big a bastard as I'd thought.

"And other stuff that will get me behind bars," he said, running an aggravated hand through his hair.

Or maybe he was.

Before I could launch into a tirade about his recklessness, Eliot made a calming gesture with his hand. "You're both cops. You know professional pickpockets don't try to access the phones. They're emptied, returned to factory settings, and sold on."

"And how would you know it, not being a cop," Danny snided.

"I'm from New York."

I snorted a laugh, feeling a bit better. And then Eliot ruined it: "And you have the contents of your phone on the cloud anyway."

I was ready to hyperventilate, but Danny gave Eliot a slow look. "I don't know if you're a cop, but you're not much of a criminal. Would I be so stupid that I'd save anything in a system that any judge can order access to if cops ask for it?"

He was right. I didn't use cloud services either. But before I could relax, thinking the video was gone for good, he patted the laptop.

"It's all here."

I leaned my forearms against the table and pressed my head between them, breathing in and out until my heart calmed and the dizzy spell eased. Eliot ran a gentle hand up and down my back—and wasn't it interesting that it was him and not my so-called husband soothing me.

I pulled myself together and straightened. "Let's get this over with so that I can go home. And then you bloody destroy that video." I pointed an accusing finger at Danny, who lifted his hands.

"I promised I will, didn't I."

I refrained from pointing out that his promises didn't mean anything to me anymore. He wasn't even in charge here.

I powered up the laptop and accessed my mail inbox through Interpol's website. I didn't tell Danny, although he should know, that it would leave a trace at the other end when I logged in. If they didn't believe my ruse about being sick, they'd know where to look for me.

Then again, I was supposed to be in London, so if they had believed me, this might ruin everything.

There were three emails from my boss, several work-related emails, and one from Laïla. I clicked it open.

> *Boss handled. You have sick leave until Monday. Answer your phone. L.*

She wasn't much of a correspondent, but it had the pertinent. I clicked the answer icon despite Danny's growing annoyance.

> *Thank you. I owe you. Can't access the phone right now, so don't call me. I'll email when I can. I'm safe, so don't worry. A.*

Safe was relative, but no one was threatening my life and I wasn't bound to the bed anymore.

I created a quick out-of-office email so that my inbox wouldn't explode by the time I returned to work—and I *would* return—before accessing the email from the archives. I downloaded the blueprints, logged off, and deleted my login information from the computer. No need to give Danny access to my mail.

I opened the blueprints. "Now, the house is from the late eighteenth century, and since it's historically valuable, the owners have had to submit new blueprints after every renovation. The latest is from five years ago."

"Provided that the owner is a law-abiding citizen who actually submits them," Eliot said dryly.

"Let's not borrow trouble, shall we."

"What changes did they make that time?" Danny asked.

We leaned closer to study the blueprints. The small laptop screen wasn't ideal for the job, but we enlarged the images section by section and managed to get a good look.

"It's basically a renovation of bathrooms and adding a new kitchen annex, and a new alarm system," I noted. "The first don't interest us, but the last does." A system this new always posed problems for me.

Eliot pointed at the screen. "And they've added an alarm on the door of the lower balcony too."

"No point trying to go through there, then…"

"There isn't an alarm on the upper balcony door though," Danny noted. "You could easily climb up there."

Great.

"We'd have to do some shopping. I didn't bring long-enough rope."

"Maybe we'll find a better way in when we go check the place," Eliot said. "Preferably one I can access as well."

"You're not going in," I stated firmly. The last thing I needed was him being caught breaking and entering with me. I couldn't live with the guilt of ruining his life.

"It's a huge house. It'll take you forever to search the place alone."

"I'll only look in two places, the study and the bedroom."

In my experience, those were the two rooms where people hid their valuables and kept things that were important to them, like college diplomas.

He wasn't convinced. "That's still two rooms, and they're large rooms."

"Where's the study?" Danny asked. I pointed at a room on the second floor.

"Here. It has a wall safe."

"Is it something you can crack?"

There was a code on the safe and I entered it in a database of a safe manufacturer. The result was promising. "Yes." Not easily, but Danny didn't need to know that.

"Surely you won't have to open it?" Eliot asked, and I shrugged.

"Depends on how valuable the key is for the owner. But more likely it's lying in a desk drawer. And don't worry, I won't risk the mission by stealing anything else that would be instantly noticed."

They had to settle with that.

We had dinner—a steak and salad, to Eliot's relief—after which we prepared to leave for our recon mission. I hadn't brought a large wardrobe with me, but I had the black clothes I'd used for breaking into this villa. They weren't exactly inconspicuous if we were spotted, but they hid me better in the dark than the white linen, and wouldn't show stains if I had to crawl in the bushes.

"Don't you look like a burglar…" Eliot quipped when I emerged from the bathroom where I'd gone to change. Not for modesty's sake. We'd seen each other naked before and he was a temptation I didn't need right now.

"If the shoe fits," I said with a smile, checking him out, because why not. He was wearing black trousers and a black tee, but both looked expensive and wouldn't cause the neighbors to call the *carabinieri* on us.

He slipped the small gun into one pocket and the secret phone into the other, and didn't take his jacket. I didn't take mine either, because the evening was sweltering.

Then he gave me a concerned look. "How are you doing?"

I hadn't expected the question and it almost brought tears to my eyes, which told me I wasn't doing entirely well. But I smiled and nodded. "This is what I do best. Let's go."

THE STREETS HAD quieted for the night when we arrived at our target, but there were a few dog walkers around, and some lights were still on in all the neighboring houses, so we had to be careful.

We left Enzo in the car—Ciro hadn't come with us— a couple of streets down and walked to the villa. It looked exactly like in Street View: large and imposing, with the main door at one end on street level, and a courtyard deep below the street level at the other end accessed by a separate gate and a ramp wide enough for a car. The new kitchen was on the below-ground floor and had a door towards the courtyard and the garage at the back corner, both visible from the street above.

The only new addition was a couple of cameras monitoring the house and a discreet plaque naming the private security that operated them on the tall brick fence that lined the street. I didn't think it was a live camera feed or that security kept a constant eye on it, but I wasn't about to risk it.

"Good thing we didn't trust the internet," I muttered as we walked casually by the house with Eliot, our arms linked like we were a couple on an evening stroll. Danny was walking on the other side of the street, which would've surprised me after the jealous act he'd pulled that day, but I knew he didn't want to be caught on camera.

He was fine risking us though. But then again, we weren't supposedly dead.

"There are no lights on in the house, so it's likely empty," Eliot said.

"Unless they're very old and go to bed early, in which case they're likely to wake up at the slightest sound."

He smiled. "You'd best be quiet, then."

We made the walk-by and then rounded the entire block, looking for the best access point to the gardens between the houses. "This one doesn't have any cameras, and the neighbor's cameras don't reach here," Eliot noted, reminding me once again that he'd been a security expert before.

"That's our way in."

We sent Danny back to the villa to watch for our approach to see if he could spot us—which, to my amazement, he did without complaint—and then slipped into the garden between the two houses, mindful of cameras and prying eyes. It was dark; the streetlights didn't reach there, but my eyes adjusted fast. Eliot had the phone with its torch, but he didn't turn it on. It would've drawn too much attention.

"I'll wear night vision goggles when I come tomorrow," I noted to him, cursing my stupidity not bringing them with me tonight. I could only blame the strain of the long day messing with my mind. I hoped I wouldn't make crucial mistakes because of it.

"I'll need a pair too. Even if you won't let me enter the house, I'll accompany you on the approach."

I had nothing against that.

We reached the first brick wall between gardens and easily scaled it, although the landing was a bit rough, as there was a box hedge on the other side.

"We'll have to avoid flowerbeds so that we don't leave footprints," I said in a low tone when we'd extradited ourselves from the hedge.

"Easier said than done…"

After ten minutes of slowly making our way through the back gardens, pausing in the shadows to study the surroundings and climbing over several tall brick walls, we reached the target. We didn't scale the wall separating it from its neighbor but crouched behind it to study the villa.

"Two cameras are monitoring the garden too," I said, annoyed.

The back garden looked different than in the satellite imagery, with a new elevated terrace taking half of it. The garden was on the level with the street and the new kitchen was underneath the terrace, with only narrow windows towards the garden. The terrace would've been an easy point of entry if it weren't for the cameras.

"But not a single camera watches the sides of the house," Eliot pointed out. "And the balconies are there, as is the kitchen door at the opposite side."

"Let's go check the kitchen door."

The building at the back of the kitchen yard had likely been a carriage house or similar, but it was now a four-car garage. The roof was flat and only half a floor above street level towards the neighboring house from where we were approaching, making it easy to climb on it.

The drop onto the courtyard on the other side was steeper, as it was below street level, but it wasn't impossible. We made sure no one was watching before lowering ourselves off the roof. Eliot landed almost as quietly as I did, which was amazing for an amateur of his size.

Eliot made to cross the yard to the kitchen door, but I pulled him back. "There may be sensors that'll turn on that light." I pointed at yard light mounted above the kitchen door. He nodded.

"It hasn't switched on yet, so the sensor's either by the gate for the approaching cars to trigger, or on the garage itself."

But no matter how hard we looked, aided by the streetlight above, we couldn't spot the sensor, so we decided to risk it. We crept along the garage wall, which continued as the wall that propped the garden above before connecting to the house itself.

We reached the kitchen door without the light turning on, and paused to study the alarm system. "It's too dark in here, I can't see it properly."

Eliot reached into the pocket of his trousers and pulled out his phone. Angling his body so that the light wouldn't be noticed from the street, he switched on the torch.

"I guess we'll know in a few moments if Danny can spot us…"

I made a quick study of the alarm and sighed in relief. I could handle it. "You can switch that off now."

Eliot did so and put the phone away. We looked around for an exit. The garage roof was too high from this direction, so we couldn't go back the way we'd come, and the brick wall that separated the kitchen yard from the street was too high up as well.

"We didn't think this through…"

"The car gate is the only way out," Eliot said.

"The camera monitoring the front door will spot us."

"Not necessarily. It's at the other end of the house, and the approach to the front door is in such an angle that the camera's range might not reach all the way here."

I wasn't convinced, because they would've added a camera to monitor the garage gate too in that case, but we didn't really have a choice. A sloping driveway led up to the gate, which was wrought iron and easy to climb over, even with the spikes on top of it.

"We can climb onto the brick fence here," I noticed, pleased, when we were by the gate. "We can land farther away from the camera, maybe even outside its range, as the street curves here."

I didn't wait for him but easily climbed onto the wall that was wide enough to walk on. I didn't though, as people might be watching from the neighboring houses, but quickly landed on the street, Eliot right behind me.

The light above the kitchen door flared on.

11

ELIOT

MY KNEES BUCKLED IN A gut reaction to flee. Instead, I crouched and pressed against the brick wall where the light didn't reach, my back to the camera that I hoped was so far away that it wouldn't catch us. Ada did the same, and I approved. Whoever was monitoring the cameras might notice a running form and become suspicious, but two lumps in the shadows might not even register.

The light took forever to switch off. Only then did we straighten and walk calmly up the street before crossing it where the camera definitely didn't reach anymore.

Danny emerged from behind a tree. "That went well," he said dryly.

"It went brilliantly, actually," Ada said. "And now we know the one weak point of the operation."

"Two," I said, pointing at the car of the security company that was in charge of the villa's security. It made a slow drive-by, but it didn't stop and no one emerged from the car. "Did they react to the light or do they monitor the house regularly?"

"We'd best wait and see if they do hourly sweeps," Danny said. "I'll fetch the car so we don't have to skulk in the bushes."

I almost asked why he didn't call Enzo, before remembering what I'd done with his phone. Then it was all I could do to keep the smug smile off my face.

I really wanted to tell Ada that she didn't have to worry about the phone and the video on it. I'd felt genuinely bad when she almost hyperventilated learning it had been stolen. But I kept my mouth shut. Her reactions had to be genuine so that Danny wouldn't become suspicious.

The car soon arrived with Danny, pulling over a little down the street in a spot where the trees created a shadow that hid it nicely. We climbed in.

"Well, is the job doable?" Danny asked.

"Yes. The kitchen door is my way in. Did you spot us?"

"Not until you climbed over the wall. What triggered the light?"

"There's a sensor by the gate somewhere," I told him. "A bit slow to react though, so if we climb faster, we could be gone by the time it switches on."

Ada gave me a stern look. "I already told you, I'm going in alone."

"I don't want you to," I stated. "What if the house isn't empty?"

"All the more reason for you to stay away. One person is more silent, and can hide more easily. And you've never done this before. You might make mistakes that'll see us both caught."

I didn't like it, but she was right. "Fine. I'll stay outside and keep watch."

"The house seems to be empty anyway," Danny said. "There were no cars in the garage and no lights came on in the house when you triggered the security light."

"Let's hope that remains true tomorrow night," Ada said.

"Or we could go in right now," I suggested.

"We're not properly equipped," Ada said, shaking her head. "No gloves or lockpicks even. Best not go in half-cocked."

"We could fetch everything you need," Danny said. "Since you don't need the rope after all."

She sighed. "Fine. But let's wait and see what their security does first."

We waited for an hour until the car returned and did another slow drive-by. It was good to know that security hadn't reacted to the garage yard light, but also bad because they might surprise us in the act.

"We'll have to time the entering right after they've done their drive-by," Ada noted. "That'll give me an hour to search the house and exit."

Enzo drove us back to Falconi's villa. It was well past midnight and I almost fell asleep in the car, my eyes trying to close no matter how hard I struggled to keep them open. It had been a long and exhausting day. I couldn't believe I'd only arrived in Rome that morning, so much had happened.

"You know what, maybe it's best we postpone the break-in," I said, stifling a yawn as we entered the villa. "I'm too exhausted to be a proper lookout, and Ada must be too."

She pursed her lips, as if listening to her body, and nodded. "You're right. We'd best have a proper rest tonight, sleep in, and then spend tomorrow preparing for the job."

Danny didn't look happy, but he gave in. "Not sleeping the whole day though. Breakfast's at nine."

"As long as someone remembers to come free us for it," I said with a pointed look at Enzo, who was seeing us to our rooms.

It wasn't until he'd locked us in that I remembered the extra mattress. Ada didn't seem to recall it either. She kicked off her shoes and disappeared into the bathroom, barely taking long enough to brush her teeth before emerging and dropping onto the bed.

By the time I'd finished the same, she'd fallen asleep. I considered being a gentleman and sleeping on the floor, but we were adults here, so I took the side she'd left empty. It was a snug fit, but I was already asleep before I could become uncomfortable.

I slept well and woke up around eight wrapped around Ada, so I had that going for me. My body was definitely happy. It had been ages since I'd woken up with a beautiful woman in my bed. In my previous life, I tended to favor one-night stands, and seldom stayed the night even in longer relationships. I savored the feeling of her warm, firm body enclosed in mine, and then carefully removed myself from the bed before I did something stupid.

I didn't want to disturb her by taking a shower that I sorely needed. Instead, I took the floor and began my morning yoga routine, stretching the muscles that had taken exception to the climbing exercise last night.

I was finishing up when a strangled snort from the bed revealed that Ada had woken up. "Are you laughing at me?" I asked, amused, my gaze on the floor and attention on maintaining the position and breathing. I didn't want to turn to look at her, in case seeing her all soft and drowsy would distract me.

"No…"

"Are you having a stroke, then? I've been informed by a reliable source that my downwards dog can cause ladies to have one." I smiled, thinking of Madame Benoit's reaction if she saw me now, dressed only in boxer briefs and a T-shirt that I'd worn to bed for Ada's sake. At least the morning wood was gone, or this would've been embarrassing.

"Yeah, let's call it a stroke…" she muttered, disappearing into the bathroom. The shower came on a little later. I finished up and straightened. I was a bit sweaty, but I'd have to wait for my shower.

Unless I joined her…

The mere memory of her naked body under the running water swept away the peace of mind yoga had brought. I could walk in, press her against the tile wall, and take her there…

But I stayed put. The shared shower had been one time only, and she'd made it clear she wasn't interested in anything more. I could respect that.

A part of me was a bit reluctant even. The lie I'd told her about why I hadn't called her when we returned from Monaco didn't sit well with me, which was a stunner. It wasn't even the first lie I told her, or the biggest, and it gave me an out that ensured she wouldn't come looking for me once I disappeared. She would maybe miss me a little, but she would move on.

Besides, I had the rule number three to think of. I couldn't get attached.

Maybe the guilty feeling was for claiming my mother had dementia, which wasn't very filial of me. She wasn't old; she'd been seventeen when I was born, and had a sharp mind. She'd box my ears if she heard about it.

The lies couldn't be helped, so there was no use feeling guilty about them. The moment I had Ada out of this situation, I'd be on my way. The countdown was on.

Ada emerged from the bathroom fully clothed, fresh and more energetic than she'd looked the previous day. "I need to go shopping. I've run out of clean underwear and tops."

I smiled, resisting the urge to pull her into a hug. I don't even know where it came from. I wasn't a hugger. "We need to buy more than that. We need to make both of us look the part for when we go to the bank tomorrow."

"I don't think Falconi will pay for our new clothes," she said dryly. "Nor do I want him to."

"Don't worry, I'll pay."

She straightened. "I can afford them myself. I was just grumbling about the work-related expenses that a boss should cover."

I laughed. "Maybe he'll pay for the break-in equipment. But I'll buy the clothes. Your boss thinks you're in London and it'll be incriminating evidence if your credit card has been used in Rome."

"Fine. But I'll pay you back when we get home."

I smiled and disappeared to the shower—and didn't tell her I wouldn't be returning with her.

VIA DEI CONDOTTI WAS a long one-lane street in central Rome. Lined with eighteenth and nineteenth century buildings that weren't entirely in prime condition, it ran from the Spanish Steps southeast toward the Tiber. The historical monumental stairs and the church above them on the hill didn't really interest me though, unlike the tourists who already swarmed the place when we arrived there mid-morning.

I was there for the luxury designer shops, Armani, Gucci, and Prada to name a few of the several that filled the neighborhood. Or only Armani, if I was being accurate, but we'd need the other shops for Ada's clothing.

"We'll start with my suit," I said to Ada and Danny. "If they need to fix it, they can do it while we shop for Ada's clothes."

"No, we'll start with a shop where I can get myself a new phone," Danny stated. "I'm not following the two of you around Rome without a phone to occupy myself with."

"You're not separating," Ciro growled, having accompanied us with Enzo again. He pointed at me. "I have nothing to keep you here."

"Yes, you do." I looked him straight in the eyes. "I'm not going anywhere until she's free."

Ada gave me a startled look, but didn't say anything.

"We're not going anywhere," I repeated in a conciliatory tone. "But fine, you come with us, and Enzo can go with him. We'll meet at the car when we're done."

Ciro didn't look happy, but he nodded. "Fine."

Danny nodded too, gesturing at Enzo to follow him. "We won't be long."

"We will…"

We'd dressed as best as we could under the circumstances, and the security at the door of the Armani shop didn't hesitate to let us in. He looked slightly impressed even, as we arrived with a bodyguard.

A shop assistant, a tall and thin middle-aged man, glided over to us and asked what he could do to help, opting for English without trying Italian first. Since I looked fairly Italian, I presumed it was the shop's policy for catering to tourists.

"I made the mistake of going on a holiday without a suit and now I need one, preferably today," I told him with an affable smile. "Anything you have off the rack will do."

He looked disappointed but nodded. "Evening or day?"

"Day, business, high-end. Summer quality."

"We have excellent light gray suits in Fresco wool that is exceptionally good for summer weather. Would you like to try those?"

"Perfect. And a couple of shirts to go with them."

"Very good. Have you shopped with us before? Do we have your measurements?"

"Yes I have, and you do. Eliot Reed."

"Very good. If you'd like to wait in the dressing room? And would madame like a glass of champagne?"

Ada smiled. "Madame would indeed."

I gestured for our watchdog to wait, as if he really was our bodyguard, and he took a post by the door, looking so natural at it that he likely was Falconi's personal guard.

We were shown to a small suite with a soft, dark gray carpet, a red divan, several full-length mirrors in elegant mahogany frames, and an area where one could strip behind a dark gray curtain. Ada sat on the divan and put her feet up.

"When I retire, I want this kind of lifestyle," she said with a sigh. I smiled.

"Why wait. Just leave. You can afford it."

"And do what for the rest of my life?"

"Travel? Drink champagne?" My hotel had been a favorite among the very rich, and they didn't seem to be doing anything worthwhile with their lives.

She straightened and gave me a level look. "Would you do that for the rest of your life if you could?"

I had that option but I hadn't taken it, opting to become a businessman instead. Now I gave it some thought as I took off my shoes. "I could become a pro gambler."

She smiled. "You're very good at baccarat at any rate. In Monaco?"

"Macao."

I hadn't realized I'd thought about it so much that I could give such a precise answer. I had no particular interest in gambling, or a yearning for Southeast Asia—Monaco was eminently more my style—but there were so many casinos in Macao that I wasn't likely to run into the pro gamblers who frequented my boss's casinos. Rule number six stated that you should keep away from the people you'd met in your previous life. You never knew who might recognize you.

"Do you speak Chinese?" she asked, curious, and I nodded.

"I do, oddly enough—a few words." Chinese tourists liked to gamble in my boss's casinos, so I had learned for them. I could get by in a casino at least.

"But whether I understand it though…"

A young woman brought the champagne, and left as discreetly as she'd arrived. Ada took a sip and nodded, impressed. Then she gave me a look over its rim, her eyes concerned.

"I'm grateful that you're here and willing to help. But you should flee. I'll distract Ciro. This isn't your mess. Danny won't hurt me."

My jaw tightened. "Falconi will."

She had nothing to say to that, and then the assistant arrived with my suits and we had to abandon the topic.

We exited the shop half an hour later, Ada a bit stunned. "I can't believe you just spent five thousand euros for clothes you wouldn't even need if it weren't for this job and will wear for fifteen minutes max."

"I can always use a good suit."

I admired my reflection in the shop windows. The suit had been perfect with only a minor shortening of the legs, which hadn't taken the tailor more than fifteen minutes. After a year with my new trim body, that still took some getting used to.

While we'd waited, I'd selected beautiful leather shoes, as well as a light pink cambric linen shirt that was maybe more holiday than work, but I didn't care. I bought a white shirt for the bank job too. That, and my old clothes were inside a couple of Armani bags.

"Let's see if we can find you a suit to match," I said, guiding her into the Gucci shop across the street, as if I hadn't understood why she was protesting. If I were to play a rich businessman, I couldn't go with a cheap suit.

"I don't need a Gucci suit."

"You're a master of disguises. You know perfectly well how to make a suitable impression. You want the clerk to remember the suit, not the face."

Nevertheless, it took an amazing amount of wrangling to get her fitted into a light pink wool and linen-blend two-piece that hugged her svelte curves but didn't look inappropriate for a PA. I made her shop for underwear there as well, despite her protests that H&M would do.

"No one will see my underwear, for crying out loud. And lace itches."

"Then buy silk," I'd said mercilessly, and the shop assistant wisely brought a selection for her to choose from that she couldn't refuse.

For her shoes and a shoulder bag large enough to hold the loot from the safe deposit box, we went to Louis Vuitton, and for our watches and jewelry to Bulgari next to it. We were looking brilliant and I was feeling great. This was how you holidayed in Rome. Ada had stopped complaining, but her eyes were slightly glazed over.

Danny and Enzo had returned while we were still in the Gucci shop, and Danny's eyes grew large when he saw us. "Who's paying for all this?"

"I am."

He cocked a sardonic brow at me. "I thought you said you're not a successful businessman."

"I didn't buy this on a cop's salary either…"

His mouth tightened. "I'm starting to look like a slob next to you."

He was, and cramping our style too. "You know, a rich man would have a bodyguard with him." Ciro had played the part admirably, but I wouldn't take him to the bank.

Danny nodded slowly, considering the possibilities. "Would a bodyguard wear Armani?"

"As if. Tod's will do."

It was well past lunch by the time we had him fitted in a black suit with a black T-shirt, which made him look like a bodyguard—or a minorly successful crook. We also made a quick stop at a drugstore to buy vinyl gloves for our nefarious activities that night, but the night vision goggles for me would require a special shop. I hadn't given up on those, even if Ada didn't want me inside the villa.

"I'm starved," I stated. "And I need to get out of this heat." Summer quality or not, a suit was not optimal for the current weather.

Ada looked around. "Good luck finding a place to eat here." There were dozens of small restaurants lining the streets in the shopping district, and they were all filled with tourists.

Danny turned to Enzo, who had followed us bemused the whole day. He knew exactly the place to drive us to, a five-star hotel next to the church atop the hill where the Spanish Steps led to.

"I'll stay here the next time," I stated when we entered the hotel's cool lobby, taking in the golden marble and mahogany interior with rows of display cases filled with luxury items. Who cared if the surveillance was tight; I needed this.

The restaurant was on the top floor with a view over Rome far below. It wasn't full—it was expensive enough to keep the budget holidayers away—so we got a good table by the window even though we didn't have a reservation. I was enjoying myself immensely, enough to forget the situation we were in.

We were halfway through an excellent lunch when a man walked in. He spotted me instantly, and a slow smile spread on his face. My insides froze.

12

ELIOT

IT TOOK ALL MY SELF-CONTROL not to choke on the expensive wine. Feigning calm, I leaned back in my chair and assessed Salvatore Bosco as he walked to our table.

He was a tall, lean man in his late thirties, with elegantly overgrown black hair, permanently tanned olive complexion, and a patrician nose; handsome—Ada had definitely shown interest before we knew what he was—and oozing understated wealth and power. In his cream summer suit, a shirt with light blue stripes on white, and white Panama hat, he looked like an artist on holiday.

A well-to-do artist. All he needed was a red carnation on his lapel.

Nothing about him pointed at organized crime. I'd been fooled by him once and had ended up drugged in a closet on Melnyk's yacht to wait for the amusing death Bosco had arranged for me. I wouldn't be fooled twice.

He paused at our table and his lip quirked as if he was amused but not surprised to see me. He'd known I'd made an escape, then. Men like him had people everywhere, like among the police in Monaco.

"Mr. Reed. I see you're doing well."

"Very well," I said, measuring him calmly. I had my body under control now. I might not be a mafia first anymore, but I was infinitely familiar with this kind of posturing. "You left Monaco rather hastily."

He spread his arms in an Italian shrug. "I'm a busy man." He nodded at Ada. "Miss Reed. Or should I say … Natasha."

I stilled. She'd been with me at the casino in Monaco in her disguise as a Russian gold digger, Natasha, when I'd gambled with Bosco. It was a good disguise and he shouldn't have recognized her. I was ready to intervene if needed, but Ada showed only mild befuddlement.

"It's Ada, actually. Have we met?"

Bosco tilted his head, taking her in, his smile appreciative. He hadn't been this interested in Natasha, who had shown a lot more skin and curves, but Ada did look wonderful in her new suit.

"Apparently not…"

"Are you staying in Rome long?" I asked, as if I were having a polite conversation and not deliberately pulling his attention away from Ada.

"No. I only came because my security company informed me someone tried to break into my villa last night." He placed a photo on the table in front of me. "For your information, my ex-wife lives there. I don't keep my secrets in that house."

I nodded, taking the photo and putting it in my pocket without looking, as if I weren't interested. "Good to know."

He sneered, nodded at Ada, and crossed the floor to his table at the other end, the maître d' at his heels.

We sat in tense silence for a moment. "Who is he?" Danny asked in a low tone, but I shook my head.

"Not here."

We continued our lunch. I could only admire Ada, who managed to look calm and have a casual conversation as if she didn't have a clue about what had just happened. But the excellent meal had lost its appeal and we skipped dessert. I paid and we left.

I couldn't help glancing at Bosco on my way out. He lifted a glass in salute to me. He wasn't even a little worried about me and what I intended to do.

"What was in the photo?" Ada asked when we were in the elevator.

I dug it out of my pocket and stopped breathing. It was a black and white photo of fairly good quality, considering it had been taken in the dark. It showed Ada and me standing at the kitchen door of the villa the previous night, studying the alarm system in the light of my phone.

Ada paled. "There was a camera in that lamp?"

"That's not even the worst of it."

"What could possibly be more horrible than more evidence of me doing a break-in?" she asked. But that wasn't what worried me. It didn't really incriminate us. *Yet.*

I gave her a grim look. "That it's Salvatore Bosco we're trying to steal from."

We were so dead.

"OKAY, HERE'S THE PLAN," I said as we exited the hotel, having spent the short ride to the lobby feverishly coming up with ideas. It wasn't a good plan—I wasn't exactly the plan guy—but we didn't have a choice.

"Danny, you stay here with Ciro and keep an eye on Bosco. Call Enzo the moment he leaves the hotel and warn us."

He pulled back, angry. "The hell I will. What are you going to do?"

"We'll go steal the key."

Ada startled. "But he said he doesn't live in the villa. I don't think the key is where his ex-wife could get her hands on it."

Bosco could've lied, but I doubted it. "We're not going to the villa," I said, climbing in the car, giving Enzo the address. "Hurry up, we don't have much time."

Bosco had found us at the restaurant and I didn't believe for a moment that it was a coincidence. He had people keeping an eye on us—or Falconi more likely. He might realize what we were up to and call security to intercept us.

The distance to our destination was a kilometer due west across the river on foot, but by car we had to detour the pedestrian districts, so it was about a ten-minute drive. I sat tensely the whole time, certain that Danny would call any moment.

"Where are we going, exactly?" Ada asked.

"The office of Bosco's shipping company. It's a shell company, so there shouldn't be many people around."

"And you just happen to know where it's located?" She inhaled, her eyes growing large. "Please, tell me you're not in Rome for him."

I'd lied a lot to her. What was one more? "I'm not a cop."

"And not a secret agent either…"

I smiled, remembering how Laïla believed I was a James Bond. "Definitely not."

"How do you know the key is in his office?"

"I don't, and it would be such a random place to hold valuable items. But it's also the only real estate in Rome that I was able to connect to him, and it could be that he keeps his Rome related items there, like the key. We'd best check the place before he suspects we'll try there."

Our destination was by the Ponte Cavour, a couple of blocks northeast of Castle Sant'Angelo, in one of the dozens of large, eighteenth-century apartment buildings that lined the river on the Vatican side of Tiber, built to accommodate the needs of Vatican personnel back in the day. It was an ornate, five-story sandstone that took the entire block, with a gateway through the south wall wide enough for a carriage to an inner courtyard. There was no visible security, even though the building housed an embassy.

Inside the gate, there was a door on each side into the building itself, with brass plaques by them depicting the names of the companies and other entities that the building housed.

"Here," I said, pointing at the name of Bosco's shipping company by the door on the right. The embassy was on the left, which hopefully meant that the tighter security was on that side.

"Are we just marching in?" Ada asked as I pushed the door open into an elegant stairwell. "With our own faces?"

"Pretty much…"

There were no cameras following us as we hurried up the sandstone stairs to the third floor where Bosco's office was. The ornate, double-leaf door on the landing was closed, and was too thick to let us detect voices inside. But we didn't have time for subtlety. I triggered the fire alarm on the landing by breaking the plastic cover with my elbow and pulling the lever, and pushed Ada to run up the stairs when the shrill sound filled the echoing stairwell.

Good thing there were no sprinklers in the old building or we would've ruined our new clothes when they went off.

In mere moments, the doors on every floor began to open and people hurried out, including those a floor up from Bosco's office in front of which we were standing, catching our breaths.

"Where's the fire?" the woman exiting asked in Italian and I shrugged, turning to follow her down with Ada as if we'd intended to do that when she showed up.

"No idea. We just got here."

Bosco's office was emptying too, and Ada and I paused to let them pass. As the door was about to bang closed after the last person, Ada deftly dropped her bag on the threshold to stop it. More people were filing down, and in the chaos and noise the alarm made, no one noticed how we slipped inside.

There was a wide hallway with doors on both sides, all of them open. Everyone had evacuated, not even one person opting to bet that it was a false alarm. In the distance, above the sound of the alarm, I could hear the sirens of approaching fire engines.

"We don't have much time."

We ran to the other end of the hallway to the only closed door, pulling on vinyl gloves as we went. I pressed the handle—and nothing happened.

Not missing a beat, I reached into the pocket of my pants and pulled out a set of lockpicks.

"Where did you get those?" Ada asked sharply.

"They're yours," I said, deftly opening the old lock on the door.

"For a non-cop, non-secret agent, you certainly have odd skills," she said dryly, not asking why I'd taken her lockpicks without telling her. I couldn't have answered anyway. They'd been on the nightstand with the rest of her break-in equipment when I emerged from the bathroom that morning, and I'd thought they might come in handy.

I'd been right.

The office was elegant with mahogany furniture and modern art on the walls. I went to the large desk by the window that faced the river below. "I'll check this, you check the safe."

She was already peeking behind the paintings and soon pulled one of them open. "There isn't even an alarm on this…" she muttered.

I couldn't spare attention for her as I began to open the drawers one by one. All but one of them opened, and most of them were empty. The rest contained perfectly ordinary office supplies in pristine condition. It looked like Bosco didn't spend much time here. The locked drawer didn't have a key, and there wasn't one on the desk either, so I utilized the lockpicks again.

The contents of the drawer didn't really merit it being locked. There were a couple of passports under different names but with Bosco's photo. I made a note of the aliases, but left them be.

There was a small bag of what I surmised was cocaine and wondered if it was a sample of his product, or if he used it personally. I guess he hadn't seen *Scarface:* "Lesson number two: Don't get high on your own supply."

Come to think of it, my idea of having rules to keep myself alive must have come from the movie. It served as a reminder, too, of what would happen if I broke them.

At the back was a large key similar to the one I had from my bank. "Found it," I said just as Ada said, "Open."

I took the key and closed and locked the drawer, before joining her at the safe. It was full of money, at least a couple of million in euros. "We don't need any of that."

"What does Bosco need the safe deposit box for when he has this?" She closed the door and put the painting back the way it had been.

"We'll soon find out."

We exited the room and I locked the door. In moments, we were out of the office and heading down the stairs. The alarm cut off abruptly, leaving my ears ringing with the absence of the noise.

People were milling in the inner courtyard and the gateway, but no one paid attention to us or asked why we were there. Fire engines were blocking the street outside and firemen were moving about, but judging by the lack of haste, they already knew the alarm was false. Slipping past them, we headed to our car.

Danny and Ciro were there. "Bosco left the hotel ten minutes ago. If he's headed here, he will arrive at any moment."

"We'd best get going, then," I said, and Enzo pulled the car into traffic.

"How did you get here so fast?" Ada asked, amazed. "Did you run?"

"No, we took rental scoots and cut through the pedestrian area. Ciro had an account."

Clever.

"Where are we going?" Enzo asked.

"The villa," Danny said, but I shook my head.

"To the bank."

"What, now?" Ada asked. "I don't even have a makeup on yet, let alone a wig, or even a hat."

She loved her disguises, and they were good. "Best go there before Bosco notices the key is gone. We have everything we need." He would know it had been us, so no need for disguises.

"Provided the key is the correct one."

I shrugged. "If it's not, we can still pay a visit to Bosco's villa and check there. The bank won't think it's odd if we return tomorrow."

"Who is this Bosco anyway?" Danny demanded. "And why are you so afraid of him?"

"Other than that he's already tried to kill me? He's a drug trafficker who intends to corner the Mediterranean smuggling routes." I couldn't know for sure, but it certainly seemed like that after what he did to the Bulgarians.

"What does Falconi want with him, then?"

"No idea. But we'll soon find out."

Enzo and Ciro glanced at each other, like they knew but wouldn't tell. I could respect the loyalty, even if it annoyed me.

Enzo drove us about half an hour downriver to a business district and pulled over outside a high-rise. Danny, Ada and I exited the car, but when Ciro looked like he would follow, I halted him. To my surprise he obeyed, but he didn't look happy about it.

I buttoned my jacket as I studied the place, my stomach tightening with unease.

I didn't want to enter the bank. I didn't want to open a safe deposit box, and I didn't want to try to break into Bosco's.

This was the worst possible move I could make, and not solely because it would enrage Bosco. I was about to break the most important rule of leaving the life of crime.

I was going back.

But it was our only way out of this situation. I squared my shoulders and crossed the street.

13

ADA

AFTER THE SUCCESS AT BOSCO'S office, completely improvised as it had been, adrenaline was coursing through me. My entire body was tingling with apprehension and I expected to be caught at any moment. I'd never tried to pull a heist with such minimal planning, in such a hurry, and with my own face.

Eliot opened the door for me. He reached into the inside pocket of his suit jacket with his other hand and gave me a passport. It was American, unlike the Italian one he'd used in the previous bank. I knew he held both nationalities, so the passport wasn't odd.

"Open the box using this name."

That caught my attention. I glanced at the ID page and my brows shot up, but I controlled my expression hastily. The face was familiar, albeit a little heavier with a crooked nose and without a beard. The name, however, was Ryan Anthony Pike. He was two years older than Eliot, and born in Boston.

My mind reeled. He'd made such a show of needing to acquire a false ID, yet here he had one. Was there a reason he hadn't wanted to use it? Was it his real name? But who, then, was Eliot Reed?

Ever since meeting him, he'd been a bit of an enigma, but now I really had to know.

I pulled myself together with an effort and smiled at the same young man behind the counter I'd spoken with earlier. Only at the last moment did I remember the Boston accent—and wasn't that a coincidence that Ryan Pike was from there.

"Good afternoon. Maybe you remember me from earlier? I want to open a safe deposit box for my client."

I indicated Eliot, who was standing a little apart from me, hands deep in his trouser pockets, calmly studying the bank as if all this was boring or beneath him. My gesture pulled the young man's attention from my cleavage to him. I'd protested the suit, but I had to admit Eliot knew what he was doing.

"Of course," the man said. "And it's always better if the client is here themself."

Eliot cocked an arrogant brow. "I do have more important things to do than run errands, so step on it." His Boston accent was much better than mine, but it would be if he was really from there.

The young man sprang into action. I gave him the passport and he began to click his keyboard. If he made an ID check, it went through without a hitch, which meant that the passport had to be genuine. But then again, Eliot's passport had worked at the previous bank too. Who had false IDs this good?

In due course, the young man gave Eliot a form to sign, which he did in a barely legible sweep. It came so naturally he must have practiced it his whole life. Once the formalities were done, the clerk held out a key and Eliot gestured for me to take it with an uninterested flicker of his hand. It was exactly like the one we'd found in Bosco's office, so the chances were good we had the right key.

We followed the clerk to the bowels of the bank, Danny keeping the rear like a good bodyguard. The young man didn't even bat an eye at his presence, so maybe it wasn't that rare to have a bodyguard around when visiting a bank.

The vault door opened with keys like the previous time. The young man gestured us in but didn't follow us. "The key opens the door and the box. The number is on the key. Yours is in the room at the rear."

I smiled at him like the good PA I was. "Thank you. We won't be long."

"Take all the time you need. I'll be here."

Eliot and Danny had already moved to the rear vault. Eliot had Bosco's key, and he was searching the wall for the number. "I can't believe you wanted us to go in blind," he noted to Danny. "We would've had to open all these boxes." There were hundreds of them.

"I'm not exactly in charge here, am I?"

Eliot located the correct box and inserted the key. I held my breath as he turned it, exhaling slowly when the door opened without a hitch or an alarm going off.

"Shouldn't we have blocked the cameras?" Danny asked as Eliot pulled out the steel box and carried it to a table at the end of the vault. There were no cameras at that end, offering the clients privacy.

"Stand a few steps behind me, side by side so that you block the view to me," Eliot said. "And face the vault, as if I'd requested privacy."

"But won't they wonder why we didn't open the correct box?" Danny wanted to know as we took post behind Eliot, keeping our faces demurely pressed down so that the cameras wouldn't have a good view of them. I shook my head in answer to Danny.

"Whoever is manning the cameras, if they're even constantly watched, will only see a person open the box with a key. They don't know it's not our box."

Behind me, I heard Eliot lift the lid of the steel box. "Huh," he said, sounding disappointed.

"What's in there?" Danny asked.

"Papers. The kind of boring shit everyone has. University diploma from a business school, old land deeds, a copy of his birth certificate—no, his child's." He sighed and his voice lowered. "The child's death certificate too."

I didn't want to feel sympathy for Bosco, but I couldn't help my heart constricting a little. You never knew the sorrows a person hid behind a cool exterior. "Are you emptying it all?"

"I should, it would be faster, but I can't imagine what Falconi would do with this." He shuffled the papers and inhaled sharply. "This is it. Give me your bag."

I extended the shoulder bag to him and he took it. A moment later he gave it back. I heard the box close and then he carried it to its slot and closed and locked the door.

"Let's go."

The young man was waiting for us outside. "Was everything satisfactory?"

"Absolutely," I smiled at him, unlike Eliot, who had marched on without so much as a nod as if a bank clerk were beneath his notice, Danny at his heels. I glanced after their retreating forms and grimaced at the young man, who gave me an understanding smile, so I bowed hastily and thanked him, before hurrying away, leaving him to lock the vault.

With any luck, we'd made a memorable but not a suspicious impression on the young man.

Eliot and Danny were already at the car when I exited the bank, walking calmly so as not to give the idea that I was fleeing. We filed into the back seat, and Enzo waited for us to put on seatbelts, as if he had all the time in the world too. I guess he was trying to give a similar impression of not fleeing.

Late afternoon traffic was starting to pick up, but it wasn't bad yet, and we reached the villa in good time. We sat in tense silence the whole ride, as if not believing we'd gotten away with it so easily.

An emerald-green Rolls Royce was parked in the driveway of the villa and my stomach clenched, wiping away the good feeling I'd had for the heist well done.

Falconi was here.

WE WENT STRAIGHT to the parlor where we'd met with Falconi the previous time. I was even more nervous now. I knew how to handle a heist; I had no idea how to deal with mafia capos. We had what he wanted, but what if he wouldn't free us?

He was seated in the same armchair, wearing a similar if not the same suit, but instead of coffee there was a glass of champagne in front of him as if he was preparing to celebrate.

But only one glass.

His brows shot up when he saw us in our expensive finery. "I hope you don't expect me to pay for those."

"Of course I do," Eliot said, even though he had claimed otherwise earlier. He held up the sheet of paper he'd taken from my bag before we entered the room, showing it without offering it to Falconi. "This is worth a million times what these clothes cost. You can certainly afford them; a small reward if you will."

I startled and turned to look at him, but I couldn't see what the paper was about. It was thick and creamy, the kind used in official certificates, but that was all I could detect.

"And here I thought the reward was your freedom," Falconi drawled, but he was starting to look annoyed. And he wasn't the kind of man you wanted to annoy.

Eliot was unfazed. "Freedom is for finishing the job. Clothes were necessary for it to happen. Cash will do."

Again, I had to wonder who Eliot was to stand so calmly in front of Falconi, negotiating as if he held the upper hand.

"I need to see that you have what I want," Falconi stated, holding out his hand, but Eliot didn't give the paper to him.

"You'll definitely want this. But not before we get what we were promised."

Falconi's brows furrowed. "I didn't authorize the expenses. You get Miss Reed's freedom and the video erased. Take it or leave it."

Eliot pressed his lips tight as he considered it. Then he nodded. I had a notion that the cost of clothes didn't matter to him at all. He'd only demanded it to give Falconi the notion of being in charge by refusing it.

"Fine." Eliot reached his free hand to Danny. "Your phone, please, unlocked. I'll delete the video myself."

Danny startled, as if about to remind him that it was a new phone and the video was gone, but he managed to keep his mouth shut. Falconi wouldn't react well to finding out his phone was stolen. He unlocked the phone and gave it to Eliot, who made a show of deleting the nonexistent video.

"And the laptop too," Eliot said when he gave the phone back. Danny looked at Falconi, who nodded, so he hurried out of the room. We waited in silence, Eliot still holding the paper.

I couldn't take it anymore. "What is it?" If the paper was worth billions, like Eliot claimed, it was easily the biggest heist I'd ever pulled.

Falconi tensed in anticipation, and Eliot's lip curled. "The deed to a casino Bosco owns in Venice. Or…" He glanced at Falconi. "…I guess our host can now lay claim to it."

The look on Falconi's face was triumphant and vicious. Whatever was between him and Bosco, it was personal. And we were about to hand him the keys to do Bosco some real damage.

No wonder Eliot was willing to give the deed up without a fuss. He could claim what he wanted; he was here to get back at Bosco for what happened in Monaco. This would certainly do. I could only hope it didn't land him in an even deeper mess with Bosco.

Who was I kidding. Of course it would.

Danny returned with the laptop and held it open for me. I didn't waste time deleting the video, making sure it was removed from the bin too. I met Danny's eyes over the screen and he gave me the barest nod.

"Satisfied?" Falconi asked, feigning boredom, but I could see he was eager to have the paper.

Eliot shook his head. "Not yet. You'll get this at the airport."

"Or I could shoot you and take it from you."

Eliot shrugged, as if it weren't even a threat if the gun wasn't out. "Naturally. But the hassle of dealing with dead bodies is disproportional to simply accompanying us to the airport and being handed the deed there."

"Fine."

To my utter amazement, Falconi rose and marched out of the room. We followed him straight out of the house, but when Danny made to follow, Falconi lifted his hand.

"Your freedom was not part of the deal."

Danny halted and his jaw flexed, but he didn't test the resolve of Ciro, who stepped in front of him. I met his eyes above the guard's shoulder. It was a fleeting gaze, but it was the goodbye we'd never had. I still didn't know what had happened five years ago, and unless a radical change in our fates occurred, I never would.

Right this moment, it didn't matter.

The door closed between us. Sighing, I climbed into the Rolls Royce. We didn't have our luggage and I doubted Falconi would return our phones, but I wasn't about to bring it up. I wasn't leaving anything I needed behind.

It wasn't the first time I'd ridden in a Rolls, but it wasn't an experience I'd had often. It was a stretched model with two seats of creamy leather facing each other at the back. Falconi and Eliot were already seated facing the front, so I took the other seat opposite Eliot. Enzo was driving again, and Ciro took a seat next to him.

Fiumicino Airport was on the west coast, a little under thirty kilometers from the villa. Traffic was slow until we reached the motorway. I was tense the whole ride, barely daring to breathe. I definitely didn't feel like talking. I wouldn't allow myself to relax until we were seated in a plane and it was off the ground.

"I confess, I'm curious to know why you sped up the timeline," Falconi said, his voice intruding, grating my already taut nerves.

Eliot shrugged minutely. "Out of necessity."

"Oh?"

"Bosco was on to us."

Falconi straightened and shot him a glare. "You told him what you were up to?"

"Do we look suicidal to you?" Eliot asked. "It turned out the villa had a security feature we hadn't anticipated. He confronted us about it this afternoon, so we had to act."

"He knows who you are? How?" Falconi demanded. "Who are you working for?"

Eliot's lip curled. "No one. I've had the pleasure of playing baccarat with Bosco and enjoying … excellent whisky on his yacht."

"You're his friend?"

"Hardly." Falconi didn't look satisfied, but Eliot moved on. "Turned out, your intel about the villa was poor. Bosco doesn't live there himself. His ex-wife does."

"There is nothing wrong with my intel," Falconi ground from between his teeth. Anger marred his face. "It's my sister he's married to and they *will* remain married."

I knew this was personal. "And you think it'll help their marriage that you steal his casino?" I asked, even though I didn't want to draw his attention, or ire, to me.

"It'll force him to do what I want."

I stifled a shudder, glad that I wouldn't have to be there for him and Bosco facing off over the casino. I could only hope that Bosco wouldn't feel like retaliating once he realized the role Eliot and I had played.

Then again, he'd tried to kill Eliot for merely believing he was a cop meddling in his businesses, so the chances weren't looking good for us.

I studied the man across me. Was Eliot a cop? I'd believed him when he denied it, and a cop wouldn't have the kind of money he'd spent today without blinking. And I sincerely doubted that a government operative would have such a vast expense account either, no matter how fast James Bond went through his funds.

He claimed to have been a security expert, and it was believable with the skillset he had. But he was too comfortable with dealing with people like Bosco and Falconi to have been anyone's underling, and the luxury lifestyle suited him like he was born to it.

Maybe he had. But the ease with which he'd handled the break-in and the heist today pointed in an entirely different direction than inherited wealth.

I froze when the realization hit, followed by a hot wave of embarrassment and anger when I finally connected the dots that I should've the moment we met.

Eliot wasn't the law-abiding citizen I'd taken him to be. He was a criminal. That's why he didn't out me to the police when he caught me red-handed—he couldn't get involved. And with his wealth, the skills, and the secret identities, one thing was clear. Eliot Reed wasn't a bit player. He was the boss.

The rest of the drive passed in a daze as I tried to recover from the revelation I'd had. Eliot sat as calm as you wish across me, giving me comforting smiles whenever our eyes happened to meet. An hour ago, his presence had helped me keep my head high and do what had to be done so that we could be free of these people. Now I found myself questioning even his smiles.

Was he playing me? Or was he genuinely what I had started to think of as my friend?

We reached the airport before I managed to work myself into a proper state and lost control of my upset and growing anger. Enzo pulled over outside the main entrance of international departures and Eliot and I filed out. I couldn't wait to get him to a quiet spot so that I could confront him. I would make him tell the truth once and for all.

Eliot reached through the open window to Falconi, giving him the deed. "Here, as we agreed."

Relieved that the nightmare was over and not wanting to dawdle, I made to head into the terminal, only to halt when I realized Eliot wasn't following. I turned back and my eyes grew large.

He was standing by the car, utterly still. Ciro stood so close behind him they were practically pressed against each other. It didn't take a genius to figure out he was holding a gun to Eliot's back.

"What's this?" Eliot asked, sounding calm. "This isn't what we agreed."

"I believe I'll keep you a while longer," Falconi said through the open window of the car, teeth bared in vicious delight. "I realized I still need insurance to keep Miss Reed quiet, so I'm altering the deal."

Pray I don't alter it further…

I almost snickered aloud, more for nerves than for finding the quote funny in this situation. Eliot met my eyes and nodded.

"You go home. You're safe and free now."

For all that I was furious with him, I didn't want to leave him behind. No matter why he'd come to Rome, he'd stayed to free me.

"But what about you?"

I took a step closer, more involuntary than for any actual purpose. Eliot jerked when Ciro ground the gun deeper.

"I'll be fine." His extraordinary eyes were reassuring, but I had a sudden feeling this would be the last time I saw them.

"You won't be coming back, will you?"

He didn't answer. Instead, he leaned down, a question in his eyes. I reached up and met his lips. I expected a brief kiss goodbye, and I closed my eyes to savor the moment. But he wrapped his arms around me and pulled me against his strong body for a deep, sensuous kiss that I felt all the way down to my toes, making me completely forget that I was angry with him.

It ended abruptly when Ciro poked Eliot with the gun again, but Eliot didn't release me. We stared at each other, slightly out of breath. Then he smiled, nodded, and leaned to murmur in my ear.

"Run."

I didn't want to, but I obeyed anyway. Twirling around, I dashed toward the terminal, ignoring the thump and groan of pain I heard behind me. If Ciro had shot Eliot, there was nothing I could do, and if he hadn't, Eliot could take care of himself.

The door opened fast enough to allow me to slip through. I heard Ciro follow, but I didn't turn to look. Pressing low, I weaved around the people milling in the huge hall, hoping they would hide me as I ran across the floor to where I knew the toilets were.

I dashed inside and straight into the only empty stall, locking the door behind me. If Ciro had followed me here, he didn't enter the loo, but I waited quietly for a long time, trying to catch my breath.

When I was calm enough, I reached into the pocket of my trousers and pulled out the packet Eliot had slipped in while he kissed me. A phone and a large wad of cash. My heart jumped.

A girl could do a lot with these.

I opened the phone that wasn't locked, and a photo of the casino deed showed up. He must have photographed it in the bank while our backs were turned.

I stared at it for a moment in indecision. I should go home. Laïla was probably worried sick already. But I wasn't done here yet. Eliot needed me, and I needed to make sure Falconi didn't come after me again.

Straightening resolutely, I exited the stall and exited the loo with a group of joyous women. I looked around carefully, but Ciro wasn't there.

The coast clear, I slipped away from the group that was shielding me. But instead of continuing to the international flights that would take me back home to France, I headed to the domestic terminal.

Venice should be lovely this time of year.

14

ELIOT

FOR A MAN WHO HAD GOT exactly what he wanted, I was curiously gloomy on our drive back to Rome, staring out of the window without seeing. Ciro's punch to my gut was part of it, though I wasn't nursing it as much as I pretended to be. I'd made a good show of clumsily stepping in front of him to give Ada a chance to flee, and I needed to make Falconi believe I was weaker than I looked.

The hurt was insubstantial for a man of my former career. What mattered was that Ada was free and the video was destroyed, which had been the main objective.

Moreover, I'd successfully manipulated Falconi to keeping me with him, a spur of the moment decision that I stood behind. He was going after Bosco. Whether he wanted to or not, he would take me with him. I should be celebrating.

Yet I couldn't help wishing I'd gone home with Ada, which was silly. I didn't even have a home to return to anymore, and hadn't planned to go back. I'd been at peace with my decision, and the reasons for it hadn't changed.

It had to be the kiss. I'd wanted to kiss Ada for a long time, and knowing this was the only chance I had, the last time I saw her, had pushed me slightly over the edge. The kiss had been deeper than I intended, and her eager response had all but scrambled my brain. I'd barely remembered to slip the phone and the cash into her pocket. She would need them to get home.

The wisdom of my rules showed their power once again. I shouldn't have become attached. It only made things harder for me.

But I had managed to help Ada, and that had to count for something too. She was free, and with less fuss than I'd originally feared. We hadn't had to break into Bosco's villa or rob a bank, both of which could've seen us behind bars.

"Why did you send us to break into the villa if your sister lives there?" I had to ask Falconi. It had nagged me the whole ride.

"She doesn't, and I don't have the key."

"The villa doesn't belong to your sister?" Had Bosco lied after all? Then again, my search for his properties hadn't brought the villa up.

Falconi shot me an angry look. "It does, it was what she got in the divorce settlement, but she has bad memories of the place and doesn't want to live there."

"So this is about revenge?"

"Salvatore should never have slighted Arianna. Belittling the whole family."

I remembered the death certificate of Bosco's child in the safe deposit box and couldn't help thinking there was a real tragedy behind the divorce. But it was none of my business. Falconi was bent on having his revenge on Bosco, and with any luck would wipe the younger man out of existence, saving me the trouble.

My objective had been to make sure Bosco didn't come after me again, but that was a futile wish after today's events. Bosco would retaliate with a vengeance. With Falconi, I might survive the encounter. Enemy of my enemy and so forth…

I sneered to myself, and it felt bitter. I'd escaped the mafia life only to land right back in the middle of it.

We drove in silence until Falconi had his anger in rein. "I must confess, Mr. Reed, I wasn't sure keeping you hostage would ensure that Miss Reed won't instantly go to the police, but after that kiss…"

Partly why I'd kissed her.

"She won't blab. She has too much at stake."

Falconi made a noncommittal sound and changed the topic. "What sort of businessman are you, Mr. Reed, to have dealings with Salvatore?"

"Legitimate," I said. "And definitely not drugs. But I only know him because I played baccarat at his table once."

"Yet you're familiar enough with him to know what his true business is. Most people think he's a wealthy philanthropist."

"He tried to kill me. I made it my business."

"Anything interesting in his office beyond the key?" Falconi asked, indicating he knew exactly how we'd pulled off the theft. I shrugged.

"If there had been, I would've taken it."

It wasn't entirely true; there had been the false IDs, but I wasn't about to give everything for Falconi, and definitely not for free.

At Falconi's villa, Ciro followed me to the room I'd shared with Ada. "Pack your things. We're leaving?"

"Oh? Where to?"

"None of your business." With that, he locked me in.

I made a quick job of packing my bag, careful not to leave anything behind. I packed Ada's things too. I didn't believe she would get them back, but I didn't want to leave evidence behind that she'd been here.

I'd given the extra phone to Ada at the airport, and I wasn't holding my breath that I'd get my own phone back any time soon. But I had money, a couple of false IDs, and two guns. I'd make do.

Ciro hadn't come for me by the time I was done, so I took a quick shower and changed my shirt before dressing in the suit again. Not because it was comfortable, but because I had to look like a person Falconi would want to take seriously. The suit was perfect for it.

It took an hour more before Ciro arrived to fetch me. I spent the time resting on the bed. It wasn't like I had anything else to do.

I took both bags, mine and Ada's, and followed Ciro out of the villa, where Danny was already waiting with Enzo. He was wearing his new suit too, and like me he'd changed his shirt. He didn't have luggage, but there was a bag in the trunk of the Rolls when I put mine there.

Falconi was in the car and Ciro made sure Danny and I were securely in before taking the seat next to Enzo. But I had no intention of fleeing. Falconi was about to deliver me what I wanted, and I didn't even have to pay the expenses.

The sun was setting and traffic was light. We drove about ten kilometers north, and I spent the time watching scenery. As I'd anticipated, a car window was the closest I got to seeing the sights on this trip. Falconi did the same on his side, and Danny had his phone. No one was talking.

Our destination was a private airport. There were no security checks, which I was grateful for because I had the weapons in my bag. The car drove straight onto the tarmac, where a small Learjet was waiting. We would be travelling in style, then. I hadn't expected anything less.

We boarded, and the plane taxied almost immediately. I still had no idea where we were going. I'd be damned if I asked.

The flight took only about an hour. I had no means of telling the direction, and the captain didn't make any handy announcements. We were served coffee, which I enjoyed gratefully, as it had been several hours and two robberies since I'd eaten anything.

We landed at another private airport. It was dark already, but I noticed during the approach that it was on a strip of land in the middle of water. As we exited the plane, the floodlights revealed that the runway was grass. Interesting.

But we weren't in the middle of nowhere, like I'd feared. As we drove out of the airport in yet another chauffeured Rolls, there were apartment buildings and grocery stores lining the streets, and we soon reached what was clearly the town center.

We drove through it, which took two minutes at most. Nothing gave me any clue as to where we were. There was the sea, but that was never far from anywhere in Italy; the cypress trees that lined the street grew everywhere too; and houses looked pretty much the same as in every Italian town.

Suburbia began again on the other side of the town center. There were larger houses here, but they were all relatively new and nothing like the opulent villas in Rome, although the architecture was clearly inspired by them.

The chauffer drove us into a neighborhood of larger villas, densely built with barely any room for gardens. At the end of the street, with only sea in front of us, the gate of the last villa on the right opened. We drove into a small courtyard that was shielded on all sides by tall cypresses and other trees. Security lights flared on.

The villa was smallish and sort of T-shaped; the vertical bar of the letter was a stump, and the horizontal bar faced the sea. It was mostly one story, though there were random second-story protrusions in the middle. Walls were white stucco, roof was red tile, and the walls had no other ornaments than brown, wooden shutters in every window. Instead of Italian, it more reminded me of Spanish ranches in California, but we hadn't flown that far. Or to Spain, for that matter.

We exited the car, took our bags, and were escorted into the house by Ciro and Enzo. The entrance hall had a terracotta tile floor and whitewashed walls with dark wooden support beams on the ceiling like in Spanish villas, adding to my sense of disorientation.

But my architectural musings were cut short when Danny and I were suddenly surrounded by six armed men, their weapons pointed at us. Falconi spread his arms and sneered.

"Welcome to Venice."

DANNY AND I WERE frisked quickly and efficiently, and Danny's phone was confiscated, much to his aggravation, but he didn't put up a fight. It would've been useless anyway.

I hadn't worn my weapons, and they didn't search the bags. If I'd been in charge of this operation, I would've done that, even if I'd presumed it had been done before.

But I kept my mouth shut and just threw the strap of my bag over one shoulder to be able to carry Ada's luggage easily too.

Nevertheless, they deemed us so dangerous that four men escorted us up the dark wooden stairs at the side of the hall, another feature that more resembled Spanish style. They were polished and slippery, and I couldn't be blamed when I stumbled as the guy at my back pushed me to the direction that he wanted at the top, making me fall against the man in front of me.

The guy I'd tackled retaliated immediately and punched me in the stomach, the same spot as Ciro had earlier but harder. Good thing I hadn't eaten anything in hours, because *oof...* I held a hand on my stomach underneath the jacket, and walked slightly bent.

The second floor was a narrow corridor with doors at both ends. We were led to a small room at the back and locked in. I straightened immediately, dropped my bags on the floor, and took in the surroundings.

The ceiling was slanted and so low at the sides that I couldn't stand straight. The only window faced the courtyard and the next-door neighbor that was barely visible above the trees. No sea view for the prisoners.

The room was elegantly furnished, but a bit impersonal, like a guest room. It had two separate beds on each side of the window under the slanted ceiling—I'd have to be careful not to hit my head when I got out of bed—a wardrobe on one side of the door, and a nice ensuite bathroom on the other.

"Isn't this bloody marvelous," Danny huffed annoyed, the first words either of us had said since entering the house.

Not that we had been very chatty during the flight or the car drive here. Up until now, we'd been sort of enemies, or people forced to work together. We had nothing to talk about. Now we were sharing a cell.

"Think of the bright side. We could be dead."

He tilted his head in acknowledgement, and his eyes sharpened. "I wonder why we aren't."

He was right. It wasn't like Falconi lacked people, so he couldn't need us. But my attention was on the phone I'd lifted from the guard that I'd stumbled against.

I switched it off, in case he activated the tracking app, and looked for a place to hide it. The obvious choice was the dark support beam that ran through the house, but on the off chance the guy was devious enough to look up there, I needed a better place.

"Where did you get that?" Danny asked, amazed, as I pushed the window up to see if the sill had room for it, but it was nonexistent.

"From the guard."

"You stole it?" He was silent for a heartbeat, then inhaled sharply. "Did you fucking steal my phone too?" I smiled and didn't say anything. He let it go, to my amazement. "He'll come for it soon."

"Hence the need to hide it."

I opened my bag and upended the toiletry bag on the bed. It was black and had enough room for my passports, the guns, my wallet, and the phone. I added Ada's lockpicks for further measure too. It wouldn't do to give the guards the notion we could open the door anytime we wanted.

"And where the fuck did those weapons come from?" Danny demanded angrily. "Not from those guards, that's for sure."

"If you were half the cop that you're a bank robber, you would've searched my bag when you had a chance."

"What?"

We didn't have time for this. "Give me your IDs and everything you don't want to lose. Hurry."

He complied and I put them in the toiletry bag too. It was too big for any other place than the rafter beam, so it would have to do.

"How much do you lift?" I asked Danny, who looked baffled. "Never mind. I'll lift you."

Luckily, he realized immediately what I was up to, and we soon had the bag hidden. In the nick of time.

The door burst open and all six guards rushed in. They forced us onto our stomachs on the floor and searched us again, more roughly this time. Two of the guys kept us secured with weapons pointed at our necks while the rest upended our bags on the floor.

"Why are there women's clothes in this one?" one of them demanded.

"I have a fetish?" I hazarded, and got kicked in the side for my trouble. That would leave a bruise.

"I'm keeping these," another said, holding Ada's night vision goggles so that I could see.

"Okay, but if we have to do another break-in for your boss, you'll have to let us borrow them."

Amazingly, that was enough for him to leave them be. But they didn't abandon the search. They pulled the bedding off the beds and even checked the tank of the toilet seat. One of them must have been a cop or a prison guard before.

But they didn't look up.

One by one, they filed out of the room, the guys securing us leaving last. "Can you bring us food!" I shouted after them. "I'm starving."

I was certain that it would see us go hungry to bed, but only ten minutes later the door opened again and two plates of risotto with plastic spoons and a plastic bottle of wine with no glasses were pushed in.

No one would blame us for emptying the whole bottle.

15

ADA

AFTER THE WEEK I'D HAD, a late, slow breakfast on the balcony of my hotel room overlooking the Canal Grande was what I sorely needed. I couldn't quite believe I was in Venice and free; the tension in my neck indicated I expected to be caught at any moment.

I don't know why. No one even knew I was here. Well, Laïla did, as I'd called her from the airport in Rome the previous day with an update and for some information. She hadn't been happy with me when I told her I was headed to Venice instead of coming home, but what could she do?

The hotel was a five-star establishment in one of the Renaissance palazzos by the largest canal that cut through Venice's main island. Gondolas with tourists determined to start their day early were gliding past my balcony, a charming sight from the third floor up. I'd been given a small suite that I didn't really need but fully intended to enjoy anyway. If I was never held captive again, it would be too soon.

I could get used to this. If I quit my job—the legal one—every morning could be like this. If I got bored, I'd simply change locations. I could easily afford it. I seldom used the money I made with my criminal career, and I had enough funds to live in style for the rest of my life.

But despite the relaxing atmosphere, I couldn't see myself doing this for long. I wasn't ready for retirement, and not because I was only thirty-two. I enjoyed my legitimate job. And while I needed the intellectual challenge and adrenaline rush of my criminal one, I couldn't see myself doing it full-time either.

Today wasn't about rest and relaxation anyway, no matter how much I needed it. I had a job to do here: saving Eliot. I wasn't entirely sure how I'd go about it, but I knew one thing. I needed to do some shopping.

I'd already bought some necessities at the airport in Rome the previous day, like a toothbrush and underwear, and a Louis Vuitton duffel bag for them to better fit in the luxury hotel. Not that it had stopped the receptionist looking down his nose at me when I arrived with only one bag. But I needed regular clothes and a few disguises too.

I'd been to Venice several times, but always for jobs. The city was full of treasures that had been owned by the same families for generations, in old palazzos that hadn't been updated in almost as long. Their security systems were often antiquated and the safes were ridiculously easy to open. A Ming vase here, an ancient Roman statuette there, and a Renaissance miniature and an antique diamond necklace in a third place. They might not sound like much, but with right buyers or commissioners, they made a good weekend's work.

I'd cased the narrow streets with their random dead-ends and the meandering canals with bridges at odd places several times, and knew the best hiding places and the fastest routes out—not always a given when everything was surrounded by water subjected to strong tides. The city held no surprises for me, and since it never changed, I could count on my intel to be accurate still. But I'd never bothered to learn where the good shopping districts were.

Luckily, I had the phone Eliot had given me and the hotel Wi-Fi was good. It didn't take me long to find what I needed, including a shop that sold quality wigs. One never knew when they would come in handy, and I preferred to be better prepared than I was in Rome.

At least when it came to disguises. I had no idea how to free Eliot, or if he even was in Venice. But the casino was, as was Bosco's yacht, which Laïla had told me when I asked. Sooner or later the players would arrive here.

I wasn't even sure Eliot wanted—or needed—my help. It was evident that Bosco was the reason he had come to Rome. He'd investigated Bosco thoroughly enough to learn about an obscure shell company, but I had no idea what his main goal was. Maybe he wanted to help Falconi take Bosco down.

I had to try anyway. He'd gone above and beyond to help me. I owed him. I wasn't as angry with him anymore either for not telling me the truth about himself. I led a double life and would lie to everyone about it. He had no reason to trust me. Moreover, it could be I'd only imagined things.

But I knew I hadn't. It took a crook to know a crook—even if I'd been a bit slow on the uptake.

The only way to find out the truth was to ask him. And for that, I had to free him from Falconi's clutches. But even the police wouldn't touch Falconi. I stood no chance, and definitely not alone. I needed backup.

And I had just the person in mind.

I headed out after breakfast. Nothing was far in Venice, and even with tourists filling the narrow streets and hogging all the water taxis, I had my shopping done by lunch. I'd taken a leaf out of Eliot's book and visited the designer shops, buying what I wanted without looking at the price tags. In my Gucci suit, I'd had brilliant service.

I returned to my room with all my bags, and took a quick shower to freshen up. It wasn't as sweltering here as it was in Rome, but I sorely needed it.

I put on a new halter-neck, knee-length, brown chiffon dress that was perfect for the weather, adding a chiffon bolero to prevent my shoulders from burning. I made up my face with new products I'd bought that morning, but I didn't aim to disguise myself. The wigs I bought had to wait their turn too.

Not that my wigs and disguises had made a difference with Bosco. I shuddered when I remembered he knew I was Natasha. I had no idea how he'd figured it out, and I didn't like it.

I'd also bought elegant sandals, as I couldn't spend the day in the high heels I'd worn with the suit. The unevenly paved streets here weren't compatible with them—the shopping trip had shown that—and I might have to run.

After adding a careful selection of accessories like pearl earrings, a large-brimmed hat, and a shoulder bag that suited the dress, I was ready for lunch. And I had just the destination in mind: *Casinò di Venezia*.

It was the first official gambling venue in Europe, established in 1638, and it operated in two locations. There was a new, enormous place next to the Marco Polo Airport on the mainland that more resembled a warehouse, with only token decorations outside the main entrance to make it seem like it wasn't, in fact, a warehouse. But I was interested in the other venue on the main island, where the casino had operated since 1950. It was a beautiful, graystone Renaissance palazzo that had housed doges and even the composer Richard Wagner at some point; his museum was still there. And it was located only a few hundred meters up the Canal Grande from my hotel.

I hadn't suddenly become a gambler. The deed we'd stolen revealed that Bosco owned the building—not the casino, like Eliot and Falconi had assumed. I'd made Laïla check the ownership of the casino for me last night. But he was paid well for allowing the casino to operate on his property, so it was lucrative for him. He wouldn't want Falconi to get his hands on it. So that's where I would start.

But when I reached the lobby of the hotel and inquired after a water taxi to take me there, the receptionist informed me that the casino wouldn't open until seven that evening.

"And I so wanted to have lunch there," I sighed. "A friend of mine recommended the restaurant there especially."

"The Wagner Museum is open and they have a café. But we have an excellent restaurant here at the hotel too. I can get you a table on the terrace by the canal."

Since I needed to eat and the casino was out of the question, I accepted gratefully. Soon, I was seated at an excellent table under a shade, the breeze from the lagoon cooling me, reading a menu. It was peak tourist season and the place was fairly full, but I was left alone.

Until I heard a delighted, "Ada," right by my table.

STARTLED, I LOOKED UP to see a familiar face. "Detective Bellamy? This is a surprise."

"A good one, I hope," René Bellamy said with a quizzical smile that made the corners of his eyes crinkle. He leaned over to kiss me on both cheeks, three times like the French did, giving me a whiff of a delicious cologne.

René was a detective with the Lyon police. About a decade older than me, he was handsome in a very French way, with a strong nose and defined features, elegantly cut black hair going gray at the temples, charming demeanor, and penchant for luxury items a cop really shouldn't be able to afford.

Today, he was dressed in light gray trousers that looked like they were made with the same expensive summer wool as Eliot's suit—and by the same designer too—with a white cambric shirt with its collar open and sleeves rolled to the elbows, revealing nicely tanned strong arms. The sunglasses he'd lifted on his head were by Gucci, and the wristwatch was an antique Patek Philippe that would fetch a pickpocket a year's pay.

It sort of was a good surprise to have him here, and then again not. I liked him, but his presence complicated matters considerably.

"And it's René," he said with an admonishing smile. "We know each other well enough for that. May I sit?"

I gestured with my hand at the chair across the table. "Yes, of course you may. And I'm sorry, I was merely baffled to see you."

I'd met him around the time I met Eliot, and for the same reason too, as he'd been investigating a murder in Eliot's building, the owner of the penthouse that I'd robbed. He'd been with us on Melnyk's yacht when we fled for our lives, and an adventure like that deserved a more familiar approach.

He took a seat and leaned back. "I'm surprised to see you too. Are you on a holiday?"

I wish.

"Only a long weekend. I arrived last night. You? Are you staying in this hotel?"

"Yes and yes. I arrived today."

At five hundred euros a night for the cheapest room, it was definitely out of a cop's pay range, but I'd already figured he had independent means. And maybe he wondered the same about me. Good thing I'd invented wealthy parents long ago for situations like this.

We exchanged some pleasantries. He'd caught a flu after our escape, so I enquired after his health as the waiter took our orders and brought us drinks.

"Have you seen Eliot lately?" he asked after we'd received our orders. I took the question as it was intended: he wanted to know if there was something between Eliot and me. As much as I would've wanted to use Eliot as an excuse to push René off, I shook my head.

"Not recently. And I understand he'll be moving away from Lyon."

His face cleared. "Ah, that would explain why he'd sold his company."

My heart constricted hearing Eliot had done that; he truly was leaving. But it wasn't what I focused on.

"You've investigated him?"

I didn't know how to take it. If he found Eliot suspicious, how long would it take before he suspected me as well?

"No, it was my brother who bought it, and it made me curious."

Not the answer I expected. "Your brother is in the tech business too?"

He smiled. "Among other industries. Denis runs the family conglomerate. Anything from vineyards to fashion and from videogames to pharmaceuticals."

Family wealth would definitely explain his luxury lifestyle.

"But you preferred to become a cop?"

"Infinitely," he said with emphasis, and we both laughed.

It was easy to talk with him, and we didn't have awkward silences. I knew he was about to ask if we could spend the weekend together, and in different circumstances I might have been pleased with the prospect. Now, though, I had to get rid of him as fast as possible.

Sure enough, as we waited for dessert, he gave me a questioning look. "Do you have plans for today? Maybe we could see the sights together?"

Despite my plans, I found myself smiling. "That would be lovely." It wasn't like I had a good excuse not to.

But he was a better reader of character than I'd anticipated. He tilted his head and studied me from under his brows. "You sound a bit reluctant. You don't want the company, or where it might lead?"

The direct question threw me, so I gave it a serious thought. I definitely didn't want his company today, but I wouldn't mind the latter as such. He was charming, and it had been years since I'd had any sort of relationship. It had been partly Danny's fault, but now that I'd found him, I was finally over him.

I was attracted to Eliot, there was no use denying it, but he was leaving. It would be foolish of me to push a good man aside for him—provided it was only a holiday fling. I couldn't become involved with a cop. It would be only a matter of time before he discovered my nightly activities.

But he couldn't know any of that. I was about to fob him off with a polite excuse, but as I opened my mouth, I realized only the truth would work if I didn't want him to become suspicious. Or a version of it, anyway.

"I wasn't entirely honest with you earlier."

His face closed, the charming smile gone, but he only lifted his brows, prompting me to continue. I hadn't planned what to say, but I had to give him something.

"I'm not here on holiday. I'm … investigating something."

"And you couldn't tell me?" He looked slightly confused, as if he hadn't expected the answer. I grimaced.

"I'm not allowed to conduct criminal investigations. It's not in the Interpol mandate. And this isn't even my country."

"So why are you?"

I spread my arms. "I … couldn't help myself."

He threw his head back and laughed, the tension gone. "And you're using a holiday as a cover?" He didn't sound like he was condemning me, so I nodded.

"Yes."

He pursed his lips and considered me in silence for a heartbeat. Then he smiled. "Do you want help?"

I pulled back. "No. Well, I mean, maybe, but I don't want to ruin your holiday."

His smile turned teasing. "I'm French. It's a perfect holiday for me if I get to spend it with a beautiful woman."

I must admit, the line worked. He saw it and pressed on, leaning closer over the table.

"So, what are we investigating and why?"

I glanced around, but no one was near enough to hear us, and we were speaking French anyway. Still, I hesitated. "I'd rather not tell you. Plausible deniability and all that."

"I've been part of one of your illicit investigations before. What's another between friends," he said, making me startle.

"You knew?"

He flashed me a bright smile. "I know now."

Bugger.

I tried to come up with a plausible explanation. "Well, this is sort of an offshoot of what happened in Monaco. But the players are dangerous, and I'd rather you weren't involved. You almost died the last time."

The reminder made him grimace. "So why are you investigating it and not leaving it to the proper authorities?"

That was a good question. I was an analyst, and I didn't have a reason to go after anyone, let alone by myself. Vigilantes weren't tolerated in the regular police force either.

"I may have told you another lie too…"

This time he looked decidedly annoyed. "Ada…"

I bit my lip, hoping for inspiration. I had to bend the truth a little.

"It's not exactly my investigation. Eliot's been tracking these mafia bosses. We were in Rome together earlier this week for it and he … went missing."

His eyes sharpened and he was very much a detective now. "Missing? How?"

"I think he was captured by one of the bosses."

"And you didn't go to the police?"

I spread my arms, exasperated. "I had no evidence. Besides, he's the kind of mafia boss the police give a wide berth to."

He nodded, knowing well how these things went. "So what do you hope to do?"

Good question. Because I still didn't have a plan. "I'm kind of hoping Eliot will show up here. The enemy of the boss who has him should be here. We believe they were gearing for a showdown of some sort. Sooner or later, the other will arrive too, and hopefully Eliot is with him."

"Provided he's not dead."

My stomach plummeted. "To put it bluntly, yes."

"And if he doesn't come here?"

I shrugged, but it didn't feel as light as I hoped. "I have until Sunday."

"Very well. Where do we start?"

His fast acceptance of my story made me feel bad, even though it was mostly true. "The marina."

"What's there?"

"The yacht of the other boss. If he's here, the other will come. And maybe I can ... persuade him to help me with Eliot's freedom."

"Will he?"

I made a face. "Considering that he already tried to kill Eliot once, I'm not holding my breath."

16

ELIOT

WE WERE BROUGHT BREAKFAST at around nine: pastries, and not enough coffee to wake me up. After the door was locked again behind the armed guy who fetched the empty breakfast tray, Danny and I were left alone. I didn't know how long that would last, so I spent the morning preparing for when Falconi's men came for us.

I did my morning yoga, much to Danny's amusement. Why was it so difficult to imagine me practicing yoga? Luckily, he headed to shower before my annoyance disrupted my concentration.

Once we were both showered and dressed in our suits again, for a powerful image, we took down the weapons and checked them and made sure they were loaded. We didn't have extra bullets, so we'd have to be careful. We put them back into their hiding place, for now. I hoped we'd have time to grab them before things started moving.

Then I dug out the stolen phone from its current hiding place under the bed. The previous evening, while we had the excellent risotto, I'd managed to unlock the phone. Either I looked like the owner or it had really lousy face recognition software.

I'd removed the security features, replaced them with my own, and switched off all the alarms and sounds, but it died before I could make any use of it, so I'd put it on a charger that the guards hadn't confiscated. I opened a map.

"We're on an island called Lido," I told Danny, showing him the map. It was a narrow strip that formed a part of the barrier against the sea, creating the lagoon where the rest of the Venice islands were. "At the farthest tip from the main island. The airfield where we landed is only a short boat trip away from there."

There was a cluster of small islands around the largest one, which was the only one connected to the mainland with a bridge. I recognized Murano, two islands east of the main island, the place where they made famous glassware, but the satellite map showed there were important buildings on all of them. The lagoon was fairly shallow, but there were deeper routes for larger ships, also visible in the satellite image in darker green.

"We'll only need a boat if we want to make a fast escape." Or any kind of escape, since the airfield didn't do commercial flights and the island wasn't connected to others.

He shot me a sharp look. "Do you think we should run?"

"It may yet come to that. I have no idea why Falconi has kept us alive. That might change at any moment."

I'd come to Italy fairly certain that I'd die going against Bosco, but not without a fight. I wasn't willing to die because of Falconi.

"Maybe he wants us to do another break-in," Danny suggested.

It was plausible. "Those geniuses with guns definitely won't be able to pull one off," I said dryly, then reconsidered. "Not that it's my area of expertise either."

"Says the man who single-handedly pulled two robberies yesterday," he countered with a pointed look.

"Technically, I only stole the key, and we didn't need anything more complicated than lockpicks for that. The bank was a perfectly legitimate retrieval."

"Right…"

I couldn't help a smug smile. For my first attempt, I'd done well. "Ada was there too."

"She's really good," Danny said, admiringly.

I studied him askance. "Yet you left her." I really couldn't fathom it. By Ada's account, they hadn't even been fighting, let alone heading for a divorce.

His face turned hard. "Would you believe if I said it was for noble reasons? For protecting her?"

"I might, if you weren't strutting around with your own name like a fool and drawing attention to her."

"I wasn't. I'm not that stupid," he said, annoyed. "But it made things easier at the hotel where Ada was staying."

"But Falconi knows the truth?" I hadn't heard him call Danny by name, but that didn't mean anything.

"Not about who I was before." He lifted his hands, as if warding off my obvious question. "And I didn't tell him about my connection to Ada. He has surveillance footage of me doing illegal things. It's proof that I'm still alive, even if he doesn't know that I'm not supposed to be."

That was bad enough. "What's your name, then?" Maybe I should've asked that earlier. I could've blown his identity by accident.

"James Allen. I go by Jimmy."

Danny, Jimmy, the guy had a thing for similar nicknames. But at least it would be easy to remember.

"How did you get caught?"

He pressed his head down, but not before I caught a brief flash of grief on his face. "I was opening a safe in a private home three weeks ago with Thom, the bloke I disappeared with. House burglaries aren't what we were used to doing, but there were only the two of us, so bank jobs were out of the question, and I figured I'd learned a thing or two from Ada. It went well for a few years. Until Falconi."

My brows shot up. "You were robbing his house?"

"Yep."

Definitely a bad move. "Not this one, I take it?"

"No, in Milan. He killed Thom outright, but he kept me alive for the gig in Rome. And since he wouldn't hesitate to kill me, and he had the footage, I had no choice but to obey. I was allowed to get one person to help me, and Ada was the only one I knew who could pull it off. So, I lured her to Rome. You know the rest."

The death of his friend only three weeks ago explained the grief and the constant harried look on his face. "Has he promised you freedom? The proof destroyed?"

He rubbed his face with both hands. "Nope. I'm his bitch for the foreseeable future."

"So even if we had a chance to flee, you can't leave."

He nodded. "Unless I die again."

"That could be arranged…"

We'd both faked our deaths once, successfully. We could manage it again.

He gave me a searching look. "Falconi's got nothing on you. And you've been armed the whole time. Why didn't you flee?"

"I needed to get Ada out safely first."

He shook his head. "With comments like that it's impossible to believe the two of you aren't closer than you claim."

My smile was a bit wistful. "We only met a month ago. But we had a life-or-death experience that brought us pretty close."

"Was it how you became involved with Bosco?" I nodded. "And now you want to get even? With Falconi's unwitting help?"

My lip curled. "That was the plan before I pissed Bosco off by stealing his casino."

"Yeah … good luck surviving that."

He was right. I was outgunned and I didn't have a plan. Even if I fled Falconi, Bosco would come after me. I could, and would, change my identity, but I had to try finding a more permanent solution for the problem first, or I'd have to spend the rest of my life watching over my shoulder. For that, I needed intel. And I knew one person who could provide.

I searched for a phone number online and placed a call. Laïla answered immediately, and since I was calling from an unknown number, I introduced myself.

"Eliot! Is everything all right?" She sounded slightly breathless, as if I'd interrupted her exercising. Though judging by the noises in the background, she was outside somewhere.

"Absolutely fine. I didn't interrupt your lunch, did I?" It was close to midday, but she kept odd hours, often working at night, so I couldn't be sure.

"No, I'm … running errands. What's up?"

"Have you heard from Ada?"

"She called yesterday from the airport. Why? Have you become separated?"

"I didn't leave Rome with her, and then I had my phone stolen…" I let the sentence hang and she sighed.

"You shouldn't be so careless."

"I know," I admitted sheepishly. "Anyway, could I get the number she called you from?"

"Of course." She gave me the number and I added it to my stolen phone's contacts.

"Thank you. And could you do me a favor too? I don't have a computer here and I need to check the location of a yacht. Could you do that for me?"

"I'm not at my desk right now, but give me the name and I'll send the info when I can."

"*Serenata*. Owner is Salvatore Bosco."

There was a pause at the other end. "That's odd. Ada wanted to know the same thing."

My brows shot up. "Did she now. And what did you tell her?"

"That it's in the marina of the Yacht Club Venice. And as it so happens, she's also in Venice."

My heart stopped. "She is?"

"Yes." She groaned. "What is going on? Are you two up to something dangerous again?"

"Would you believe me if I said no?"

"I wouldn't, but don't worry, I'm on it."

That sounded ominous. But before I had a chance to ask what she meant, the call abruptly cut, and when I tried again, she wouldn't answer.

Danny noticed my worried look. "I don't speak French. What's up?"

"Laïla cut off." But her phone could've died, so I tried not to worry.

"Who is she anyway?"

"She's Ada's best friend at Interpol, a tech genius."

He looked impressed. "What did you want to know?"

"Where Bosco's yacht is, and it's here in Venice."

"How will that help us?"

I put the phone in my breast pocket—on mute. "Because he's usually on his yacht. And Ada is in Venice too."

"She didn't go home?" He didn't look happy. I wasn't entirely pleased either, but not terribly surprised.

"Apparently not. But I have her phone number now, so we can coordinate." But before I could try, sounds from the hallway made us stop talking. The door opened and the guard pointed a gun at us.

"Lunch. Let's go."

I jumped up from the bed, almost hitting my head on the low ceiling. "Thank fuck. I'm starving."

Danny and I followed him to a dining room on the ground floor. It had two large windows facing the lagoon that was glistening in the midday sun, competing with crystal chandeliers hanging above a long dining table that was set for four, but otherwise the room was plain. None of the expensive displays of art here like in the villa in Rome.

Falconi was sitting at the head of the table. A woman was about to take a seat cornerwise to him, and she straightened when we entered, turning to face us. Her spine was rigid, and she frowned, displeased.

She was average height and slightly plump, and maybe in her late thirties, although it was difficult to tell for sure under her heavy makeup. Her nose was strong, her eyes were dark, and her mouth was large, which made her look more striking than beautiful. Her hair was dark mahogany and in a long braid that fell down her chest, and she was dressed in a pink, two-piece Chanel skirt suit.

I thought she might be Falconi's wife, but the resemblance between the two told me the truth before Falconi spoke.

"This is my sister, Arianna Falconi-Bosco." Then he indicated to us. "These are the men that got you the casino."

She gave us a cold look. "You should've saved yourselves from the trouble. I don't need the casino. I need Salvatore dead."

DANNY AND I GLANCED at each other carefully, but controlled our faces. "We don't do wet work," I said, and she rolled her eyes, sitting down.

"As if I'd trust strangers to do it." Her English was heavily accented but understandable.

Falconi patted her hand in a patronizing manner, like she was a child. Anger and deep-rooted contempt flashed in her eyes, but he didn't seem to notice.

"You need him to rescind the annulment first and then challenge the divorce. There's no point in killing him if you can't lay a claim on his assets."

Charming family.

I took a seat across her, and Danny—Jimmy—sat next to me. "If you're divorced, why does he want an annulment?" Was it even possible?

Her face distorted with fury that could rise only from the rawest emotions. "To hurt me. And I'm going to hurt him back."

Her vicious tone made me imagine a medieval torture chamber. I cleared my throat. "Bosco is a powerful man. You'll need force to go against him."

Falconi sneered. "I have a powerful organization."

"You'll go to war?" A mafia war was the last thing I wanted to get in the middle of, even if it would deliver me what I wanted.

"If he won't listen to reason."

The lunch was served by a middle-aged woman in a light blue maid's outfit. It was rich Italian food again, and I resigned to my fate. Then again, I was a prisoner; a healthy lifestyle was the first thing to suffer. I should be grateful it wasn't moldy bread and water.

After she'd gone, I picked up my utensils and gave Falconi a questioning look. "What is our role here?"

"Mediators."

"Between you and...?"

"Salvatore. I'm not sacrificing my people, and these things can't be handled over the phone."

I took a bite of my food and had to stifle a hum of pleasure that would've been inappropriate for the situation, briefly losing focus. "And the objective is?" I managed to ask.

"To lure him where I can kill him," Ms. Falconi said, but her brother ignored her. He was likely used to her anger, but it made me uneasy. It seemed so deep and personal, more than a mere divorce would cause. I wouldn't want to be the target of it.

I remembered the death certificate of her child, and her rage became more understandable. The child drowned when he was four. Maybe they blamed each other for it.

"The casino deed in exchange of him calling off the annulment and the divorce," Falconi told me. As far as objectives went, that sounded doable. In theory anyway.

"And as a reward we get our freedom?"

He sneered. "You'll get to live, provided Salvatore won't kill you. We'll see about freedom later."

It wasn't what I'd hoped to hear, but we didn't have anything to negotiate with.

"When do you want us to start?"

"This afternoon, once the low tide is over. Salvatore is on his yacht and I want you to push with this before he realizes I hold the upper hand."

"I'm going with them," Ms. Falconi said in Italian.

"Absolutely not," her brother stated in the same language. "This is no business for women. You stay out of it. You're useless and can't be trusted with something this important."

A flash of fury was the only warning we had. She shot up, pulled a thin filleting knife from her sleeve, and slashed her brother's throat open in one smooth move.

The surprised look on his face as he died matched ours.

Jimmy and I sat absolutely still, muscles tense, barely daring to breathe. This wasn't the first violent outburst I'd ever witnessed, not even by a woman, but the victim had never been a capo of a powerful crime organization before. If his soldiers retaliated, we'd be dead before we could leave the dining room.

She studied her handiwork with a satisfied look on her blood-splattered face. "I should've done that years ago."

I wet my lips with my tongue to be able to speak, and it still took an effort. "I take it the men are on your side?" The armed soldier in the room hadn't reacted at all.

Her eyes were cold, the anger gone like it had been switched off. She nodded at the guard. "Of course. The men in this house are mine. And those who aren't have been dealt with."

She'd planned for this? It had seemed like a spur of a moment act, but the knife had been in her sleeve, which pointed at premeditation.

"And the rest of the organization?"

She shrugged, as if it wasn't an issue. "Once I bring down Salvatore, they'll be mine too."

I hoped I lived to see it, but I wasn't confident even she would. For some minions in a crime organization, killing the boss was a show of strength, but for others it was a betrayal that couldn't be rewarded with loyalty. Those people would come at her with force.

"What's the plan?"

I didn't expect her to answer, but she smiled, sat down, and placed the bloody knife next to her plate like it was tableware, staining the white placemat. Then she picked up her utensils with bloody hands and began to eat as if her brother hadn't just died, his body slumped on his chair, blood soaking the front of his shirt. I wasn't squeamish but I found myself unable to look.

"The moment the tide turns, we'll go to Salvatore's yacht with a peace offering."

My brows shot up. It didn't sound like she intended to kill him after all. "And what would that be?"

"You two, the men who stole his casino."

Fuck.

Her smile was satisfied. "You'll be our Trojan horse, of course. He'll be too distracted by you to suspect me." She looked at the guard behind us. "Take the men back to their room. We'll leave in half an hour."

It wasn't like I'd be able to eat anyway.

We exited the dining room, only to halt. The guard poked me with the weapon and I walked to the stairs, but my attention was on the scene in front of me.

Enzo and a man I didn't know were on their knees in the middle of the hall, hands bound behind their backs and heads pressed down, each with a soldier standing behind them, weapons pressed at the back of their heads. Half a dozen men were surrounding them, making sure they didn't flee.

Ciro wasn't among them. Either they'd already killed him or he was hiding. Could be he'd switched sides too. Falconi wasn't anyone to die for.

It didn't take a life in a mafia organization to recognize an execution scene. Arianna's men were getting rid of Falconi's loyals. And since it had happened while she was killing Falconi, it made this a planned coup.

There was a time when I would've been standing at the head of the execution squad, giving the order to fire, but that was well past me. I wasn't fond of Enzo, but he was someone I knew, however briefly. I didn't want to watch him die.

Enzo lifted his face just then and our gazes met. I nodded and he gave a wan smile in return. Then I was already pushed up the stairs.

Two shots sounded behind me when I reached the top.

17

ADA

THE MARINA WHERE *SERENATA* was berthed was at the southern tip of the main island. It wasn't far from the hotel; nothing here was, even if the canals, winding streets, and bridges at random places made straight routes impossible. A water taxi would've taken us there in no time, but the tide was at its lowest and there was no water in the canals.

And I'd thought the Tiber smelled bad.

René and I walked like tourists enjoying the sights, having pleasant conversation that revealed he was a cultured person whose talents and interests were probably wasted in the police. We chose a route that took us past the most famous landmarks, like St. Mark's Square, even though it was a short detour. I likely wouldn't have another chance to see the sights anyway.

Not that we were able to enjoy them much, as all the tourists had found their way onto the huge square and were now stranded by the low tide. I heard some of them complain about it, as if it were a personal affront that they couldn't get where they wanted when they wanted and had to walk. I bet there were a few one-star reviews on TripAdvisor because of it.

We were in no hurry. Bosco's yacht was going nowhere until the water was at its highest again. This was a scouting mission anyway, and we didn't have a plan. But even with several pauses for photos and a coffee break, it took less than an hour to reach the marina where the largest yachts were.

"Why do I have a feeling of déjà-vu?" René said dryly when he saw the yachts.

The marina sat in a large man-made cove, with a rectangular pier built towards the sea on two sides, shielding the yachts from the tide in the lagoon. We walked down it to where the familiar superyacht rose above the others, easily three times larger than the next largest yacht.

"Melnyk's yacht won't be here," I said wryly, and he made a face. He'd been accidentally drugged on it when he drank the water meant for a woman targeted for human trafficking. The French police had the yacht now.

"I should hope not. So which one is it?"

I pointed at *Serenata* at the other end, outside the pier as it wouldn't fit inside it. "That one."

"I remember that from Monaco. You say it belongs to a crime boss? Who?"

"Salvatore Bosco."

"The name doesn't ring a bell."

"He's very discreet, with a solid businessman front, and doesn't run an old school mafia family. But I believe he's trying to corner the Mediterranean drug smuggling route. That's why he set Dobrev and Melnyk against each other."

"So this does connect with your investigation," he pointed out. I nodded, even though the investigation itself was partly a smokescreen that I'd created to hide that I'd broken into the house of a victim whose murder he'd been investigating, to give him evidence he needed without implicating me.

"Yes. But I didn't come here for that. I'm not interested in Bosco, or Falconi, the other boss. And Falconi is after Bosco for personal reasons."

He grimaced. "With mafia, those can get ugly. What do you want to do here?"

"I'm hoping to gain some goodwill with Bosco so that he may be would be willing to help me free Eliot."

He pursed his lips, considering. "It's a longshot and might get us killed."

"Yeah…"

To his credit, he didn't turn back. I almost wanted to, but Eliot had gone to great lengths to free me. And I had Danny to think of too. I didn't owe him anything—it was his fault we were in this mess—but we'd been married once and I didn't want to leave him in Falconi's hands.

We walked past the yacht. No lights were on inside that I could see through the darkened windows, so Bosco probably wasn't there yet. I had no idea what I would do if he didn't arrive at all. Maybe he and Falconi were facing off in Rome and I was in the wrong location entirely.

At the end of the pier, we turned back and walked past Bosco's yacht again. From the corner of my eye, I detected movement there and turned to look. A face looked straight at me through a cabin window, eyes growing large with surprise. A familiar face.

"Laïla?"

I halted with a jerk. René gave me a baffled look, but the face had disappeared. "What is it?"

"I saw my colleague inside," I said, barely believing it myself. I wanted to press my face against the window to get a better look, but there was a gap between the pier and the yacht and I couldn't quite reach.

He startled. "Are you sure?"

"Honestly, no. She's not the kind to leave her computers, but she hasn't been happy with me for investigating alone. And I told her I'd be here." I took out my phone and placed a call to her, but it wouldn't connect. I began to worry.

"Let's go check."

We hurried to the stern, where we could board the yacht, not giving a thought that we were trespassing. No one came to see what we were up to, and the first deck with a dining room and a kitchen was empty. We went through it to the bow and took stairs down to the cabin level where I'd seen her. No one confronted us there either, and there was no sign of Laila. Everything was quiet.

"Surely she would've come to meet us halfway…"

"Maybe she went up the steps at the stern thinking we'd be there." René pointed at the opposite end of the long corridor.

"Or I imagined seeing her."

"No harm in looking. The place seems empty."

We checked the cabins on both sides of the corridor as we went, but they were all empty. Opulent, but empty. We climbed the steps to the dining room, but Laïla wasn't there. She wasn't waiting for us on the pier either. But a sound above us made us glance up.

"Could she be there?" René asked, already heading up the spiraling stairs.

I followed, even though I was fairly sure Laïla wouldn't be that silly. He reached the top and came to an abrupt halt. I peered around him and stopped too. My gut clenched in fear.

A very pro-looking guard in black combat gear was pointing a weapon at us, and we lifted our hands slowly up. He gestured for us to step out of the stairs and into the lounge, and we obeyed. It was a beautiful space with cream leather, teak and brass, perfect for the purpose, but the charm was lost on me.

On one soft sofa, Salvatore Bosco sat facing us, a calm, slightly amused smile on his handsome face. He would've looked charming if it weren't for the situation. There were armed guards everywhere, and in the middle of the floor, held at gunpoint by one of them, was Laïla. My gut clenched painfully.

She was dressed in knee-length jean shorts and a yellow tank top, which made her look like a street urchin and not much older either. She seemed unharmed, but her full-sleeve tattoos could hide bruises. I knew that from years of martial arts training with her.

She grimaced in apology when our gazes met, and I gave her a calm smile, like I knew how to get us out of this situation.

The guard patted us down quickly, as if my dress had any place to hide a weapon, and checked my bag, but let me keep it. Then he pushed us forward.

I walked to Laïla with stiff legs. Bosco gestured for us to take a seat, and we dropped on the wide sofa across him, Laïla on my left and René on the right.

Bosco smiled politely. "Welcome, Miss Reed, and Detective Bellamy," he said in perfect French. His English had been perfect too when we first met him at the casino in Monaco.

René startled. "Do you know me?"

"I make it my business to know the names of the police who sniff around my yacht."

I felt René tense against my leg, but his voice was calm. "And then you kill them?"

"We'll see," Bosco said with a small shrug, as if discussing casual plans.

I took Laïla's hand and she squeezed it tightly. I kind of wanted to take René's hand as well, but he was holding his together on his lap, seemingly calm, but the tension in his body where it brushed against mine said otherwise.

Bosco tilted his head, studying us. "I must say I'm curious to hear what all you law abiding citizens are doing on my yacht uninvited." He put a slight emphasis on *law abiding*, looking straight at me.

But this wasn't the first time I was lying about who and what I was. Even under pressure, I could pretend I didn't understand what he meant. And any rate, he could only be referring to that security photo outside his villa, and that could be police work. I nodded, calmly.

"I was hoping to meet you, Signor Bosco."

He cocked a brow in polite inquiry. Nothing about him was sinister, from his tan trousers and white shirt to the charming expression on his face, yet my gut tightened.

"Were you now…" he drawled. "Voluntarily?"

"Out of necessity," I conceded.

"And you brought backup?"

I made a minute shrug, as if I were as calm as him. "It's only prudent, when meeting a person of your … caliber."

"And Miss … Diab, was it … is the vanguard?"

"Laïla has nothing to do with this," I stated, squeezing her hand to keep her silent when she was about to protest. Bosco's eyes turned hard.

"When I find a member of law enforcement nosing around my property, I get to decide whether or not they have anything to do with things."

Shivers ran down my spine. I wanted to demand Laïla tell me what she had been thinking boarding the yacht, but now wasn't the time for it. Besides, we'd done the same.

Bosco leaned back on his seat, stretched an arm on the backrest, and crossed his legs, by all appearances relaxed, as if this were a casual visit.

"And what is it, Miss Reed, that you wanted to meet me for?"

This conversation had sprung on me so fast I hadn't had a chance to come up with a strategy. Truth, or a version of it, would have to suffice.

"A few days ago, Eliot, I, and a fellow Brit, crossed paths with Aristide Falconi."

Bosco's face turned into a tight mask, the amusement gone. "Crossed how?"

This was the tricky part. Even if we'd been alone, I wouldn't have revealed my shady business to him, and it was imperative that Laïla and René didn't learn about it.

"In a manner that required us to perform a certain service for him in exchange for our liberty."

He dipped his chin. "I take it you were successful, since you're here?"

"Yes and no. We delivered, but he only freed me."

Laïla inhaled sharply, figuring out what I meant, but I couldn't have her interrupt, so I squeezed her hand again.

"I see. Is the service rendered why you were sniffing around my property in Rome?"

"I was given to understand it's Falconi property now," I countered. "Nothing illegal in checking the security measures of his sister's house."

The real question was, why was Bosco still in charge of the security, if he didn't even own the villa anymore? But I wasn't going to antagonize him by asking.

"And what is it that you want from me now, Miss Reed?"

My stomach tightened painfully. I didn't want to do this, but I had no choice. "I was hoping you had something I could use as a leverage against Falconi to free my friends."

HIS EYES GREW LARGE. "What made you believe I'd help you in any way?"

"I figured you owe Eliot," I said with a small shrug that masked the panicky fluttering of my insides.

"For what?" he asked, incredulous.

"For trying to kill him without cause." I don't know where I found the nerve to state it. "He's not a cop, you know."

"Yet he's investigating me."

I knew it!

"You tried to kill him. He's vexed."

That was an understatement.

"I'm not a philanthropist."

"I thought that's exactly what you are," I said in a passable lazy drawl. His brows furrowed and my palm holding Laïla's hand started to sweat.

"I'd need something in return."

I pointed at my bag that sat at my feet. "May I?" The question was for him, but it was the armed guards I was afraid of. He nodded and I fished my phone out of the bag.

I unlocked the phone, opened the photo of the deed, and reached the phone to Bosco over the low table between us. He took a look—and his face went slack in shock, the first genuine emotion I'd seen him express.

"How … did you get this? It's in a safe deposit box in a bank. How did you even learn about it?"

"Your ex-wife is a good source of information." It was a guess, but only a wife could know about Bosco's private matters.

"You robbed a bank?"

"Of course not. We had the key." It was an easy enough admission that wouldn't give Laïla and René any incriminating information. The key could easily have come from his ex-wife.

His face hardened in anger. "Did you empty the box?"

"No. We only took the deed." I tried to keep my face emotionless—he didn't need my sympathy over the death of his child—but I didn't quite manage.

Bosco blinked several times, inhaling and exhaling slowly as he stared at the photo. I hoped he wasn't about to explode into violence. Laïla leaned closer to me and we huddled together. René wrapped an arm around us and it made me feel slightly better, even though there was nothing he could do to help.

My phone beeped. Bosco read the display and his jaw flexed. Since it wasn't originally my phone but Eliot's, the message wasn't for me, but whatever it was about, it made him pull himself together.

"This is certainly a bargaining chip, Miss Reed," he said, throwing the phone back to me. I managed to catch it, and I put it away, though I itched to read the message.

"Who has the original?" He shook his head. "Falconi, of course. What does he want for it?"

I drew a calming breath. "I believe he's unhappy with the divorce settlement between you and his sister."

Understanding dawned on his face. "It's not about the divorce, it's about annulment. Arianna wants me to call it off."

"It seems to me like a small price for getting your deed back," I said carefully, not really comprehending the issue. "They've gone to quite a length to force your hand."

He sneered. "Of course they have. She's livid about it. The annulment will prevent the soul of our child from going to heaven."

I blinked, not following, but René, the only Catholic among us, understood. "The child would be illegitimate if the marriage is annulled."

Bosco nodded. "Any living children would still be considered legitimate, but ours is dead and it doesn't apply."

"And that would be fine with you?" I asked. He'd secured the death certificate; it mattered to him. He shrugged.

"I'm not religious. Luca is dead, has been for three years. Nothing will bring him back. But I will have no trace of that woman in my life to remind me of him."

He seemed cold, but the demand for annulment rose out of grief. Nothing we did would be able to counter it.

"You're not willing to call off the annulment, then? Even for the deed?"

"No. But I do want the deed back."

I nodded. "Help me free Eliot and we'll make it happen."

He snorted a laugh, which dispelled some of his anger. "That's optimistic of you. But I'm afraid it's already too late. Isn't it, Roberto?"

A steward in white, the only unarmed man in the room, startled. "Sir?"

"You've been leaking information about me to Aristide for months, haven't you?" A nod from Bosco made all the armed guards surround the steward, who paled.

"No, I haven't done anything."

"I've read all your messages, so it's no use denying."

The man looked desperate. "Please, I have information."

"Do tell."

"Miss Falconi is about to take over and she doesn't care about the deed. She'll come here with force the moment the tide turns to kill you."

Bosco's brows rose, but he didn't seem surprised. "That's an odd turn of events." He glanced at his watch. "We'd best hurry, then."

He nodded at his men, and the one standing in front of the steward shot him without preamble. I startled, and René jumped like he was about to surge up and intervene, only to remember that he wasn't here as a cop.

Bosco got up and gave us a cold look. "I suggest you follow me, unless you want to be here when my vindictive ex arrives with her soldiers."

Since none of us wanted that, we pushed up on tottering legs and followed him to a speedboat attached to the yacht. Two guards were already there, and that wasn't all. My luggage and what I presumed were René's and Laila's too were piled between the seats.

My body turned to ice and I dropped heavily onto the seat behind me. Bosco had known about us from the start. We were so dead.

18

ELIOT

MY KNEES ALMOST BUCKLED IN relief when the door to our room closed. Jimmy dropped heavily on his bed and leaned elbows on his knees, head dropped.

"Bloody hell. I knew I was going to die here, but this really brings it home."

"…yeah…"

I'd lived with the threat of death hanging above me my whole life. This past year without had been wonderfully relaxing, which I only appreciated now that the tension had returned.

We didn't have time to dwell on our impending death. We took the toiletry bag down from the rafter beam, and I pulled out the contents.

"I want the Makarov," Jimmy said. I didn't want to give it up, but the 9mm was easier to hide in my pants pocket so I handed the larger weapon to him.

Jimmy checked it with professional expertise, even though we'd done it that morning, and put it under the waistband of his pants at the small of his back. It was an uncomfortable place to wear it, but the only one where it wouldn't instantly show when he put the suit jacket on.

I took the IDs and put them in the pocked of my suit jacket with the phone. As a finishing touch, I slipped Ada's lockpicks into my pants pocket. I didn't know what I would need them for, but it felt like a good luck charm.

We packed our bags, just in case, and wiped the surfaces of our fingerprints. There wouldn't be any prints connecting us to this place if we didn't survive.

Since we had a little time, I tried to call Ada, but she wouldn't answer her phone. I sent her a warning message instead, telling her what had happened and to stay away from Bosco's yacht. The mere thought that she would be caught in Arianna Falconi's revenge made my insides turn cold.

I was about to put the phone away when a message arrived for the owner of the phone. I'd skimmed some of his messages before, and found him uninteresting, but now my brows shot up.

"It appears Falconi has an inside man on Bosco's yacht. He wants to know when the attack will take place."

Jimmy looked impressed but not terribly surprised. "Can we use the info?"

"We could use it to buy goodwill with Bosco." We'd need more, but it was a start.

"I don't think we'll get a chance to talk with him," Jimmy said dryly. If he was afraid, he didn't show it.

I rubbed my face, thinking furiously. "Should we use it to warn him anyway?"

"Are we on his side in this?"

"I'm mainly on my side."

He tilted his head wryly. "If we don't warn him, Arianna might kill him and our troubles would be over."

I gave him a questioning look. "Do you really think she'll be able to pull it off?" The execution of Falconi and his men had been swift, but Bosco was a ruthless man and likely better prepared for her.

"Hell hath no fury and so forth."

She was definitely furious, but that might prevent her from thinking clearly. It would lead to mistakes, and they might be fatal.

But we had to do something. The guards were already climbing up the stairs, their steps loud. Out of time, I simply wrote, *Now*, and pressed send.

The bodies were still in the entrance hall when Arianna's soldiers escorted us out and to a paved promenade that ran between the houses and the lagoon. There were small yachts and outboard engine boats docked along it, each neighbor having their own vessel. Boats were more useful here than cars.

We were shoved into a speedboat with white leather seats for six and two powerful engines at the back, already on, churning the water of the lagoon. Half of the soldiers boarded with us and the rest went with Arianna. All were armed to their teeth as befit the soldiers of an arms dealer.

So much for the peace mission.

The tide had turned and water was pushing into the lagoon from the sea with a force I'd never witnessed before. But the guy handling the boat knew how to navigate the waters and it didn't take him long to cross the lagoon to a marina at the tip of the main island.

I recognized Bosco's *Serenata* from afar. A 170-foot superyacht with three decks above and two below was difficult to miss. It was docked outside the pier that rounded the marina, the only place with enough room and depth for it. It didn't look like anyone was in, and there were no visible guards.

"I don't think he's there," I said when we pulled over by the yacht, not even trying a stealth approach. A guard would've opened fire already, or at least come to check.

"He's here. We have a man inside," a soldier said, verifying what we already knew, but I had to wonder if the inside man was a double agent who had evacuated the yacht after my warning.

He hopped onto the platform at the back of the yacht to secure our boat into it. The soldiers made Jimmy and me disembark next before following suit.

There were a dozen soldiers and Arianna, now dressed in black leggings and a sleeveless tunic that looked like it hid a bulletproof vest. She was armed too. Jimmy and I were a clear weak point in our suits, which made me uncomfortable.

Their weapons weren't drawn, but they were visible in the holsters on their hips. I kept mine hidden, as did Jimmy. No need to tip our hand just yet.

The yacht remained quiet, and no one came to check as we filed onto the back deck. I didn't like the quiet. I glanced at Jimmy, and we went into a cop mode—yeah, even I—as we followed the soldiers, walking sideways to present a smaller target, our backs against the wall when possible.

The first deck with a dining room was empty, so we climbed to the next while half the men went below. The upper deck held the lounge, which brought instant bad memories. It was empty too.

Arianna didn't look pleased. "Where is he?" she demanded in Italian. "You said he would be here."

The soldier she addressed looked baffled. "Roby assured us he was here."

Jimmy pointed at something behind the low couch I'd sat on during my previous visit. "Would this be your guy?" He didn't even speak Italian, but it didn't take much to figure out what had happened, especially since he already knew about the inside guy.

A man in a formerly white steward's uniform was lying dead on the deck, the chest of his shirt red with drying blood. I tried to feel bad for him; it was probably my fault that he was dead, but I couldn't muster the sentiment.

Arianna took one look and let out a string of colorful curses in Italian. But my attention was already elsewhere.

There was a bar desk at the back of the lounge, and on it was an open laptop. Movement on the display drew me there, and my mouth dropped open as I saw the contents.

It was video from inside a private plane. Bosco sneered at me from the screen when he saw me, startling me. "I'm sorry I couldn't be there to receive you in person, Mr. Reed," he said in English. "If you survive what's to come, we'll see you in Milan. Bring the deed."

The camera turned around to show people opposite him, and I went cold all over. Ada was there, looking beautiful and composed as always, but her eyes were worried. And next to her were Laïla and René to my utter bafflement. All three had guns pointed at their heads.

FURY SURGED UP INSIDE me, the deadly kind I hadn't had to control in my previous life. I squeezed my hands into tight fists, wanting to let it loose now, to punch something, someone.

I was furious at Bosco for daring to take my friends hostage. But I was furious at myself too.

This was exactly why I'd wanted to deal with Bosco before I left. Yet all I'd managed to do was to draw his attention to those I'd tried to protect.

I took a hold of the laptop lid and hurled it across the lounge like a Frisbee with a force that shattered it against the window at the opposite side of the room. Six guns were instantly pointed at me, and my hand went in the pocket where my 9mm was.

Jimmy grabbed my arm before I could pull it out, a foolish act in my current state of mind, but his attention wasn't on me. He looked tense.

"Is it me or is it too silent in here?"

I forced myself to relax. I wouldn't have stood a chance against the semis of the soldiers anyway, and I couldn't afford to die before Ada, Laila, and René were free. I cocked my head, listening.

"What's holding the men who went to search the yacht?"

Jimmy shook his head. "Wanna bet Bosco didn't take all his men with him?"

Fuck.

"It's an ambush. Take cover!" I barked in Italian, as if these were my men. To my amazement, they dropped instantly behind the low lounge chairs.

Before I could follow suit, Arianna swirled to me, furious. "What do you think you're doing?"

"I don't know, not dying?"

"Too late for that." She lifted her weapon and aimed it at my chest. Even across the floor, she might actually hit me.

I dove behind the bar, but the shot never came. Instead, a dozen armed men filed into the lounge through all the doors and the stairs behind me—an *I told you so* moment if any was, but I was too busy hiding to gloat.

Someone fired and it was all the situation needed. Bullets started to fly, filling the room with a rattling cacophony. The teak lining of the bar wasn't a match against them. I had to change locations, and fast, before a stray bullet found me.

The attention of the man closest to me was on the firefight, so I took the chance and lunged face-first down the spiral staircase behind the bar. It wasn't elegant or painless, but it landed me on the deck below fast and without bullet holes.

It landed Jimmy on me as well. "Up, up, up," I urged him and we scrambled to our feet and through the dining room to the back deck.

An armed man was detaching the ropes of one of Falconi's boats, but I had no way of knowing if he was Falconi's or Bosco's man. When he pointed a weapon at us, it didn't matter.

My hand went into my pocket, but Jimmy was already holding his and he shot the man without pausing, dropping the guard with one shot to his head.

"Good job…" I muttered, impressed, jumping on board the boat the guy had been working on. I went straight to the steering console while Jimmy detached the other rope. I had the engine running before he'd followed me.

"Keep an eye out for pursuit," I said as I maneuvered the boat away from the yacht and onto the open water of the lagoon.

"Gun it! They've spotted us and they're rushing to the other boat."

We should've disabled it, but it was too late now.

We'd be easy targets on the lagoon, so I headed in the opposite direction, between the main island and the one closest to it on the right. The tide was still rising, but not gushing in with full force anymore, and water traffic had returned to normal. There were a lot of boats and water buses about, shuttling between the islands. I hoped we would disappear among them.

A spray of shots hit the water behind us and I ducked by instinct.

"Drive faster," Jimmy shouted. "I'll handle the pursuit."

"Okay, but you only have so many bullets, the range of the Makarov isn't much, and there are innocent people around, so aim before shooting."

"Oh, I'm not using the Makarov…"

I risked a glance and saw him holding a semi he'd taken from the guard he'd shot. That would work.

A canal through the main island opened on my left. The narrow waterways crisscrossing the islands could be good places to ditch our pursuers, but then again not. This canal was narrow and straight; we'd be like targets at a shooting range. And there was a lot of traffic. We might get stuck.

Instead, I steered right, along the coastline of the island there, and came to a wider canal through it that had less traffic. I pushed the gas and the engine roared as we picked up speed.

After a couple of hundred meters, the canal made a steep turn to the right again, and I found myself within sight of the yacht club we'd just left, though mercifully at least a hundred meters away. There was a commotion on *Serenata*'s deck, with Bosco's men clearly in charge. I couldn't spot Arianna.

A shot rang again and Jimmy cursed. "Are you hit?" I asked, not daring to turn to look.

"Just a scrape and not on my weapon arm." A moment later, he fired his weapon. "I hit the driver. They're slowing down. Floor it!"

I pushed the lever to full speed. Ignoring the dozens upon dozens of boats and yachts filling the lagoon, I headed round the tip of the main island and immediately towards the island left of it. The water traffic was even heavier there, but I couldn't slow down.

"They're around the tip," Jimmy shouted.

I steered the boat between two waterbuses, creating a wake that made them shake and the people on them scream loud enough to hear over the noise of our engines. Another boat had to make a sharp turn not to collide with us, making it collide with a different boat. It was only a matter of time before we had the police on our tail too. We needed to hide.

A canal opened on our left through the smaller island, with small boats docked on one side. Shielded by the commotion I'd created, I made a sharp turn there, almost losing control of the boat before I managed to cut speed. Our momentum carried us straight into the canal, lifting the water level and making the boats there sway violently.

There was barely room to move past the boats at minimum speed, but I managed it without scraping our boat against the wall on the other side. I spotted an opening between the docked boats and maneuvered ours there.

The wake hadn't even settled when the boat of our pursuers drove at full speed past the canal's mouth. I didn't wait for them to circle back. I pulled out and headed south through the canal.

The lagoon opened there and I sped straight across it toward the sea, keeping on the deeper paths that were visible through the water.

"Where are you going?"

"Back to Falconi's house before Arianna returns." She didn't have a boat, but there were plenty of those in this city. It wouldn't take long. Provided she was still alive.

"Are you insane?"

"Possibly. But we need the deed if we want to go after Bosco."

And I definitely intended to do so.

Falconi's house was empty, unless you counted the bodies in the hall and Falconi's in the dining room with the lunch still on the table. The maid had finally found the courage to clear it, but she took one look at us when we let ourselves in through the unlocked front door and stiffened.

"Don't touch anything," I told her sternly in Italian, and she nodded and fled to the kitchen.

"Fetch our bags, Ada's included, I'll check the study," I told Jimmy, heading to the room on the left of the hall with a writing desk and some bookshelves I'd spied through the partially open door.

"We don't need the luggage."

"If the police come, I don't want there to be anything of ours around."

And the police would come, because I'd call them myself.

He didn't argue but shot up the stairs. I went to Falconi's desk, hoping the deed was here and not with Arianna. And I hoped it was visible somewhere and not inside the safe. Jimmy would likely be able to open it, but it would slow us down.

The desk was clear so I pulled the drawers open. One of them was locked, and I took out Ada's lockpicks, pleased that I'd thought to take them with me, though I would've broken the lock if I'd had to.

The old lock yielded to me in no time, and at the top of the drawer was the deed. I grabbed it and closed the drawer, not bothering to lock it again.

Jimmy was already coming down the stairs with the luggage. "Good thing we packed them or I'd have left them."

I gave him a brief once-over, but there was no visible blood, so I just took the bag he carried on his injured side and rushed out of the door.

As we boarded the boat again, I glimpsed one in the distance heading fast our way. It might be our pursuers—Bosco's men would believe we worked for Falconi and would come to check—but I wasn't about to stay and find out.

I gunned the engine and headed another direction.

19

ELIOT

IT WAS A THREE-HOUR-DRIVE to Milan, the biggest commercial hub of Italy, northwest of Venice near the border to Switzerland. We made it in two and a half.

Our escape to the mainland had been uneventful. We'd left the boat at a dock there, after wiping it clean of our prints, and hopped into a taxi that took us to a car rental.

We made a brief visit to a pharmacy to buy a dressing for Jimmy's wound, and another to a post office next to it. The cut was shallow and had almost stopped bleeding by then, so the biggest damage was to his new suit jacket. He wasn't as upset by it as I was.

If the situation hadn't been so dire, I would've enjoyed the drive in the Audi R8 sports car. It handled well on the motorway, allowing me to test its limits. Now I merely gritted my teeth and pressed on, grateful that there were no traffic police around to stop us.

Milano was a center of fashion and some of the most luxurious five-star hotels there were owned by fashion houses, which I learned when I had the phone service provided by my credit card company to book a room for us. To my disappointment, the Armani Hotel was fully booked, but Bulgari Hotel had a suite available.

"Bloody hell, that's two thousand euros a night," Jimmy said, appalled, when I ended the call that had been on speaker while I drove. "Why would you spend that much on a hotel room you probably won't even use?"

"What do you use all your money for, then?"

"Who says I have any? Laundering money from bank heists isn't easy, you know."

"It is if you know how…"

He shot me a sharp look, but I answered the first question.

"I like luxury. Those hotels have movie stars staying in them, so they're absolutely discreet. And most importantly, they're not owned by Falconi or Bosco."

"As long as you're paying…" he said dryly.

"These may be our last days, and I have no one to leave my money to. Might as well enjoy them."

"That's one way to look at things." He was quiet for a stretch. "If I survive, I'll have to die again."

He was right. Falconi was dead, but Arianna would find the footage eventually. Or if she was dead and Bosco took over, he would.

"Do you have new IDs ready?"

"No."

"That's sloppy of you."

I felt him give me a slow look, but I didn't take my attention from the road. "Getting one set of genuine fake IDs was difficult enough, you know."

I did know.

"I might have a person who'll get them for you." I'd intended never to contact the guy who had helped me with mine, but he was the only one who was good enough.

"The same you were going to use in Rome?" he asked,

his tone indicating he was on to me, whatever that was.

"Maybe. Pick a name and birthdate."

"What, now?"

"Do you have anything better to do?" I had no idea why I was helping him. Maybe the shared near-death experience had brought us closer.

He gave it a brief thought. "Francis Hart, Frank. August 4th."

"That was quick." I had several IDs ready and I hadn't been able to choose between them. I liked being Eliot Reed.

"Frank was Ada's dad's name and Hart was my mum's maiden name. August 4th is Ada's birthday. I'll use my own year."

Practical. "And what will you say if they ask your mother's maiden name as a security question?"

"The same. Frank Hart is a son of a single mum from Manchester."

That would work. Now we only had to make him die. And while we were at it, I might as well die too. Again.

The evening rush was at its peak when we arrived in Milan around half past five, and it took us a while to navigate to the city center where the hotel was. It was a new, six-story building built around an old six-story building, with an entirely new wing attached to them. It was completely hidden by a block of other old buildings and accessed through a side alley you couldn't find accidentally. Two blocks south were La Scala opera house and other cultural landmarks.

My attention was on the orange Bugatti Veyron parked by the main entrance.

A porter came to take our luggage, and a parking valet took the car key. He would see it back to the car rental. If we needed a car, we'd get a less flashy one.

In due order, we were shown to our suite on the top floor. The bedrooms and the sitting room between were fairly small but beautifully furnished in a mix of old and new that we'd aspired to with the casino-spa hotel of my old boss but hadn't quite pulled off. The canopy bed was large enough for me, which was the most important feature. The balcony was huge, and the view to the inner courtyard was excellent.

"What's the plan?" Jimmy asked when the porter had left.

I'd done research on Bosco and knew he had businesses and a penthouse in Milan, but it didn't give me much to work on. First things first.

"I'll take a shower and change my shirt. Then we'll have dinner."

I'd asked the receptionist to send me a shirt from the shop on the ground floor selling designer clothes. It would be delivered after they'd steamed the wrinkles off.

I loved luxury hotels.

"Do you have a clean shirt?" I asked him. The one he was wearing had blood staining it.

"Yes. But I'll have to ditch the jacket." The bullet had torn the upper arm of the sleeve beyond repair.

"You can borrow my blazer, but it won't be as fine."

He shook his head, amused, and disappeared into his room.

Once I was feeling more like myself again, I sat down on the balcony and took out my stolen phone, decidedly not thinking if the owner was still alive to want it back.

I had the contact address of my hacker memorized. It wasn't something I could store on any devices, and we had code words established to ensure we both knew who we were dealing with. But I hadn't contacted him since letting him know I was safe, and I had no way of knowing if he'd be able to do what I asked.

"Is your current passport genuine?" I asked Jimmy when he emerged, showered, shaved, and in clean clothes. I wished I could shave too, but I would need the disguise soon enough. He nodded, giving the passport to me, and I added the passport number to my request.

"If my contact comes through, he'll replace the existing info in the database with the new one. That way the biometric data on your passport will match."

He shook his head, amazed. "If that's actually possible, I'll … I don't know, eat my proverbial hat."

"Just write down the passport number like a good tourist. If he comes through, you'll march to the nearest British embassy, tell them your passport was stolen and request a new one. And destroy all evidence of your current life."

"It's as if you've done this before."

I shrugged and he straightened, as if having an epiphany.

"You're FBI, aren't you? Handling witness protection programs?"

"If it makes you sleep better…"

We went through a host of security questions the passport officials would ask and I added them to my email too. Then I put the phone back into my pocket, checked the weapon already there, and we headed for dinner.

The restaurant on the top floor of the new wing was almost full when we walked in. We hadn't made a reservation, and I was prepared to negotiate with the maître d' for a table, but to my amazement he smiled politely and gestured with his hand.

"This way, signori. Your host has already arrived."

Jimmy and I glanced at each other, but we didn't say anything as we followed the maître d' across the restaurant to a discreet table at the back. I had an uneasy feeling in my stomach, but I pretty much knew who was waiting for us.

I turned out to be right.

"I WAS BEGINNING TO fear you wouldn't show up at all," Bosco said affably, gesturing at the chairs across the table. We took seats and a waiter showed up with menus. I opened it to gather myself, but I couldn't say I understood a word I was pretending to read even though it was in English.

I pointed at items in random. Jimmy said he'd take the same, and the waiter left. Then I levelled a look at our surprise host.

"I expect my friends to be unharmed."

"Do you, now?" Bosco drawled. "Mightily optimistic of you." He glanced at Jimmy. "And who would this be?"

"James Allen, a security expert," I stated, deadpan, and Jimmy didn't twitch a muscle to contradict me.

"The way you are a security expert?" He asked it like he too thought it was a euphemism for a cop. Since Jimmy actually was a cop—or used to be—I made a minute shrug.

"He's the one who handles the day-to-day security. I was more a moneyman, though not in the same company as him."

"I see." He tilted his head, considering us. "As it so happens, I'm in need of a security expert."

"We've retired."

"I'm sure you'd be willing to consider my offer in

order to free your friends."

I leaned towards him over the table. "I'm willing to hand you the deed in exchange for their freedom."

"I find it's not quite enough anymore…"

"A casino worth hundreds of millions isn't enough?" I shook my head, stunned. "Would you even have considered exchanging it for calling off the annulment?"

"Ah, you know about it?"

"Falconi was vocal about it."

"He always held it against me that I divorced his sister." He shook his head as if sad. "But I never would've guessed Arianna would act against him like that."

"She wasn't insane when you were married?"

Genuine sadness flashed on his face. "Grief changes a person. But the seed of her hatred of her brother springs from their childhood."

"Still, she doesn't seem like a woman you would marry."

It wasn't that I expected him to date supermodels—although he could, with his looks and wealth. But Arianna hadn't struck me as a woman who would suit an important businessman either.

"I'm Italian," he said with an elaborate shrug. "All women have their charms. In her case, it was the possibility of taking over her brother's business—or having our son to inherit it." His face tightened again.

"She's not handing it over to you now."

"She doesn't have to. You will help me to take it from her."

I tensed. "We're not getting involved in mafia takeovers. The best I can offer is your deed in exchange for my friends."

"I'm getting that back regardless."

The waiter arrived with our food, giving me a chance to gather my thoughts. I seemed to have chosen some sort of fish, which looked delicious, but I didn't have much appetite anymore. I forced myself to eat anyway. I'd already skipped most of my lunch.

"I'm not the only one who will want his hands in Aristide's organization once the word gets around that he's dead," Bosco said when the waiter had left. "Arianna has no control over his soldiers and definitely not the vassals. They'll try to take over, which will lead to infighting and the entire organization breaking apart."

I nodded, because I knew how these things went. Arianna was angry and determined, but her brother hadn't respected her, and his men would have adopted the same attitude. They would not concede the power to her even if she had the manpower, which she likely didn't. Even if she'd survived the firefight on the yacht, the men loyal to her hadn't.

"He hadn't chosen a successor?"

"He didn't expect to die quite so young."

"Or at the hands of his sister," I said dryly, and he grimaced.

"Aristide's organization needs the casino here in Milano. Whoever controls the casino has the best chance to win."

"And who does currently control the casino?" Jimmy asked. He'd let me handle the conversation so far. "Falconi's number one?"

"I presume so. It's not Arianna, at any rate. Aristide didn't trust her with his businesses."

"I'm surprised to hear he even trusted his number one with it." I'd had access to all of my boss's businesses when I rose to his number one, and I'd repaid the trust with skimming quite a lot of his ill-gained goods for myself before faking my death and disappearing.

"You have to trust someone," Bosco said with a shrug.

"And you chose us?" I asked, incredulous.

He sneered. "Hardly. But you proved yourselves resourceful for Aristide. Now you'll be useful for me."

My jaw flexed. "Or maybe I'll just keep the deed to your casino and disappear."

"I could take it by force."

"Good luck with that. It's currently in the care of the Italian postal services." The detour to a post office in Venice had been about that. I'd needed a quick way to hide the deed and that had been the first solution I came up with.

His fork paused midway to his mouth. "On its way to…?"

"Macao. I have a hotel reservation there for the next week. It should arrive there by then."

It wasn't true, but I kept my face calm so he couldn't read the lie on it.

He lowered the fork and leaned back. "Well played. Now I can't kill you."

"Not yet anyway. And any harm done to my friends will ensure the deed ends up in very appreciative hands. However, the good news for you is that you will absolutely get it back the moment I have what I need."

He tilted his head. "The bad news for you is you won't get what you need until I've got what I need."

"I guess we're at impasse, then."

"The deed won't be much use for you," he said. "It's not about the casino. I don't own the gambling enterprise, only the building it operates from."

I hadn't studied the deed closely enough to realize it. "Falconi seemed to think you'd be willing to move the Earth for it."

"And now he's dead."

My eyes turned hard. "I don't need to use the deed. I just need to make sure you can't."

He dipped his chin, studying me from under his brows. "You do understand that while I hold your friends, you will do exactly what I want."

My food threatened to push back, but I nodded. "Touch them and you'd better kill me too, because I will end you."

He only sneered. "That can be arranged."

I was amazed that Bosco let us leave after dinner. I'd been sure he'd have his armed bodyguard take us with him. He wouldn't have succeeded, but shooting in a luxury hotel would've derailed matters considerably.

We dropped on the couches in our lounge and I lay down, legs hanging over the armrest, an arm over my eyes. I was exhausted in a way I hadn't been in a long time.

"I have no idea how we'll deliver what Bosco wants."

"Getting our hands on Falconi's casino is the easy part," Jimmy said, to my amazement. "It's making Bosco keep his word afterwards that worries me."

"Yeah…"

We clearly didn't have enough leverage against Bosco. We'd need something more to force his hand.

"What are the chances that we could bring down his organization?"

"Zero," Jimmy said with conviction. "We'd better just deliver."

I sighed. "Are you prepared to break into Falconi's house again?"

20

ADA

BOSCO'S PENTHOUSE IN MILAN was luxurious and spacious enough for the three of us to have our own rooms with baths that looked like they'd never been used before. I found it kind of sad, to be honest, but I also understood how he couldn't trust anyone to stay over. I'd never had overnight guests either.

Or it could be he didn't live here, as he spent most of his time on his yacht.

He also had enough men that the bedroom doors weren't locked. I checked, only to come face to face with the muzzle of a semi, held by a sneering twenty-year-old who I didn't trust not to pull the trigger. It would've been easier to merely guard the exit of the penthouse, but I guess they thought we were a serious flight risk.

I definitely was.

After the day I'd had, I wanted to lie down on the soft bed and not rise until everything was solved. But I took a shower instead and changed into clean clothes I'd bought in Venice. Was it only this morning?

I'd had no idea Bosco was powerful enough to have the kind of operation that could keep an eye on random people like the three of us should've been. And that he had the clout to have his men march into a hotel and walk out with the luggage of random guests.

Unless, he owned the hotel…

There was a knock on the door, but no one entered, so I went to open it. The guard—not the same boy—nodded politely and without pointing a gun at my face. "Dinner."

I wasn't sure I'd be able to eat, but I didn't want to spend the evening alone in my room either, so I followed him to an elegant dining room with a view over whichever part of city we were in.

It was dark already, and lights on hundreds of windows outside revealed that this was an area of modern high-rises. We were staying at the top of the tallest of them. I'd been to Milan several times—like Venice, it had plenty to steal—but I wasn't familiar enough with the newer parts of the city to know where we were.

The table was set for three, and the realization that Bosco wouldn't be joining us was such a relief that I nearly had tears in my eyes as I took a seat. Laïla and René soon arrived too, both in clean clothes.

"I simply can't understand how Bosco could know about me so far in advance that he had my bags fetched," René mused, studying his clean clothes, tan trousers and a white T-shirt.

We hadn't been able to speak on the plane, and I wasn't sure we'd be able to do so here either, even though the guards left the room the moment the housekeeper had served the food. I didn't have an answer for him anyway.

"Maybe he's kept an eye on you since Monaco," I said. "He likely has people everywhere. As an intimidation tactic, it really works."

I couldn't decide if I should commend Eliot for figuring out that Bosco was the main player, or chide him for his stupidity for going after the man alone.

The dinner looked delicious, so I picked up my utensils and began to eat like my guts weren't in a knot. "How are you holding up?" I asked Laïla, who shrugged.

"Not exactly how I pictured this going." She hadn't bothered to fix up her blue faux-hawk after showering, and the way it drooped seemed to reflect her mood.

I shook my head in fond exasperation. "I can't believe you came to Venice on a whim like that. What did you think you could achieve?"

"I had a hunch you needed me," she said defensively, then gave me an accusing glare. "And I was right. You were held captive."

I'd hoped she would've forgotten about that part, but no such luck. "That was in Rome." As if that made it better.

"How did it happen anyway? And how did Eliot get caught?" René wanted to know as well, luckily not bringing up the lie I'd told earlier. I had no idea what to tell them. The only explanation that made sense was the truth, and I couldn't reveal it.

"I was nosing around where I shouldn't have and was captured," I settled with, hoping I sounded casual enough. "I was held in my hotel room though, and the security there was a bit lax. Eliot had booked a room there too for his private business and the receptionist thought we were there together, because we have the same last name. They gave him my room number and he was captured when he came to check on me."

Laïla grimaced. "It's my fault for sending him after you."

"No, you did the right thing. Besides, he didn't know I was in Rome until you told him." The lies were piling up. "And I got in trouble all by myself."

"Teaches you to investigate on your own," Laïla stated, pointing an accusatory fork at me. "Even if you were a cop, you still wouldn't be allowed to go on a mission like this alone."

"You're right. But I was acting on a hunch, and surveillance operations cost money and require firm intel to get approved. And I couldn't bring anyone in on it and risk their careers."

"Did you at least find anything useful?" René asked, and I shook my head.

"Not to my knowledge. I wasn't investigating Falconi, but I must've stumbled on his businesses by accident."

His gaze sharpened. "And you had to steal the deed to Bosco's casino to be freed?"

"Yes." There was no sugarcoating that. I could only hope he wouldn't ask why Falconi thought I'd be able to—or how we actually pulled it off. "Falconi provided all the intel. All we had to do was walk into a bank, gain access to the safe deposit vault, which we did legally, and use the key we had." I hoped they wouldn't ask why Falconi didn't use the key himself, if it was that easy.

"Now all we need is Eliot to show up with the deed and we can be free," Laïla said, but I didn't share her optimism.

"He's still Falconi's captive and won't be able to get his hands on it." I didn't add *if he was even alive*, because I wouldn't entertain that possibility. If Falconi's sister had taken over like Bosco believed, she might have got rid of him and Danny.

"Moreover, Bosco tried to kill Eliot just because he thought Eliot was a cop. I don't think he'll spare our lives even if he gets the deed back. We know too much."

She paled, and put down her utensils as if she'd lost her appetite, but René shook his head. "He would've killed us already. He needs us for something, even if it's just leverage."

I hoped he was right.

We were finishing our dessert—excellent tiramisu—when Bosco walked into the dining room. My body tensed instantly, acid pushing up.

"Good, you're all here. I've had a chat with Mr. Reed and Mr. … Allen, was it?" The latter was for me. A brief panic flared because I didn't know who he was referring to, before I realized it had to be Danny's current name. I don't know why I hadn't come to think of that he would've changed it, other than that he'd used his old name at the hotel.

"They're alive?"

He nodded and I went almost limp with relief, and had to steel myself with effort. I wouldn't show any weakness in front of him.

"My men tell me they escaped in a speedboat during a firefight on my yacht. After killing two of my men."

I found myself not caring about the latter. Danny was an excellent shot, and Eliot could handle a weapon well too. "And they have your deed?"

His brows furrowed. "Not quite. At any rate, I'm not settling for getting it back anymore."

I didn't like the sound of that. René and I exchanged glances over the table. He looked resigned, and his lip curled as if he'd tasted something foul. "What do you want, then?"

"My ex-wife, Arianna, has killed Aristide and is trying to take over his organization. I can't let that happen. So Mr. Reed and Mr. Allen are going to help me defeat her."

We sat in stunned silence. "How?" René managed to ask.

"They're going to help me get my hands on the casino Aristide owned here in Milano." His lip curled. "They've proven adept at stealing deeds."

"Is it also in a safe deposit vault in a bank where they can simply walk in with a key?" I asked. He smiled.

"I have no idea. But I'm sure resourceful people like you can find out."

"You expect us to participate?" René asked, appalled.

"I'm not feeding idle hands. Or freeing them."

That didn't sound good. I drew a resolute breath. "Just free Laïla and René. I've already participated in one crime. It won't make a difference if I commit another."

"That's very commendable of you, but surely you understand I need them as leverage."

I wanted to slump over the table and weep, but I steeled my spine. "Just as long as they don't have to do anything illegal."

"I can help," Laïla stated, her pleading eyes on me. "You'll need intel for this, and you don't have my skills."

"No one has your skills, but we'll just have to manage without. I can't have either of you losing your jobs for what is ultimately my mess."

René rubbed his face, looking tired. "I'm not terribly worried about my job. But I can't have anything to tarnish the reputation of my family's business."

I doubted any of this would make headlines, but I nodded. "You'll keep Laïla safe, then."

She looked mulish. "I'm perfectly capable of defending myself."

"I know you are. I'd just rather you didn't have to."

BACK IN MY ROOM, I dug out my phone and locked myself in the bathroom with it, hoping it was the one place that wasn't spied on. I felt a bit silly for my paranoia, thinking Bosco would have listening devices in his own home, but he clearly believed in the power of information. I wasn't going to take any risks.

I'd been curious about the message sent to my phone, but I hadn't dared to even touch my phone so that Bosco's men wouldn't remember I had it and confiscate it. I opened it now and felt both stunned and touched after I read it.

It was from Eliot, warning me to stay away from Bosco's yacht. Too late for that. But now I had his phone number. I considered sending a message, as it would be more difficult to spy on, but I wanted to see with my own eyes that he was all right, so I placed a video call.

His face filled my screen, concerned and relieved. "Ada? Are you all right?"

Tears sprang to my eyes and I wiped them away. "Yes. We all are. You?"

I could see he was well and unharmed, but I had to ask anyway. Danny showed up over Eliot's shoulder and I couldn't help the wave of relief that washed through me. I was mad at him for getting me into this mess, but I didn't want to see him harmed.

"Jimmy was shot in the arm when we escaped, but it's just a superficial flesh wound and is already healing."

I didn't ask who Jimmy was, just in case I was wrong about the listening devices. I didn't have to. Danny's dad had been called Jimmy. Danny showed me his upper left arm where a bandage showed under the sleeve of his T-shirt.

"Where are you?" I asked.

"In Milan, at the Bulgari Hotel. You?"

"At Bosco's penthouse in Milan, but I don't know where it is." I hadn't checked the map yet.

Eliot's smile was satisfied. "Don't worry, I do. If things turn sour, we'll release you ourselves."

It warmed me to hear it, but I shook my head. "Don't. There are armed guards everywhere."

"We'll think of something," he said, as if it was that easy.

"What's the plan?"

The men glanced at each other. "We don't have one yet. We need intel."

I sighed. "I wish I could involve Laïla. She'd get us everything we need."

Eliot gave me a stern look. "We're not involving you either."

"You'll need me if you have to open a safe," I reminded him, but Danny—or Jimmy, I guess—shook his head.

"I'm perfectly capable of doing it. And how would you even flee the armed guards?"

"I'll think of something," I said, mirroring Eliot's line. Eliot shook his head.

"Just stay where you are. I'm much happier if I know you're safe."

"Safe is an odd word for this." But I knew what he meant.

We ended the call, and I held the phone tightly against my chest, as if it would bring me comfort. Eliot was only a call away, and I couldn't lose that lifeline.

I SLEPT TOLERABLY WELL, considering I was a captive once again. But I had a soft bed, the room had air conditioning, and I didn't have the large form of Eliot wrapped around me to keep me awake, pretending I was asleep.

I wouldn't have minded waking up to watching him do a downwards dog again though. *Can cause a stroke* indeed…

I was feeling refreshed when the guard fetched us for breakfast. It was served in a smaller room adjacent to the kitchen. Bosco was already there, and although he was looking put-together and charming as always, his presence wiped away my good mood. I forced myself to fill a plate from a lavish spread on the table anyway, knowing I'd need the strength. Laïla and René followed suit.

A small line appeared between Bosco's brows when he read something on his phone, as if he was displeased, and I almost lost the shreds of my appetite. "It appears my ex-wife not only survived yesterday, she managed to escape."

"Is she coming here?" I asked, taking a bite of a slice of melon I'd deemed something I could eat.

"That would be foolish of her. No, she's barricaded herself in Aristide's office at the casino. Aristide's loyals have gathered outside it, but they're holding back from attacking for now."

"They have the manpower though?" I didn't really care, but we needed all the intel he would give.

"Yes. If they want to, they'll take over."

I wasn't a military historian, but I knew sieges usually worked better for those on the outside of the barricades, as they had access to resources, like food. "But if the deed is there, she has the upper hand."

Bosco sneered. "Only if she can access it."

René tilted his head. "She can't open the safe?"

"That's what my informant tells me." He sounded satisfied. I gave him a questioning look.

"And there isn't a single safe-cracker in Falconi's organization?"

He folded his napkin on the table, indicating he had finished eating. "The soldiers aren't usually chosen by their skills or finesse. But whether or not Falconi employed one, *she* doesn't have access to those skills. And even if she did, she would still have to get out of the office alive with the deed."

"What are you going to do, then?" René asked, the only question that mattered.

"I'm going to march in there with some men and see what happens."

I could picture exactly what would happen. "You'll shoot your way through Falconi's men and then deal with those inside the office."

Bosco dipped his chin, his eyes fixed on my face. "Or I'll wait until they become hungry and they'll leave voluntarily."

That was wise, but would take longer.

"You'll need to go in with your own safe-cracker, otherwise you lose the advantage," Laïla suggested, to my surprise. Bosco considered her with narrowed eyes.

"Let me guess, you?"

She nodded. "It's a hobby of mine."

I hadn't known that, but I'd bet she was better at it than me, though where she found safes to practice on, I had no idea. That didn't mean I liked her suggestion.

"Those people won't let you simply waltz in to open the safe," I said, worried. She looked surprised.

"I'll wait until Signor Bosco has the place secured, of course."

Bosco was looking at her like a cat does a mouse. He wouldn't hesitate to use her, whether it was safe for her or not.

"Let's find out first if it's a model you can actually open," I suggested to play for time.

"Okay, but I can open most modern safes, especially if I have the right equipment."

"We can get you everything you need," Bosco promised, and she perked.

"What I need is intel. Can I get a computer?"

"No."

Her shoulders slumped. "How about my phone back, then?"

"No."

"Come now," I said, not wanting to lose the opportunity. "Operations like this depend on accurate information."

"And how would upstanding members of law enforcement such as yourselves know what information is required?"

Touché.

He rose. "Is there anything else?"

We all shook our heads, and he smiled. "I'll call on Miss Diab when we're ready for her." With that, he left the room, leaving us to enjoy breakfast in peace.

After we were done, a guard came to escort us back to our rooms, and he didn't stay to guard the doors of our rooms. I checked. Maybe Bosco had taken everyone he could spare with him.

I took out my phone and called Eliot. "Bosco is on his way to storm into Falconi's casino with force. Stay out of the place."

"Good to know. We'll go to Falconi's home instead."

"Good call. Do you know where he lives?"

"Jimmy does."

I startled. "How?"

"How do you think he was caught in the first place?"

I hadn't given it any thought. "He knows how to open the safe there?"

Eliot relayed the question. "He says he didn't have the chance to try the first time, but it's doable."

"I can open it faster, especially if I had the tools I had in Rome."

"Good thing we brought your bag, then."

I smiled. "Text me the address. I'll be there."

After ending the call, I peeked out of the door. The corridor outside the guest bedrooms was empty, so I tiptoed to Laïla's room and quietly rapped on the door. "Laïla."

She opened immediately, her eyes large with worry. "What are you doing here?"

"I'm sneaking out to help Eliot. Can you create a distraction in about half an hour?"

"Help him how?"

I shrugged. "No idea."

"Take me too. You'll get in trouble again."

Most likely. But I shook my head. "Then you'd be in trouble, and I can't have that. Besides, you need to be here when Bosco returns for you."

"And if he asks for you and you're not here? What do I tell him then?"

"Let's hope that will not happen."

Back in my room, I set out to disguise myself. I would not make another house burglary with my own face ever again. I'd learned that lesson well. Besides, I was about to do a daylight entry, which made it even more imperative that I didn't look like myself.

Good thing I'd gone shopping in Venice.

When I was done, I didn't even recognize myself. Now I only needed to make my escape.

I crept through the corridors of the penthouse to a spot between the lounge and the bar where I could see to the front door without being seen. Only one guard sat there, looking bored as he read something on his phone.

I didn't have long to wait before Laila showed up and went to him. She said something to him in Italian, her tone whiny. I hadn't known she spoke the language, but I wasn't surprised.

"No," the guard said curtly, one of the few words I understood. She slumped and begged some more, until the guard rose with a huff, took her by the arm, and walked her down the corridor towards her room. I slipped out of my hiding place.

A moment later, I was free.

21

ELIOT

FALCONI'S CASINO WAS IN Chinatown, in a beautifully restored eighteenth century building in the middle of a huge courtyard formed within tall apartment buildings from the same era that lined the streets. The courtyard was accessed only via a car-wide gateway through one of the buildings toward the main shopping street. If you didn't know the casino was there, you wouldn't be able to find it.

The courtyard was its own world hidden from eyes, large enough for two houses, several parking spaces, and plenty of greenery. Restaurants and cafés that lined the shopping streets outside served customers also to the courtyard, creating an air of exclusivity.

Jimmy and I had been sitting on the terrace of the café closest to the casino since the early morning, but I hadn't told Ada so that she wouldn't worry. The unusual activity in and out of the establishment that was supposed to be closed for the day had been enough for us to merely observe instead of trying to break in as had been our original plan.

Bosco and at least two dozen of his men in black vans arrived not long after I'd ended the call with Ada. They pulled over outside the casino, blocking its exits.

They were dressed for business with the best protective gear on the market and the kind of weaponry you couldn't legally get in this country. People on the terraces and those living in the buildings lining the courtyard took one look at them and hid themselves. They might even call the cops, but I doubted law enforcement would show up. Not until the dust had settled anyway.

I hadn't spotted anyone keeping an eye on us, but the moment Bosco exited his car, he crossed the courtyard over to us and took a leisurely seat. A waiter hurried to bring him an espresso, indicating that this wasn't the first time he'd been here.

Unlike his men, he was wearing a suit, but I caught a glimpse of a bulletproof vest and a weapon underneath the jacket, so he wasn't entirely stupid.

"Are you storming the place?" I asked, wanting the conversation to happen on my terms for a change. He took an unhurried sip of his cup.

"Yes. Arianna has locked herself in Aristide's office, and his men are now sieging the place." That explained the activity.

He put the cup down and gave us a questioning look. "Would you care to join us?"

"Will you give us weapons?" Jimmy asked, looking almost hopeful for the prospect, and Bosco snorted.

"No."

"We'll stay here, then, if it's just the same," I said.

"Good." He rose, buttoned the jacket of his suit, and calmly crossed the yard to where his men waited, as if he were headed to a business meeting instead of preparing to attack a bunch of mafia soldiers.

I had no doubt he would win, having observed the preparations of Falconi's men the whole morning. Falconi's men were well-equipped as befit an arms dealer, but they'd lost their leader, and they weren't prepared to die for whoever was currently in charge. Falconi's vassals hadn't showed up, each of them likely waiting to find out who would win before making their move.

"I think it's time we vacate the premises," I noted dryly, tossing a twenty on the table that would cover Bosco's coffee too.

Jimmy emptied his cup and got up. "Yep."

Arianna and Bosco might be right, and what they needed was in the casino. But I had a hunch Falconi had been a man who kept important things closer to his heart, and so we would check his home while everyone's attention was here.

Falconi's main residence was in San Siro, west of the old town center, the home of the football stadium—soccer to my countrymen—that hosted both of the city's prides, AC Milan and Inter. It was only six kilometers from Falconi's casino, and we took a taxi there.

Well, we took the first taxi in a random direction and then switched to another, on the off-chance that Bosco had people keeping an eye on us.

The house was a huge, cream-colored Palladian villa, three stories high and seven windows wide, with a large, lush garden. The neighborhood around it was filled with modern apartment blocks, the more expensive kind that each looked unique and only had a few units to a building with verdant gardens around them.

Guarded only by a brick fence the same color as the house, the place practically demanded attention, which I wouldn't have thought a crime boss craved. But Falconi's family had owned it for a couple of decades already, his father the first successful capo of the family as I'd learned from Jimmy, who had done his research prior to the first break-in.

Pity they hadn't realized who it really was they were trying to rob.

I could understand the need of a mafia capo to ditch his humble origins in a Sicilian slum and boast of his newfound wealth. My old boss had done the same, except he was from New Jersey and he'd settled in Brooklyn, which wasn't quite the same improvement.

"How do we go in?" I asked Jimmy after the taxi had left us outside one of the apartment buildings a little down the street. This was only my second ever attempt at house burglary, and he knew the place.

He studied the neighborhood with a sharp eye. "Two options. We'll either walk through the gate and pretend we have legitimate business here, or we'll slip over the fence at the back."

"Let's try the gate. We're dressed for the part, and that way we'll get the hang of the security currently present."

The front gate was an elegant wrought iron edifice wide enough for a car. There were no visible security measures beyond a camera on the fencepost that didn't look entirely up to date. We rang the intercom buzzer by the gate. Nothing happened.

"Maybe they're all at the casino," Jimmy suggested.

Since no one in need of guarding was in the house, it was plausible. "Let's show ourselves in, then."

There was an old gatehouse at the corner of the lot, with a regular sized door for pedestrian traffic. We went there, and tried to doorbell again, just in case. Again, nothing happened.

Jimmy tried the door and found it locked but not alarmed, so I took out Ada's lockpicks and opened the door. His brows shot up.

"For a businessman, you're handy with those." He hadn't witnessed me use them before.

"The things you learn when you're in the security business…"

"Did you learn to pick pockets in that business too? I'm starting to question exactly what kind of security it was you provided."

"What, am I not an FBI agent after all?"

He gestured for me to enter first. "I've yet to meet a cop who can use lockpicks that well. Or who would pick pockets."

"I'm definitely not a cop," I said with emphasis as he closed the door behind us.

We crossed the front garden to a side door, staying behind the shrubbery lining the gravel-topped paths. Jimmy sneered, pointing at the cut wires of the security system of the door.

"It's been three weeks and they haven't fixed this."

I pursed my mouth in disappointment. "It could mean this house isn't their priority. Maybe the deed isn't here after all."

"There's something important here. Thom's intel was never wrong. But do Falconi's soldiers know it? That is another matter entirely."

"They wouldn't have abandoned the place for the casino if they did."

With the help of Ada's lockpicks, we let ourselves into a small corridor that had a servants' staircase on the left and kitchen on the right. It was empty and the house was quiet. We took a peek at the ground floor and found it empty.

"What were you here to steal?" I asked in a low tone as I followed him up the narrow stairs. The old steps creaked every now and then, but not so loudly it would attract attention.

"Cash. We don't—didn't—have the connections to move stolen goods, and the cash here would've been clean."

"How did you learn about it in the first place?"

His smile was sad. "Thom was really good with people. He could make almost anyone reveal anything over a pint. He didn't even speak Italian." He paused and reconsidered. "Though the guy he spoke to must have told his boss everything…"

Falconi's men wouldn't have been waiting for them otherwise, not with security this lax.

"Let's make sure we're not surprised this time round."

We reached the landing of the middle floor and paused to listen. It was quiet, and we proceeded to check every room as thoroughly as possible, finding a library, a salon, and a large ballroom, all empty. No cameras or other security measures were following our approach.

We left the study last, but it was empty too. "The safe is here," Jimmy said, going to a painting of a man that looked like an old version of Falconi on the wall that separated the study from the library. With gloves on, he checked the painting for wiring, but shook his head.

"They haven't fixed this either."

"That doesn't sound promising…"

If there was anything to protect here, they would've upped the security by now, even with Falconi's attention in Rome. Or maybe his number one was even less competent than the preparations at the casino indicated.

Jimmy moved the painting aside and took out a device Ada had had in her luggage that could decipher complex number codes in minutes. He set it over the keypad and pressed a button that made numbers run down on its display.

It was kind of fascinating to watch, but I had a job to do. I checked the hallway and then crossed the floor to the windows. They faced the front of the house and the gates to the street. I startled in surprise.

A woman was walking down the side path.

"SOMEONE'S COMING," I said to Jimmy.

I couldn't see the woman's face from this angle, but her hair was long and black; she was slim, and she wore elegant clothes, so she likely wasn't household staff. She didn't skulk behind bushes like we had, so she didn't fear being detected. Did Falconi have another sister? Or was she a lawyer or similar?

Jimmy's attention was on the safe. "You go deal with it."

I hurried to the servants' stairs and down them as fast as I could without making noise, which isn't easy for a man my size. I took cover in the kitchen by the side door and pulled out my 9mm.

I didn't have long to wait. There was a brief rattle, like a key turning in the lock, and the door opened. But she didn't enter. She waited, as if trying to detect sounds. I held my breath.

I couldn't see her from my hiding place behind the wall, but I heard a soft click as the door closed behind her. A moment later, she peeked into the kitchen.

Seizing the moment, I stepped flush against her back, wrapped an arm around her throat and put the gun against her temple. The safety was on, but she wouldn't know.

"Don't move."

She stiffened and lifted her hands, slowly. I could feel the frantic pulse on her throat. She swallowed hard.

"Eliot?"

Stupefied, I released her immediately and stepped back. "Ada? What the fuck?"

She turned around and I saw it really was her, though she had taken care to alter her looks. Gone was the English rose, replaced with someone you wouldn't look at twice. She gave me a tremorous smile.

"You scared the living daylights out of me."

"Serves you right, creeping in," I said, putting my weapon away. "Why are you here?"

She brushed a hand down her clothes, the gesture more about helping her calm herself than for any actual need to tidy herself up. "You texted me the address. I thought it was self-evident I'd come. When I couldn't immediately see you, I decided to check the place myself." She lifted a bunch of lockpicks, having restocked at some point.

I shook my head, exasperated. Then I opened my arms to her and she stepped into a hug. I held her as tightly as I could, and she squeezed me back with the strength of her fright. It had been only two days since we'd been separated at the airport, but it felt like an eternity.

"I'm so glad you're well," I said against her hair—or wig. At least it was real hair and not plastic. I pulled back, and gave her a questioning look. "How did you know it was me anyway?"

She chuckled. "For one, I recognized your cologne. For another, you spoke English."

I hadn't realized I'd done that—or that people would pay attention to how I smelled. I would have to change the cologne too.

I released her and studied her, marveling at the change. Her eyes were dark, almost black, and they slanted down a bit in the corners, a clever makeup trick. Her lips were thin and her features were almost gaunt, and she must've bound her chest, because her curves were gone.

"Let's go upstairs. Jimmy's opening the safe."

"Have you dealt with the security?" she asked as she followed me to the next floor.

"There wasn't any. All Falconi's men are at the casino." I'd be surprised if any of them would be able to return.

We entered the study just as Jimmy uttered a triumphant, "Yes!" and pulled open the safe door.

"Look who I found," I told him, and he spared a glance from his task. A smile lit up his face.

"Ada!"

"How did you recognize me so fast?" she asked, crossing the floor to him. He rolled his eyes and huffed.

"Please…" He looked like he wanted to hug her too, but she merely peeked into the safe.

"It's just money," she said, disappointed. I echoed the sentiment, although it was a lot of money. Easily several million euros.

"This is what Thom and I were after last time," Jimmy said, briefly sad. If they'd been deliberately lured in here, this would definitely do the trick. Ada gave his shoulder a consoling squeeze, before dropping her hand.

"How did you escape from Bosco?" I asked as Jimmy opened a large duffel bag he'd brought for the purpose and began to fill it with as much money as it could hold. It was laundered money and his partner had already died for it. He deserved to take it.

"Laïla created a diversion," she told me, looking around the room.

"How is she here anyway? And René?"

"Who's René?" Jimmy asked, pausing what he was doing, but he didn't look quite as jealous as he had earlier that week.

"He's a homicide detective from Lyon. He's here— well, in Venice on holiday, and I asked for his help." She grimaced. "I shouldn't have. Now he's in this mess with us, and I think he's starting to suspect I'm lying to him."

That wasn't good.

"Let's get you freed first and worry about him when you're back at home," I said calmly, but my mind was already racing, planning to contact my hacker again for new IDs for her.

"So he's not your boyfriend?" Jimmy asked, still hung up on the notion. Ada's mouth twisted annoyed.

"He could be though. But I can't date a cop."

"You could if you stopped being a criminal," I said with a pointed look. The idea of the two of them together didn't sit well with me, but I was leaving and she deserved to be happy. She shrugged.

"It's what I'm good at…"

Jimmy finished filling the bag, which was about quarter of the safe's contents. He studied the safe, annoyed. "I would've thought there would be other things than money in here too."

"I guess not." I sighed and looked around. "Maybe he keeps the papers in his desk drawers."

I was about to head there when Ada snorted.

"Amateurs."

"What?" Jimmy asked.

"This is the more obvious safe. He has another elsewhere in the house. More private, more discreet."

"How would you know?" I asked, and she gave me a slow look.

"I've done this before, you know. Where's the master bedroom?"

"Not on this floor," I told her. "Let's check upstairs."

Jimmy closed the safe and put the painting back. Then we headed up the main stairs. The master bedroom was in the middle, facing the garden. It was a large, elegant room full of antique furniture that with the walk-in closet and the bathroom took as much space as the ballroom below.

Ada took a quick peek under the canopy bed, and then marched into the walk-in closet. Suits and other clothes filled both sides, and at the back were shoes and accessories on neat shelves and racks. She looked behind the clothes and I remembered the hidden door in her closet, but she didn't find anything interesting and went to the back wall.

She studied the custom-built cedar shelves with her head tilted and eyes narrowed. Reaching into her pocket, she put on gloves and pulled open the drawer in the middle. To my amazement, the one above and below opened too.

"It's a false panel," I said admiringly. "How did you guess?"

"Not the first one I've encountered," she muttered, her attention already on what was inside.

The drawer held a small safe, lying on its back the door at the top. It didn't have an electronic keypad like the one in the study, but it looked modern to my inexpert eyes. Ada smiled, pleased.

"My favorite." She ran her hands gently around the safe and peeked under the drawer. Her brows shot up. "No alarm."

"Could be inside the safe," Jimmy said, and she nodded. Then she set out to open it.

I would've loved to watch her work, to see the concentrated expression on her face as she listened to the tumblers turn inside the lock when she turned the wheel. But Jimmy and I had to be on the lookout for Falconi's men, so I went to the window and Jimmy stood at the door to the hallway.

"Open," she shouted, sooner than I could've imagined.

I had to go look myself. She lifted out several files and other papers and put them on the floor. "I think all his assets are here," she said. "But I don't read Italian, so…"

I kneeled next to her and skimmed them quickly. I didn't read Italian well either, but one thing was obvious.

"The casino deed isn't here." My heart sank.

She shot me a worried look. "What do we do now?"

Our freedom and safety hinged on us delivering the deed, which didn't leave us with many options. "It must be in Falconi's casino after all, but it's under siege and there's no point in trying to get there."

"He needs someone to open the safe though. Laïla already volunteered."

My brows shot up. "Why?"

Her shrug was very French. "It's an intellectual exercise for her. She gets bored really fast if she can't flex her brain."

I could believe it, but I wasn't about to let Laïla put herself in danger. She wasn't a field operative.

"Bosco will have to find someone else, then. You have to get her and René to safety before he returns."

She nodded. "What will you do?"

I gathered the papers. "I'll go through these and hope there's something we can use as leverage."

"And if there isn't?"

My gut tightened. "Then I'll have to make something up."

"What, lie?"

"I prefer to think of it as sleight of hand."

Her gaze sharpened. "I'm beginning to think you know everything about hoaxing people."

I had no idea what I'd done to make her suspect me, but I met her eyes calmly. "Takes one to know one, I guess…"

I'd never thought of my life in terms of hoaxing people, but that was what I was doing. And I'd done it perfectly—until I met her. I should never have become involved. Attached.

"Come, we have to get you to safety." I reached a hand to her and, smiling, she took it.

"Let me worry about me. You handle Bosco."

I nodded, with more assurance than I felt. And then, because I apparently hadn't messed up my life properly yet, I leaned closer, placed a hand lightly on her neck, thumb caressing her cheek, and kissed her.

And then I kissed her some more.

22

ADA

I STILL FELT ELIOT'S KISS ON my lips when the taxi left me a block from Bosco's building. I'd wanted him to kiss me, but I was irked by it too. He was leaving. I didn't need to know what his kisses felt like when he took the time to really make it work.

They felt great, by the way. But I had to push it out of my mind. I wasn't a teenager whose entire life was turned upside down by a kiss anymore.

I paused at the corner and studied the twenty-story building. There were no armed men milling outside it. Either Bosco wasn't back yet or they hadn't noticed my absence.

My mind slightly eased, I made my way to the front door, only to realize that I had no idea how I could get back in. There was an electric lock on the main entrance, and likely on Bosco's penthouse door too. And even if I could open the locks with the decoder Jimmy had returned to me—doubtful—the guard would be sitting right inside the door. Moreover, the lift needed a key to make it go to the top floor, and I didn't fancy climbing twenty floors up.

I hated modern houses.

As I was mulling my options, a delivery van drove to the building. But instead of pulling over by the main door where I was standing, offering me a chance to slip in behind the delivery person, it rounded the corner. I hurried after it and saw it disappear into the garage under the house.

Hastening my steps, I managed to slip in before the steel door rolled down. I walked down the ramp to the garage and saw the van parked in front of a large goods lift at the back. The cage was already heading up, so I had to wait a bit, but the good news was it didn't require keys to take me to the top floor.

There was a small, bare landing at the top that wasn't even monitored with a camera. Careless of them. Across the lift was a door. I pressed my ear against it, but couldn't hear anything. I knew the kitchen wasn't on this side of the house, but there had to be other maintenance rooms like the laundry, where the housekeeper might be.

I'd have to risk it. I could handle the housekeeper if the need arose.

The lock on the door was modern and difficult to pick, but at least it wasn't electric. It took longer than I was happy with before the lock finally yielded, but since no one came to see who was rattling the lock, I was fairly confident there wasn't a guard on the other side when I cracked the door open.

There was only a dark corridor on the other side and it was empty, so I slipped in. An alarm display blinked on my left, but it wasn't armed, so I ignored it as I went down the corridor deeper into the house. It was dark, but a light ahead helped me to navigate without hitting the walls.

I found the kitchen—and the housekeeper—and managed to slip past her. But I would have to go past the front door before I could get to my room.

The guard was still there, looking as bored as when I left. I crouched behind the bar at the edge of the lounge, and as silently as possible crept into the hallway that led to my room.

I was about to hurry down it when a small table at the side caught my attention. It was one of those occasional tables where people dropped their housekeys when they came in, and where the housekeeper apparently left the mail for Bosco to find.

A large envelope lay there addressed to him—in Danny's hand! I'd recognize his scrawls anywhere. My heart tightened. What was this about?

I didn't second-guess my actions. I took the envelope and ran to my room. As the door closed behind me, I sighed in relief, but I couldn't let my guard down yet.

I pulled off the wig and dropped it on the bed with the envelope, before heading to the bathroom to remove my face. I'd just applied the removal lotion when there was a knock on the door. "Lunch."

I startled. Was it only midday?

"Just a minute!" I shouted through the door, and quickly wiped my face clean. The rest would have to wait until after I'd eaten.

LAÏLA WAS ALREADY IN the small breakfast room, and she visibly relaxed when she saw me enter. René soon followed, looking tired and bored.

"Italian daytime TV is horrible," he stated, taking a seat. "I'd give anything for some relief of boredom."

Since the guard wasn't in the room, I leaned closer and lowered my voice. "How about escaping? The back door isn't guarded."

"Then why did you need me to distract the guard?" Laïla asked, miffed.

"I didn't know there was a back door," I said apologetically. "I had to return through there."

René startled. "You went out?"

"Yes."

He shot me a sharp look that definitely revealed he was starting to suspect my actions. "Why? And how exactly did you return?"

"I followed a delivery guy," I said evasively, but he didn't look convinced.

"How did it go? Did you find anything?" Laïla wanted to know.

"We went to Falconi's house, but it was completely empty. I think all his men are at the casino getting killed."

"Was the deed there?"

I shook my head and they looked disappointed.

"Now what?" René asked.

"We escape."

He looked reluctant. "What's stopping Bosco from coming after us?"

I could only shrug. "Eliot promised to think of something."

"And if it doesn't work?"

René was a cop; he knew the answer as well as I did.

"He still wants the deed," Laïla said. "If I open the safe at the casino, that will buy us goodwill."

She was right, but I couldn't let her stay. My stomach tightened painfully for what I was about to say. "I'll do it, then. You flee." Two protesting faces turned to me and I lifted my hand. "There's absolutely no need to give him more hostages than necessary, and this is my mess."

"But can you open it?" Laïla asked. René looked dubious, and slightly suspicious too. I spread my arms, appetite gone.

"I have no idea, but the longer I'll try it, the farther you have a chance to flee. We don't have much time. Pack your things. I'll call a taxi and you'll leave right after lunch."

The guard saw us to our rooms after we'd eaten. I packed my bag quickly. I would give it to the others to take with them. If I had to flee, I wouldn't be burdened by it, but I couldn't leave it for Bosco to find incriminating evidence inside it.

As I packed, I found the key to Bosco's safe deposit box in the pocket of my suit jacket. I hadn't wanted to give it Falconi—hadn't had a chance either. I didn't need it, so I should return it.

My eyes landed on the envelope on the bed. I should probably return that too. But I wanted to see what was inside. Why was Danny sending mail to Bosco? Disregarding all privacy issues and good police practices, I opened it.

My mouth dropped open.

It was the deed to Bosco's casino building in Venice. Why had Danny posted it to him? Or was it Eliot, and Danny had merely been the scribe? Had they hoped the postal service would be slow enough for it to be delivered some later date when it would work to their advantage better?

Would this be enough to buy us our freedom?

But I didn't trust Bosco any more than the men had. I had to find a way to return it that would force him to free us. I looked around the room and considered hiding it under the mattress, but there was no need to make this too easy for him.

I couldn't dawdle anyway; the taxi was already on its way and Bosco could be too. I crept out of the room and the others emerged from theirs too.

"Let's not try past the guard and the kitchen," I said in a low tone. "This corridor must lead to the back too."

It took a couple of twists and turns—the place was huge—but we found the back door. It was dark, but I fumbled the door open and light from the landing flooded in.

"Quickly," I urged them, and they obeyed. Laïla hurried to call the lift.

"The taxi will wait for you at the corner," I told them. "Do you have money?"

René rolled his eyes. "It's one thing I always have. And don't worry. I'll see Laïla safely home."

"You'd better."

Laïla looked like she would protest again, but the lift car arrived and she stepped in. René took my bag and then leaned down.

"Stay safe. If you haven't returned by Monday, I'll come back with force." Then he kissed me.

It was a nice kiss, but it was more comforting than exciting. I smiled.

"Don't worry about me. Go straight to the train station. Don't take a plane. Bosco might have people at the airport."

With that, I closed the door and leaned heavily against it. A brief panic flared that I should've gone with them, but I pushed the emotion aside. I was a professional criminal. I operated best when adrenaline and fear were driving me.

I found Bosco's bedroom at the other end of the house. It wasn't as large as Falconi's, and although it was elegantly furnished with dark grays and cream, it looked like it hadn't been used much. The walk-in closet confirmed my notion, as it was almost empty of clothes.

I found the safe behind a false panel next to where the shoes would be. It was the same model as Falconi's, though mounted upright with the door at the front, and I smiled as I began to open it. It went faster than that morning, but the payoff was a disappointment, as the safe turned out to be empty.

No matter. I wasn't here to steal anything.

I put the deed and the key in and locked the door again. I was about to get up when a man cleared his throat behind me, frightening me out of my skin.

"Well, well, the law-abiding citizen trying to break into my safe," Bosco drawled. "I admire the initiative, but that's empty."

Not anymore.

I swallowed hard and got up to face him. His shoulder was propped against the doorjamb, and he was looking at me with an amused smirk. I wasn't fooled by it. "Good to know."

"What brought this about?"

I considered lying, but there was no point. "I thought I would practice opening the safe at the casino with your safe."

He cocked a brow. "And you knew where to find it?"

I shrugged. "I used to be a detective. One learns the oddest things in that profession, like where rich people keep their safes."

He didn't look surprised. Had he made a background check on me? How thorough had he been?

"I thought Miss Diab would open it."

"I sent René and Laïla home." I sounded calm, but my mouth was dry. His jaw flexed.

"I wish you hadn't done that."

"You don't need them."

"You'd best deliver, then." He straightened and headed out of the room.

One of the three men with him walked me to the front door by my arm, but at least his weapon wasn't out. The guard at the door stood in attention, the earlier boredom wiped away. Bosco walked past him to the door, ignoring him, then paused with his hand on the door handle and turned to me, as if remembering something.

"Tell me, Miss Reed, where did you go this morning?"

I staggered to a halt. "I'm sorry?"

"I admit, the wig threw me a little, but not for long. I have met Natasha, after all." He gave a signal and his men pulled out their weapons.

My knees went feeble with fear, only my escort's hand around my arm propping me up. But the weapons weren't pointed at me. They were aimed at the door guard, who inhaled in shock and started babbling in Italian.

Bosco gave me an admonishing look. "You do understand that I have to punish Marco for letting you slip out."

I shivered with sudden cold, and I had to swallow heavily to keep the contents of my stomach in. I wetted my lips to be able to speak, my mind racing.

"So far, I haven't seen or witnessed anything that would demand I take interest in you as the police," I managed to say. "I could even argue that you saved our lives in Venice by taking us away before your yacht was boarded. But watching a man being shot in cold blood would put a serious crimp in my belief that you are an upstanding businessman."

I held my breath as Bosco contemplated my words, his gaze never leaving mine. Then he shrugged and tilted his head in unconcerned acknowledgment, as if it didn't matter either way. The men put their weapons away, but Marco didn't dare to relax and neither did I.

One wrong move and I'd be where he was.

23

ADA

THE CASINO WAS IN CHINATOWN, so named for reasons I didn't know. Perhaps it was in memory of Marco Polo, whose travels to China gave him life-long fame, even though he was from Venice and not Milan. Mainly, the neighborhood had a lot of Asian shops and restaurants.

That was as Chinese as it got. The four- and five-story buildings were from the nineteenth century and perfectly average European, with modern estates in random places with no regard for how well they fit architecturally. The streets were narrow and lined with small retail stores. Nothing looked like it would lure in wealthy people to gamble their money away.

"Why do you want Falconi's casino?" I asked, mostly out of curiosity.

Bosco was sitting next to me at the back of the car and he gave me a look that said he couldn't believe a prisoner would question his decisions. "I don't own one. They're useful, so I want it."

"Along with the rest of Falconi's organization."

He dipped his chin. "I certainly won't let Arianna have it, or any of Falconi's vassals."

I couldn't fathom it. "But you're in the drug trade. Falconi was an arms dealer."

His eyes turned flinty. "Why would you say I'm in the drug business?" Before I could say something that would ensure I'd never walk away here alive, he leaned closer. "And who says Aristide wasn't in the drug trade?"

I blinked, baffled. Then it dawned on me and I inhaled sharply. "Falconi was teaming up with Dobrev, wasn't he? You weren't trying to take down Dobrev's operation. You were trying to destroy Falconi's."

I had no idea why I hadn't thought of it, other than that I hadn't been here investigating it, and it would've required a random jump in logic. I wished René and Laïla were here to hear this. I felt vindicated, even though they hadn't voiced their suspicions of my actions.

His smile was smug. "Close enough, though it wasn't Dobrev but that right-hand man of his. Melnyk wanted to branch out to arms, to start his own business, and Aristide promised to deliver in exchange for Melnyk giving him an in with the drug business."

"That explains the arsenal on Melnyk's yacht," I said, remembering what we'd found there.

He nodded. "They were a good match, and with Aristide's help Melnyk would've taken over Dobrev's organization. I couldn't have that."

It certainly made more sense than that Bosco would've been branching out into human trafficking, which had been my original theory.

I tried to come up with a way to tie this new information with my actual investigation on Dobrev—other than falsifying evidence, again—but before I could, the car made a turn into a pedestrian street full of cafés and restaurants, heedless of the sign that forbade such action. On the left was a long yellow building, four stories tall and the entire block wide. In the middle of it was a gateway through the building large enough for a car, and we took it. I looked around in awe.

We were in a huge courtyard with parking spaces and green areas, completely secluded from the noises and buzz of the city by tall buildings on all four sides. In the middle were two beautifully restored eighteenth century houses, built corner to corner so that they formed an L. They were three stories high with mansard roofs, and four windows wide, one of them light blue and white, and the other cream with red trimmings. The car pulled over by the latter and we exited.

The courtyard had its own restaurants and cafés that all looked expensive, but the surroundings and the quiet atmosphere would make it worth the extra cost, if one didn't mind it came with a mafia-owned casino.

I followed Bosco into the casino, his men keeping the rear with their weapons drawn. There was an expensive looking restaurant and a wine bar on the ground floor. Both were closed, but there was a group of people in waiting staff uniforms standing in the middle of the restaurant, looking worried. Some were crying.

The forceful change in ownership must have come as a huge shock.

We headed up a mahogany staircase at the side of the entrance foyer. The casino occupied the two upper floors and it was formed of consecutive rooms that could be seen through the open double leaf doors all the way to the back. There were three or four tables in each room for various games of chance, and it looked elegant and expensive. Not a slot machine in sight.

We continued to the top floor. It was the erstwhile attic under the mansard roof, with skylights at regular intervals letting in light. It was mostly open space with writing desks and other office furniture, as if this was a perfectly normal office.

The illusion was ruined by the dead bodies.

My step faltered and I almost turned back. This was where the battle had taken place. There were at least a dozen bodies scattered around the floor. Blood and other fluids spread around them, and the debris of gunfire that had hit shelves and computers littered all the surfaces. It smelled horrible. I was a former homicide detective, but I'd never witnessed a massacre like this.

"How are you going to clean this mess up without involving the police?" I blurted out, unable to curb my tongue.

Bosco only shrugged. "We have our ways."

I didn't like how blasé he was about me witnessing this, especially after the speech I'd given at the penthouse.

I picked my way gingerly across the floor, and the same guard that had walked me earlier took a post next to me, as if fearing I would faint or flee. He wasn't entirely wrong on either score.

We entered a large office at the back. The mess continued there, but with fewer dead people. Filing cabinets and other furniture stood near the door, having been used as a barricade.

Sitting in the middle of the floor was a woman in black, in her late thirties and spitting mad. She was restrained with handcuffs and watched over by two armed guards.

The moment Bosco entered, she began to curse and yell at him, but I didn't speak Italian so I didn't understand. It wasn't a great loss.

"Arianna Falconi," Bosco said, gesturing at the woman. "My ex-wife."

I would've guessed that without introduction. I gave her a curious glance, but her face was distorted with rage and I couldn't really tell what she looked like.

The furious woman taking my attention, it took me a moment to notice that there were other prisoners on the opposite side of the room. My legs almost gave out under me.

"AH, YES, I FORGOT to tell you," Bosco said with a mocking smirk. "We found your friends as they were entering a taxi outside my building."

Laïla and René were sitting side by side in a corner behind the filing cabinets, leaning against the wall with their hands behind their backs and their mouths gagged. They looked unharmed, but René was scowling at Bosco, and Laïla had tears in her eyes. I'd never seen her cry, and my heart constricted in upset and anger.

I wanted to rush to them to remove their gags, but Bosco crossed the floor to the back of the room, ignoring my friends, and the guard next to me pushed me after him. I gave them an apologetic grimace as I went past. I would open the safe and hope Bosco would let us go.

A huge oaken writing desk stood under one of the skylights at the back. Judging by the scrapes on the hardwood floor, they'd tried to move it to barricade the door, but had given up. There had been easier furniture to move. A lot of it. I looked around.

"How did you get in here?"

He smiled and pointed up. "Skylights."

Clever. No way to block them, and there was a clear sightline inside from the roof. And with all the furniture piled against the door, not many hiding places either.

Bosco rounded the desk and leaned down to press a spot on the wooden cassette paneling on the side wall that was so low he had to almost bend double. It slid aside, revealing a large safe. He pulled back, straightened and gestured at it. His eyes were mocking.

"You bet the safety and freedom of your friends on your ability to open this, Miss Reed. Now it's time to deliver."

It hadn't been much of a bet on my side. I was confident with my skills. But that was before Laïla and René had been recaptured and brought here to witness what I could do.

My guts in a knot, I stared at the safe, dithering. I had two options and both were bad. I could protect my double life and save my reputation as a cop by failing to open the safe, but then my friends would suffer. Or I could open the safe, save my friends, and out myself as a criminal.

I'd be screwed either way, but in the end, the decision was easy.

Inhaling to steady my nerves, I kneeled in front of the safe to study it. It was the same model Falconi had had in his study, and would open with the decoder I had in my bag. If I'd been alone, I would've used it too. Now, it would be too difficult to explain where I'd got it. They weren't exactly sold in regular electronics shops. I had to think of something else first.

I wanted to put on gloves, but that would've caused too much attention as well. I was beginning to sweat a little. I'd never had to do this with an audience while pretending I didn't know what I was doing.

"Is this thing alarmed?"

"Why, are you afraid the police will come?" Bosco asked, mocking. I bit my lips to keep a retort in, because that was exactly what I'd been afraid of, but I couldn't think like a criminal here. And if the police did come, we'd be freed.

"In movies, there's always an alarm in these."

"We've disabled it already."

Good to know…

Hesitantly, as if unsure of what I was doing, I pressed the start button on the electronic keypad and eight yellow zeros flared to life on the digital display. I pursed my lips, thinking. That many digits were impossible to guess, and even the decoder would take its time. But there were other options.

"What's Falconi's birthday?"

Bosco crouched next to me, too close to my comfort, leaning elbows to his knees to study the display too. "You think he was that stupid?"

I shrugged. He'd be amazed how often people used their birthdates, but I couldn't reveal that. "It's a start." The system would allow three tries, if it was the kind I thought.

"October 4th, 1970."

I entered 04101970 to the system and held my breath. The display turned red to indicate a wrong code, and my stomach tightened, but I wasn't about to give up this easily.

Since Falconi was Italian, I doubted he would've entered the month before the date like Americans—I'd made that mistake once on a job in the States, before remembering they liked the dates backwards; a panic-inducing thirty seconds if anything was. But the numbers could be otherwise reversed.

People were seldom that complicated though.

"What's his sister's birthday?"

He snorted. "Aristide didn't value her. It won't be that."

I felt headache coming. "Was he close to his mother?"

"Is the Pope Catholic?"

The stupid saying made me roll my eyes. "Do you know his mother's birthday?"

He shook his head. I glanced at Arianna Falconi, who was still fuming, and he shuddered, making me smile despite the situation.

"Do you want this open or not?"

He closed his eyes briefly, and his face settled into a tight mask. He moved me aside by my shoulders and entered a code himself. The colors on the display turned green and the lock clicked.

"It was his mother's birthday?"

His voice was grim. "My son's."

Shit.

He pulled the door open to reveal at least as much cash as had been in Falconi's home safe in neat piles. I stared at it, amazed. "Did he keep the casino's reserves here?"

He shook his head, disbelieving. "I hope not, with security this lax." He reached into the safe and took out a sheet of paper, looking satisfied as he showed it to me.

"Behold, the deed."

"Congratulations," I said dryly. "Now you only need to win over Falconi's vassals and all this is yours. How about freeing us?"

His smile was devilish. "How about not."

My heart sank. "You promised."

"Did I?" He shrugged and put the deed on the desk before turning to close the safe. He could keep it locked, now that he knew the code. With that much money inside, he'd better keep it locked. "You still need to give me back *my* casino."

I swallowed. This was it, the only ace up my sleeve. But I'd be buggered if I negotiated on my knees in front of him.

I was about to rise when a dark shadow passed above us. A shot rang out, and glass broke.

Bewildered, I looked around, only to have Bosco push me under the desk, following me in as the room filled with bullets. We huddled in the tight space between drawers, hands on our ears as bullets rained on the desktop above us, the heavy oak holding against them. I had no idea who was shooting, but they'd taken a page out of Bosco's book and come through the skylights.

Silence fell as suddenly as the shooting had begun. Bosco waited a moment before leaving our shelter and getting up. He cursed. "They took Arianna."

I crawled out too and pushed up on tottering legs. I propped my hands on the desk and leaned heavily on them, staring at the ruined top with unseeing eyes, gathering my wits and strength to face the room. It smelled of burned metal and blood.

I blinked, my focus sharpening on the desk. Empty desk. "She's not the only thing they took. The deed is gone too."

Bosco cursed. His men were filing in to look after their comrades, and he barked sharp commands at them in Italian, before storming out of the room with them at his heels.

With him gone, I finally found the courage to take stock of the office—and my friends. They'd been completely unshielded and I didn't want to see what had happened to them.

Behind a low metal filing cabinet on wheels was a pile of people, unmoving. A sob caught in my throat, and I staggered toward them, tears blurring my vision.

The pile began to move as I reached them, and the guard who had walked me here pushed himself to his knees off the top of it. His brown eyes were large and he was sweating, and there were a couple of tears in his shirt at the back, but he was otherwise unharmed.

"Bulletproof vest," he said in English, reaching to help René off Laïla, who was the bottom of the pile. He removed their gags but left the handcuffs on, before moving to check his comrades. I dropped on my bottom next to my friends and leaned against the filing cabinet, which rolled away. I almost fell on my back, the last bit of strength leaving me.

René was sitting on his legs, hands still behind his back. His mouth was in a tight line and his face was pale. Laïla had tears in her eyes and her whole body shook when I pulled her into a tight hug.

I checked her for injuries, but she was unharmed. René didn't have visible wounds anywhere either.

"What happened?" he asked, bewildered. "There were men on the roof, shooting down from the skylights. If the guard hadn't thought to pull that cabinet to shield us and thrown himself on us, we'd be dead."

The mere thought made me close my eyes. "They were people loyal to Arianna, or Falconi men who oppose Bosco. They took her away—and the deed to this casino."

Anger brought some color to his cheeks. "*Mérde.* We're back where we were, with nothing to bargain with."

"Let's call the police before Bosco returns," Laila pleaded, and I squeezed her tighter. It was the best solution but I shook my head.

"If the events here don't make them show up on their own, nothing will," I said, sounding as tired as I felt. She looked unhappy.

"We'll never get out of here."

I feared she was right, but I wasn't giving up just yet. "I have one more ace up my sleeve."

"Will it work?" René asked and I could only shrug.

"Has anything so far? Besides, I know too much about his operation now. He might not let me go."

He gave me a sharp look. "Do you have evidence that'll hold in court?"

Trust a cop to ask that.

"Not yet, but I know where to look for it."

Before I could elaborate, Bosco returned. He looked furious, and I feared the odds of him showing us leniency were nonexistent.

"They're gone. I don't know how, but there isn't a trace of them."

"Helicopter?" I suggested feebly, and his jaw flexed.

"That would indicate that some of Aristide's vassals are now on her side."

"You did kill quite a lot of his men. Between the two of you, she's the lesser evil."

"And now they have the deed to this casino and I still don't have the deed to mine."

I pushed up and helped Laïla on her feet too. "I can give it to you."

He pulled back, disbelieving. "What, you'll travel to Macao to fetch it from Eliot's hotel there?"

I blinked, trying to comprehend his words. Then I smiled, amused, which I hadn't thought possible after the events today. "Is that what Eliot told you?"

His brows furrowed. "Where is it, then?" he demanded, but before I could answer, his phone rang. "What?" he barked into it. A brief conversation in Italian followed and he put the phone away. He pointed at the door.

"Let's go. Mr. Reed is ready to negotiate for your freedom."

24

ELIOT

THERE WAS A LARGE OUTDOORS area west of Milano-Linate airport about ten kilometers east of the city, a forested park full of trails for hiking. You couldn't drive a car there, which was why Jimmy and I had chosen it for our meeting spot with Bosco.

In the middle of the park was a manmade lake. It was mostly meant for paddleboarding and kayaking, but you could rent flatbottomed aluminum boats similar to those used in the marshlands in the US, though they came with soundless, fairly inefficient, electric outboard engines.

As far as a getaway vehicle was concerned, it wasn't exactly fast, but it would do. Especially when we made sure Bosco didn't have access to a boat.

Our meeting spot was by the lake at the end of a narrower path that wouldn't lure hikers. It was lined with overgrown shrubbery and trees, which wasn't optimal, as we couldn't see people coming, but it would force everyone to approach down the path.

Jimmy and I were sitting on a short wooden dock where we'd tied our boat, legs hanging over the water. It would take a while for Bosco to arrive and all we could do was wait, a brief respite that felt almost bizarre after the week we'd had, but I couldn't relax. My stomach was churning with nerves. I'd need antacids before the day was over—provided I was alive to need them.

"Will this work?" Jimmy asked. He was wearing jeans now, and I'd given up my suit too, but we were both wearing jackets to hide our weapons and bulletproof vests.

We'd searched Falconi's house after Ada left and found a weapons cache that we'd made liberal use of. We'd had to appropriate one of Falconi's cars to move everything, but it's not like he needed it anymore. We'd chucked it for a rental later, just in case the police were more efficient than we believed and were keeping an eye on it—not that Falconi's men were in any position to report it stolen.

"We've done our preparations. We can only wait and see."

I wasn't entirely as confident as I tried to sound. But we had Falconi's papers, which Bosco would need if he wanted to take over, and we'd found our ace in the hole among them too. We'd also found the video of Jimmy and Thom breaking into the safe, which we'd destroyed. And if Bosco didn't want the papers, we could always give them to the police and see where that led us.

"I can't believe we're about to help Bosco to become even more powerful," Jimmy said, shaking his head in disbelief. Or maybe I should call him Frank now, as he'd acquired his new passport today after my hacker friend had informed me that he'd handled everything.

Then again, maybe I'd best forget I knew about Frank. I wouldn't meet him after today. So, Jimmy it was, as if I didn't know about the new identity.

I wasn't entirely sure either why I was helping Bosco. I'd come to Italy to take him down, yet here I was about to hand him Falconi's operations on a silver platter—legally. It didn't sit well with me, but I had no other choice. I'd lost the fight before I'd even started.

"He's the lesser evil." And I even sort of believed it, having met the greater evils.

"He's a drug trafficker," Jimmy said, disgusted.

"But not a human trafficker or arms dealer."

I'd been in the drug trade all my life and had justified it for myself ages ago. I was well aware of its impact and the damage the drugs did, but I'd seen it as a choice people made. I'd had to regard it as a lesser evil in order to do my job. I'd only faked my death after my boss teamed up with a human trafficker. That's where I'd drawn the line.

He gave me a pointed look. "He'll be an arms dealer too after he takes over Falconi's operation."

He was right, but I couldn't bring myself to care. "That's such a cop way to see things. We could take down one organization and two more would spring up while we were still congratulating ourselves."

He gave me an exasperated look. "You definitely aren't a cop."

"Nope." I shook my head, giving in. "I'm not happy about it either, but it's what I'm prepared to do for Ada's and her friends' freedom."

I wasn't worried about Jimmy and me. We would change our identities and disappear, but Ada and the others didn't have that option. Although, I was seriously contemplating contacting my hacker friend for IDs for Ada too. If things went south today, I'd take her with me.

"Do you know where you're going?" I asked him. I wouldn't ask the specifics. We would part our ways today and never contact each other again.

He spread his arms. "Anywhere I want. I have money for it."

And it was clean, thanks to Falconi's casino operation. I wouldn't have minded having some of it myself, but I'd sold my company for a hefty sum, and it was clean and legal money. And I still had the money I'd stashed away all over the world.

We were silent for a moment. He was opening and closing his fists, as if trying to make a decision or find courage to say something. Eventually, he found it: "I wish I could've told Ada why Thom and I had to die back then."

I was curious to know too, but it was none of my business. "Write her an email."

He startled, as if that option had never occurred to him. "What, now?"

"Do you have anything better to do?"

A brief panic rose to his face, but he took out his phone, a new one we'd purchased that afternoon. He'd gone through quite a few this week.

"It's been a weird week," I said aloud, and he tilted his head in wry acknowledgement, his attention on the phone. The message was fairly short, considering the things he surely needed to tell her. Or perhaps it wasn't that complicated.

Then we were out of time. I could hear people approaching. A large group. We'd chosen a spot not far from the nearest parking lot. No need to aggravate Bosco more than I already had.

We stepped onto the boat and made sure the fastening was so loose we could open it with a quick tug.

Three of Bosco's soldiers, all in tactical gear, emerged around the bend carrying assault weapons, scanning the surroundings for threats. They spotted us in the boat, and pointed the weapons at us in such a coordinated move they must've had training for it. Ex-military, then.

We spread our arms to show we weren't hiding any weapons—though we were. They stepped aside, but didn't lower their guard.

Bosco walked unhurriedly down the path to the dock. He was wearing the same suit as that morning, and I was sure the bulletproof vest was still underneath too, despite the late afternoon heat making it uncomfortable. I knew that for a fact, as I was wearing one too, sweat running down my spine.

"Gentlemen," Bosco drawled in English. "Let's talk shop."

I shook my head. "Not until I can see Ada."

He gestured and the guards walked her to us— followed by Laïla and René. She hadn't managed to free them after all. But it didn't matter, as we'd anticipated that option.

Their hands were bound behind them, but they were otherwise unharmed. My eyes met Ada's and she gave a reassuring smile. Tightness inside me eased, but only a little.

"Well?" Bosco demanded.

This was it.

"I have the legal documents of all Falconi's assets. Free my friends and forget we exist, and they're yours."

He crossed arms over his chest, leaning slightly forward to look down at us where we stood on the boat. "And if I don't agree?"

"Everything goes to the police. Some DA will have a field day and a sure promotion. You'll spend the rest of your life behind bars."

"Provided they can connect me with Aristide's operation."

I shrugged. "You'd have to let his vassals take over in that case, and the heat that goes with it." I held up my phone. "But I have something to sweeten the deal. I'm sending you a photo."

A moment later, Bosco's phone beeped. He opened it and his brows furrowed in puzzlement. "What is this?"

The ace, the jackpot, and the royal flush in one.

"It's the last will and testament of Aristide Falconi." I paused for a dramatic effect. "Where he leaves everything to you."

Falconi really hadn't valued his sister at all. The will was dated after the divorce even. Arianna might try to challenge it—though how you challenged someone for a criminal organization in court was anybody's guess—but she wouldn't be successful. Not that she could inherit her brother's estate anyway, having killed him.

A stunned silence fell. You could hear the birds singing and the distant hum of traffic and the planes taxiing on the other side of the lake.

"Where is the original?" Bosco demanded.

"In a safe deposit box in a bank, with the rest of the papers." It had worked for us before. No reason why it wouldn't now.

"And I'll only get access for the freedom of your friends?"

"Exactly."

I showed him the key. Jimmy gave me a Ziplock plastic bag containing the power of attorney in Bosco's name that gave him access to the safe deposit box. Well, it was in one of the aliases I'd found in his office, because I'd memorized the birthdate on that one. Let him chew on the knowledge that I knew about them.

I put the key in the bag. Then Jimmy lifted up a radio-controlled boat and I put the bag inside it.

"Release my friends and allow them to come to the boat. Once we're off the dock, we'll send the boat to you."

"Or I'll shoot you and take the key." All the soldiers pointed their weapons at us in unison.

As if we hadn't anticipated that. "All Falconi's papers have been digitized and an email to Ada's boss with them as attachment has been scheduled for Monday. If I'm not there to cancel it, Interpol will go to town with your new assets."

His jaw flexed with anger and his eyes were hard. Then he nodded and the soldiers lowered their weapons. Those holding my friends removed their handcuffs. One by one, without a word, we helped them onto the boat, making it sway a bit, and they took seats.

I started the engine, Jimmy removed the rope, and I backed the boat out, slowly. Everything was going according to the plan.

Until it wasn't.

HALF A DOZEN HEAVILY armed men emerged from the bushes, weapons pointed at Bosco's men, who had no choice but to drop theirs. One of them was Ciro, and I found myself wanting to congratulate him for surviving the past couple of days.

Arianna Falconi walked around the bend, her gun pointed at Bosco, face calm and hand unwavering. He took a step back, which brought him to the end of the short dock. One more step and he'd drop into the lake.

I had no idea where they'd come from or how they'd found us, but I wasn't about to stay to find out. I added more speed and made to turn the boat around when Arianna switched her weapon at me.

"I want the key."

She'd heard everything, then. How long had they been there, listening without anyone noticing?

"It won't do you any good," I said, but I returned to the dock. I kept the engine running, but since the electric motor was silent, I doubt they noticed. "The will is clear. And you killed your brother. You can't inherit his estate anyway."

"No one would dare to touch me," she snorted with derision, but I shook my head, calmly.

"No one dared to touch your brother. You are nobody."

My disparaging words, so alike what she'd heard all her life, made her face distort with anger, but she controlled herself.

"They'd have to prove it. If I kill you, there won't be any witnesses."

"They don't need witnesses when you left the bloody knife with your fingerprints on it right next to the dead body of your brother. Now in the hands of the Venice police."

I'd alerted the police before we left Venice, posing as a concerned neighbor who had heard gunshots. Since there had been nothing on the news, I'd thought they hadn't done anything about it. But when I called the local police this afternoon to invite them here, they'd been very eager to come.

As if on cue, I heard the sound of approaching sirens nearing the parking lot. Calling the police had been a gamble, mostly a failsafe against Bosco in case he wouldn't cooperate, but it had paid off.

I sneered. "And here they are now."

She twirled to face the path. That was all Bosco needed. He turned around and jumped onto the boat, making it sway wildly, almost pushing me overboard.

"Go!" he commanded, throwing himself onto the bottom of the boat. Ada, Laïla, and René smartly followed suit as Arianna faced us again, ready to shoot.

The shot never game. As her men took new positions to aim at us instead of securing Bosco's men, Ciro pushed Arianna out of balance, almost making her fall. Bosco's men seized the opportunity to attack hers. A tousle broke out with punches and kicks instead of weapons, the grunts the men uttered carrying over the water.

I didn't stay to look how that turned out. I sped up the boat as fast as I dared, crouching low. But it wasn't fast enough. Even if those on the shore wouldn't be able to reach us, bullets could.

Jimmy was about to throw himself on the floor too when Arianna freed herself and fired in our direction. He jerked, as if hit, and the force of the impact combined with his and the boat's motion threw him overboard. He disappeared under the water in a blink.

"Danny!" Ada screeched, trying to stand up, only to be pulled back down by René and Bosco. "We have to save him!"

But there was nothing to save. Some of Arianna's men had opened fire at us too, the rapid shots echoing around the lake. I kept my back bent, hoping the bulletproof vest would shield me, but the boat wasn't as sturdy. Already there were holes in the aluminum hull that were letting water in. If I didn't get us to safety, we'd all drown.

I pushed the engine as fast as it would go and we were finally out of range. I rounded a small island in the middle of the lake and sighed in relief. Arianna and his men couldn't get to us and the police would be on them in moments.

But we weren't safe yet. The water was coming in faster. "Start bailing or we won't make it."

Ada was sitting in the rising water, her eyes large from shock. Laïla put a hand around her and helped her onto the bench, while Bosco and René tried their best to bail the water. But without proper tools, there was nothing much they could do.

Our destination wasn't far, but we wouldn't be able to make it. I gunned the weak engine and managed to bring us almost to the shore before I had to admit defeat. The boat sank.

I pushed to my feet and realized there was only a meter or so of water and we could stand. I took the radio-controlled boat and grabbed Ada by the waist with my other hand, and helped her onto the shore.

"Come on, not far now," I coaxed her. Like an automaton, she followed me to a nearby parking lot, where I had a car waiting.

We were soaking wet from the waist down, but we couldn't care about it now. I helped Ada into the front seat, and Laïla and René sat in the back. I gave Bosco a reluctant look.

"Can I give you a drive somewhere?" The day had taken an odd turn, but I could be polite. He smirked.

"My men will fetch me in a few moments. If you wait, they'll bring everyone's luggage."

I blinked. I was about to decline when a black Mercedes pulled into the parking lot and paused by us. Bosco's soldier emerged from the front passenger seat to open the back door for him. Bosco gestured at the trunk.

"Move our guests' luggage to the other car." Then he reached a hand to me. "The key."

I took the plastic bag with the key and the power of the attorney out of the little boat. I gave him a steady look. "You will stay out of our lives."

It wasn't a question.

"With the sword of Damocles hanging over me? Absolutely."

We nodded at each other, understanding. I gave him the bag and he turned to Ada.

"And the deed to my casino?"

The question startled me. I'd sent it to Bosco's address, hoping it would arrive next week. I was about to say so, when Ada gave him a wan smile.

"It's in the safe in your bedroom closet. With the key to your safe deposit box in Rome too."

He looked as stunned as I felt. Then he nodded and got into his car, which drove off immediately. If I never saw Bosco again, that would be too soon.

But I wouldn't let down my guard until I had everyone to safety.

* * *

I GOT US A SUITE at the airport hotel so that we wouldn't have to travel in our soaked clothes. René and I shared a room and took turns showering, and Ada and Laïla shared another.

I couldn't help remembering showering with Ada in

Monaco after our previous adventure, but that wouldn't happen today. Or ever.

When I emerged in clean clothes, warm again, the food René had ordered when we checked in had arrived, and everyone was gathered in the lounge area to eat. Ada was sitting huddled, feet on the couch, hugging her bent knees, staring into the distance. Laila gave me a concerned look, and I sat next to Ada, but she turned away from me.

"You could've gone back." Her tone was angry and accusing.

I sighed inwardly. I'd underestimated how badly this would hit her. She'd gone through Jimmy's death once already, but back then she'd known it wasn't real.

"I couldn't, the gunfire was too intense. But the police are on the scene. They'll help him." I didn't add if he was there to be helped. I picked up the remote. "Let's check the news."

We watched TV while we had dinner. The news about Arianna and the great mafia arrest was just breaking, and one thing was clear: she would definitely go down. The reporters and the police were downright gleeful.

"Pity Bosco didn't fall with her," René said, annoyed, and I shrugged.

"I prioritized your safety."

His mouth pressed in a tight line, but he nodded. "It was the only call that saw us out alive. And now he owes you for saving his life."

I could only hope so.

Ada snorted, bitter. "Trust criminals to stick together."

Awkward silence fell. René and I glanced each other, and he looked a bit hurt, as if he thought Ada had meant him. I would have to defuse her anger before she accidentally ousted herself too.

Sighing, I pushed some plates aside on the coffee table and took a seat on it in front of her. I reached to take her hand, but she wouldn't let me.

I lowered mine. "I'm sorry I didn't turn back." We both knew it hadn't been possible, but she wasn't in the right headspace to hear it. "Jimmy was wearing a bulletproof vest and he's fit. I bet he dove deep to avoid the bullets and then swam to shore."

"We could've picked him up there."

"Not with our leaking boat," I said dryly. But she only crossed her arms and sank deeper into the couch. René cleared his throat.

"Who is Jimmy?"

I glanced at Ada but she wasn't ready to talk. And she couldn't tell the truth either, though in her current state she might, and everything else with it. I had to come up with something.

"He was her partner at the Metropolitan Police. He disappeared one day, presumed dead, only to surface in Rome last week."

René gave Ada a sharp look. "Is that what you were really investigating in Rome?"

It was an out for her and she took it, with a disgusted twist of her lips, the sentiment likely directed at my lie. "Falconi had him. I went to check the lead and was captured too."

It was a neat explanation and I would've left it at that when she roused herself a little. "Though it turned out Falconi was connected with my case too. He'd teamed up with Melnyk, who wanted to become an arms dealer."

That explained the cache on Melnyk's yacht. "Did Bosco tell you that?"

"Yes. He'd deliberately taken Melnyk out of the picture to make sure Falconi couldn't branch out."

"And now he's in charge of the operation…"

"Why couldn't you tell me that's what you were doing in Rome?" Laïla asked, upset. Ada sighed.

"I'd … insisted with my boss at the Met that Jimmy was alive and got ridiculed for it. I didn't want to bring it up until I was sure."

For all that it was a lie, she went with it easily enough.

"Will you tell your old boss of this?" René asked, and she shook her head.

"What's the point. He's definitely dead now."

I kept my mouth shut. Rule number nine of faking your death was clear: *Don't tell anyone you've faked your death.* Even if it was someone you trusted or someone else who died.

It wasn't easy though. I felt genuinely bad watching Ada's grief, not solely for her, but for my mother too, whom I'd put through this.

By the time she recovered, I'd be gone.

On that note: "We'd best head to the train station. I have tickets for us to the overnight train."

Ada lifted her gaze to meet mine, her eyes angry and full of contempt. "I'm not travelling with you."

I closed my eyes briefly. Then I nodded, ignoring Laïla's upset gasp. "I'll travel home alone."

Wherever home would be.

Whoever *I* would be.

I would start anew, and this time I would stick to my rules. But their priorities had changed. From now on, the most important rule of leaving a life of crime was this:

Never get attached.

EPILOGUE

ADA

I RETURNED TO WORK ON Monday as if nothing had happened, an hour early because the thought of sitting in a bus full of commuters of my regular schedule was too much to face. I was neat and put-together like always, but I was tired to my core. Not for the lack of rest. I'd slept the entire Sunday.

We arrived in Lyon on Saturday afternoon after an uneventful train ride that had required two changes. Flying would've been faster, but I'd needed the slow transition to normal the journey offered.

At the station, we'd taken separate taxis home. As René had seen me to mine, he'd smiled a little ruefully. "Next time I want to help you with your investigation, just kick me."

I was fairly certain he was over me.

Laïla and I had had a talk and we'd agreed it would be best if we stuck to the original story of my illness in London.

"It's not like we're the heroes of this story," she'd said dryly. "We helped a bad man to become even more powerful."

She didn't have to worry about explaining things to her boss; she'd been on a legitimate leave of absence. But

I'd claimed—or she had claimed for me—that I had pneumonia. I'd need a good explanation for why I didn't have a note from my doctor stating so.

At my desk, I checked my emails first like always, hoping routine would see me out of my funk. It wasn't solely sadness over Danny. It was everything that had happened, being captured and shot at. I was suffering from acute PTSD. And I couldn't even go to the Interpol counselor for it without blowing my story.

My out-of-office message had worked and my inbox was manageable. Nevertheless, the email from St. Thomas' Hospital in London would've stood out. My heart thumped heavily as I clicked it open. Had something happened to my mother?

The contents were nothing I expected, and I had to read it three times to make sense of it. It was a genuine-looking message from Dr. Halston with a brief summary of my illness—not pneumonia after all to his relief—with a PDF file of the official medical certificate.

I stared at it with my mouth open. I had no clue where it could've come from. Had Laïla hacked the hospital system? But she would definitely have told me about it herself, and even though she had the hacking skills, she wasn't one to break the law.

Gift horses and their mouths echoing in my mind, I printed the certificate and carried it to my boss, Laurent Paget, the head of the crime division who had just arrived at work. He studied me with a critical eye as he accepted the note.

"You look a bit tired still."

"Thanks," I said dryly. "Just what a girl wants to hear first thing Monday morning."

He smiled. "All I'm saying is that if you need a couple more days, you can have them."

I felt wretched for his kindness, but I nodded. "I'll keep that in mind."

Back at my desk, I had to field dozens of questions from my colleagues about my health as they arrived at work one by one. Apparently, I truly looked pale and tired, because they all commented on it. And I hadn't even tried for that look when I made my face that morning.

When they finally left me alone, I continued with the emails. But the mere thought of tackling whatever they demanded of me made the exhaustion worse. So, when I spotted another curious email, I clicked it without hesitation, even though the sender only said *Danny*. Subject line said, "I'm sorry."

My mouth was dry and tears threatened to spill as I read the short message.

> *I should've explained face to face while I had a chance, but better late than never. Remember Barry's gang? The one who fancied becoming the kings of London bank robbers? They got their clutches on your dad somehow. He came to me; I helped him out. And then I was in their clutches, and Thom too. Death was the only way out. I'm sorry I couldn't tell you, but your reaction had to be believable lest they came after you next. I changed my identity and I decided it was best I didn't bother you again.*
>
> *I have another new identity. Eliot knows a world-class hacker, so it's sound. I won't share it with you. It's best you think I'm dead.*
> *Bosco's coming. I've got to go.*

The message ended there. I stared at it, and the tears dried on their own. I hadn't known about my dad. He died a year before Danny, so the whole mess had been going on for at least that long, a third of our marriage. I tried to feel grateful for Danny for handling it, but mostly I was miffed that he hadn't confided in me. That was not how a marriage was supposed to work.

The bit about Eliot aggravated me. Why had he helped Danny get a new identity? Knowing about the hacker explained the quality IDs he had, but why did he have them? Had he arranged for the sick note too? I didn't want to owe him more than I already did.

And what did Danny mean it was best I thought he was dead? He died. I'd witnessed it myself.

Like I'd witnessed him die at the bank…

My anger began to rise. Had the two of them played me? Had I been left out of the loop on purpose, as if I didn't matter? Eliot's behavior at the lake and later in the hotel began to make much better sense now. Why would he be worried about Danny when he knew everything was fake?

My anger energized me so much that when Laïla came to ask if I was up to attending the self-defense class after work that she taught, I said yes. I was supposed to be recovering from almost-pneumonia, but none of my coworkers attended the class, so they wouldn't know.

At the back of my mind, I must have hoped Eliot would be there too so I could confront him. I don't know why; he hadn't attended after the first class.

Still, I felt a pang of disappointment when I entered the dojo and he wasn't there. The three old ladies that were the life of the class were and they rushed to us immediately, distraught and loud.

"Monsieur Reed is gone," they all but wailed.

Laïla was instantly upset. "Gone where?"

I swallowed to remove the foul taste in my mouth. "Back home," I told her, the explanation he'd given me. I had no idea if it was true, but it would have to suffice.

"To look after his mother," Madame Benoit sighed, her eyes gleaming with what I suspected was hero worship. Some hero.

"He was so lovely too, bringing us chocolate and wonderful Marsala wine from his trip to Italy," Mademoiselle Morel said, equally sad.

"I don't know if I'll bother going to yoga anymore," Madame Fabien added with a quiver. "Watching him bend and stretch was the highlight of my week."

I wanted to tell them Eliot wasn't anyone to pine over. He was a scammer and a hoaxer. A con artist. That he hadn't stolen their money to boot was a miracle.

And he hadn't stolen my heart, dammit.

I was furious with him for abandoning the old ladies. Abandoning me. I wanted to confront him. I wanted the truth.

But it would be impossible to try to find Eliot Reed. He no longer existed, just like Danny Reed and Jimmy Allen no longer existed. I probably wouldn't get far researching Ryan Pike either, the alias Eliot had used in Rome.

I wasn't completely without clues though. I had the key to his safe deposit box in Rome, the one he'd given me himself with permission to look. First chance I had, I would.

Eliot had better watch out. Because I was coming after him. And I wouldn't fail.

ACKNOWLEDGEMENTS

I spent a month in Rome in 1996, studying ancient history, and the city has stayed with me since. I haven't had a chance to go back, but writing this book was a small substitute that brought back wonderful memories. Who knows, maybe one day I'll return there.

All the usual suspects are to thank for this book. The failings are all mine.

I would like to thank all of you for reading and liking *The Perfect Scam*, encouraging me to write more about Eliot and Ada. They will return in *The Perfect Heist*.

ABOUT THE AUTHOR

Susanna Shore is an independent author. She writes *Two-Natured London* paranormal romance series about vampires and wolf-shifters that roam London, *P.I. Tracy Hayes* series of a Brooklyn waitress turned private investigator, *The Reed Files* crime capers, and *House of Magic* paranormal mysteries set in London. She also writes stand-alone thrillers and contemporary romances. When she's not writing, she's reading or—should her husband manage to drag her outdoors—taking long walks.

WWW.SUSANNASHORE.COM